Romancing the Kicker

Catherine Lane

ACKNOWLEDGMENTS

Thank you: Tina Minns for answering all my athletic trainer questions so quickly and even sending me a video that inspired the stretching scene between Parker and Carly.

My wonderful beta readers Ann Etter, Boz, and Danielle Zion. To Anne, Becky, Mary, and Claire for their last-minute help.

Celeste Castro for jumping in repeatedly when I needed her. And Susan X Meagher, who somehow keeps me grounded and encourages me to soar as a writer all at the same time.

Thank you: Astrid Ohletz and the amazing team at Ylva for the wonderful cover and so much more.

And then, Sandra Gerth. As usual, words just aren't enough. Thank you so very much for taking me on this journey to "better than fine." Although I know we still have a long way to go, I am so lucky to walk down the path with you.

And, of course, my wife. She inspired Parker's love of movement and countless other things in my life.

*For every young girl who's kicked a ball
around a field and dreamed of more.*

CHAPTER 1

PARKER SHERBOURNE WOKE UP IN a strange bed with two pillows pressed into her upper back. For a second, she didn't know where she was. She took in the plush mattress, the freshly cut flowers on the bedside table, and finally, the Eiffel Tower framed in the huge picture window. The monument's golden lights threw a romantic glow into the luxury hotel room.

Of course.

She knew exactly where she was.

Sin City—the Las Vegas Strip. Over five thousand miles away from the real city of lights, the tower across the street was only half the size of the original in Paris. Parker sighed deeply. This one shone silly and fake, like a teenager who had raided her mother's closet for more grown-up clothes.

Today, she would try out as a point-after-touchdown kicker for the High Rollers—the NFL expansion team that had landed in Las Vegas when the deal from California had fallen apart. Then she would be the outsider. Did a woman, even if she could kick the stuffing out of any ball, really have a chance at the most macho sport on the planet? This whole thing was a publicity stunt at best and a fool's errand at worst. No one in the game was ready for a woman—and an out lesbian at that—to suit up in the NFL...no one but her.

Parker scooted over to the bedside table and fumbled for her phone and the time—almost three in the morning. The pillows at her back traveled with her.

Wait. They weren't pillows.

Rolling over, Parker fell into breasts so perky and full that a girl could get lost in them. Tanya, her shiny new agent with Gridiron Sports Management. She had jumped on Parker when the Rollers had started sniffing around. Not literally, of course…until last night.

Parker bit her lip. She could have sworn that Tanya had gotten up to leave after their bump-and-run activities, but the nipple resting on her cheek clearly said otherwise.

Tanya stirred, and the nipple slipped closer to her mouth. Parker resisted the urge to wrap her lips around it…again. Sex with Tanya had been fun, but Parker had only asked Tanya in for one reason: to unwind. She always played better on the field when something, or usually *someone*, had drained her nervous energy the night before.

Parker slid a hand under Tanya's shapely behind and tried to ease her to the other side of the bed without waking her up. She needed her sleep, and she always slept best with no one crowding her.

Just as she maneuvered Tanya far enough away, Tanya's eyes fluttered open. A hungry smile lit up her face. "Hi, there."

"Hi, yourself." Parker pushed the words out. The last thing she wanted was to talk.

"You made the touchdown last night." Tanya scooted back and up, raising her mouth to Parker's. "Don't you want to try for the point after?" Apparently, talking was the last thing Tanya wanted as well.

"Look." Parker slid back to the edge of the bed. "That's very tempting. It really is. But I need to get some more sleep. You know, be ready for today and all."

Tanya's gaze clouded over. Instantly, she was the very picture of professionalism. "Don't worry. I don't U-Haul." She grabbed the sheet and pulled it up over her nakedness.

"No, it's not that. I really enjoyed last night." Truth be told, she already missed the sight of those perfect breasts. "But—"

Tanya ran a hand through her short hair and eased from the bed with the sheet still wrapped around her. "You're right. We shouldn't muddy the waters until we find out if there's actually something to wade into. Let's see what happens today." She found her clothes on the floor and turned her back as she started to throw them on. "Then we can figure out if this is something."

"Yeah. Okay." Parker wasn't sure about the metaphor. But she got the tone. Tanya had leaped through Parker's door earlier only because she was certain tomorrow would be a total bust. She was way too smart and polished to sleep with a client, and after a failed tryout, Gridiron wouldn't even field a phone call from Parker. Tanya was playing the odds and just getting some while she could.

Parker ran a hand through her long hair, sweeping it behind her shoulders. Shit. She had thought she was in control, the one writing the story of their night. She jumped out of the bed and strutted across the room without bothering to reach for her clothes. Years in the gym and on one field or another had toned her body to absolute perfection, and she knew it. She'd give Tanya one last look at exactly what she was betting against.

The energy in the room stilled, and Tanya stopped rustling with her clothes.

Parker could almost feel the heat from her gaze, like Supergirl's X-ray vision, moving up and down her body. She would take the small victory.

Parker walked to the front door and pulled it open. The hall outside was empty at this late hour, thank God. She just wanted to make a point, not provide a free peep show to anyone in the hallway.

"What time's the car to the stadium?" Parker swung to face Tanya in a full reveal.

Tanya stared for a moment and then closed her mouth with a soft pop. "Noon. I'll meet you in the lobby at noon. By those jack-o'-lanterns made of…"

"Chrysanthemums."

"Yeah, the Halloween exhibit." After bending down to grab her purse, she headed out but paused before she stepped over the threshold and raised her hand to Parker's cheek. "Of course, you know that just trying out for an NFL team is a very big deal, even if you never play. To be the first at anything is a great honor. You'll open the door. Play this right, and you'll make contacts. We'll both make some money, and maybe we can do all this again when—"

Parker caught the hand and pulled it off her cheek. "Hey, I thought you were supposed to be on my side."

"This is being on your side." Tanya's brow furrowed. "You know the likelihood of this crazy stunt working out is pretty slim."

Parker's hackles rose. "Don't count me out yet. I could be the one to walk through that door. I may just surprise you."

"Oh, you've surprised me already." She ran a glance up and down Parker's body one last time. "Get that sleep."

Parker closed the door behind her and flipped the privacy lock with a hard snap. The room was still awash with the lights of a city that never slept. Crossing to the mirrored picture window, Parker looked out on perhaps the finest view of the Strip. The Eiffel Tower and the Arc de Triomphe straight ahead, the glorious dancing fountains of the Bellagio to the left, and the brilliant neon of fantasies and dreams as far as the eye could see.

She yanked the blackout curtain across the window, and the room sank into darkness. A view for suckers. The bright colors and all the bling gave people false hope. There were far too many people in this city standing alone in hotel rooms in the middle of the night with broken dreams. Behind all the glitz, Vegas was a brittle place. She had never liked it much.

The Sherbourne Hotel, of course, was the one exception. She had to hand it to her father. He sure knew how to choose a location. He got five stars for that and, in fact, for the entire hotel. Dozens of guidebooks had called him a genius for the way he had created such intimacy in a property with over two thousand rooms. The hotel rose like an island of elegance in a sea of extravagance.

Parker sighed. She wished for the umpteenth time that he would work as hard on their relationship. Lately, she would give him one star, if that. When she was a kid and there was a football game on TV, they would grab a couple of Dr. Peppers and chill out in the media room. But she couldn't remember the last time that happened. She had learned the hard way people never hung around when you wanted them to. It was better to kick them out before they walked away and chase your dreams alone—and that's what she would do at the tryout later.

Not far away in Paradise Valley—a neighborhood off the Strip with no glitzy neon or shrunken French monuments—Carly Bartlet was also wide-awake. She tossed and turned in her twin bed, twisting the blankets up under her chin and then pushing them back down.

"Can't sleep?" Her grandmother's soft Southern drawl drifted over from her side of the room.

"Oh goodness. Did I wake you?" Carly raised her head and peered into the semi-darkness. A lone streetlamp outside their bedroom window cast a sickly yellow light into the room. She could barely see her grandmother's pale figure.

Minnie Lee sat in her own twin bed propped up against several pillows. "No. Not at all. When you're my age, you chase sleep at night. Not the other way around."

"Seventy-three is not that old." Carly pulled herself up as well. "And if sleeping badly is the criteria for age, tonight I must be a hundred and twelve."

"You're just nervous, sweetheart."

"It's more than that." She bit her lip as the panic rose like bile in her stomach. "I'm afraid that I won't be able to make this work."

"That's the silliest thing I've ever heard. Who was hired by UNLV the second she graduated?"

"Yeah, but this is the pros, and you didn't see the Rollers' head athletic trainer when Mrs. Fisher brought him into her office and announced I was his newest assistant. Buck was so mad, steam would've come out of his ears if he were a cartoon character."

"I'm sure that's not true. And if it is, you just show him what you're made of, and then he'll blow a different tune."

"Maybe." Her shoulders dropped as her grandmother's unwavering confidence washed over her. In a way, she didn't blame Buck Johnson. When Marina Fisher had inherited the High Rollers after her husband's death, she had gone on record as saying she would find a way to change the league.

Carly had signed the contract before she had a chance to sit down with Buck and lay out her philosophy and expectations of medical care on the sports field. Knots tightened in her stomach. How was she supposed to navigate treatment with the players when she didn't even have the head athletic trainer on her side?

"You might as well get up if you're just going to sit over there and fret." Her grandmother broke into her thoughts.

Carly looked at the clock on her bedside table. Three forty-eight. She wanted to be at the stadium by five thirty, a half hour before the training room opened. It was almost time to get up anyway. "Okay. Do you think I'll wake up Teddy if I take a shower?"

"That boy could sleep through one of his zombie apocalypses."

Laughing, Carly threw back the covers and climbed out of bed. "Tonight, when I get home, we should talk about me moving out into the main room, though. I don't want to wake either of you up if I come in late or get up early. Who knows what my hours are going to be?"

"I'd rather talk about how your first day went." Her grandmother snuggled back into the pillows.

"Thanks, Grandma." She slipped from the room.

What Carly really wanted to talk about, however, was her grandmother dropping a few shifts at the diner or maybe looking for an affordable used car. She shook her head to clear her mind. She shouldn't get ahead of herself. To get the bigger paycheck that could change their lives, she actually had to keep the job.

After getting out of the shower, she swiped a towel across the steamed-up mirror and caught a glimpse of herself. *Who am I to think I can do this?*

The pretty, light-brown face staring back at her held no answers. She looked younger than her twenty-six years. Maybe she would one day be grateful for that genetic gift from the father she had never met, but right now, it was a liability. No one at the Rollers was going to take her seriously. They would treat her like an intern, for sure. The knots in her stomach tightened. She pulled her loose waves up into a high ponytail. No, that was even worse; now she looked like a teenager.

She yanked the hair band out and nodded at her reflection in the mirror. "You can do this."

Her grandmother waited for her in the main room of the tiny apartment. She sat on a barstool at the breakfast bar, wrapped up in a thick bathrobe. October mornings in the Valley were still mild, but Minnie Lee, thin as a rail, was always cold. And thanks to the cost, they almost never ran the heat until December.

"Wish me luck." Carly grabbed her backpack and a new, quilted Rollers jacket off the sofa.

"Exactly." Minnie Lee pointed to the vintage cake carrier beside her. "You didn't think that I'd let you go off to your dream job without Sweet Luck, did you?"

Carly's heart melted. The cake tin was almost as old as her grandmother, and with its faded red roses and broken hinges, it had certainly seen better days. But ever since her grandmother had arrived in Vegas from Alabama, this cake tin had appeared at all the big moments in their lives. A family tradition. Sweet Luck. Her grandmother meant it literally.

"I told you. You're not going to need it." Minnie Lee's eyes crinkled with a smile. "But it doesn't hurt to hedge your bets, does it?"

Carly shook her head and grinned back. "Thanks." She flipped the latch at the bottom of the tin and raised it to reveal a serving of her grandmother's famous banana pudding: fresh bananas smothered in vanilla pudding with butter cookies on top.

"Is that Sweet Luck?" Her half brother stood in the hallway, barely awake. His dark hair was tousled, and his warm eyes still sleepy. "I could use some Sweet Luck." And when they both looked at him, he added, "Seriously, I have an important science lab today."

Laughing, Carly held out the fork. "You finish it, then. I got to go anyway."

"Score." Teddy held out his clenched palm for a fist bump. "You too, Grandma."

When her grandmother added her fist to the mix, Carly marveled at the different colors of their knuckles—white, tan, and a darker brown. They didn't look like family, and that was why their grandmother always worked so hard to make them feel like one.

Teddy pulled his fist back, wiggling his fingers in some move he had probably picked up at school, and slid onto the barstool to attack the pudding.

Carly kissed her grandmother on the cheek and gave her brother a quick side hug.

"See you later, sis," he said.

"Goodbye, sweetheart." Minnie Lee raised her hand.

"Oh! Wait!" Teddy dropped his fork on the plate. "Did you hear? There's a new way to put players' muscles back together when they hurt them."

"Oh really?"

"Yeah. With super gluteus." Teddy glanced back and forth between them. "Get it? Super glu…teus."

Minnie Lee laughed.

Carly groaned and rolled her eyes. "Seriously?"

"There's a lot more where that came from."

"Then I'm super gluteously happy I'm going to work."

On the way out, she caught their reflection in the mirror of the coatrack by the door. They sat at the bar, the smiles from the joke still playing at their lips.

Laughter and love. They had plenty of that.

<hr />

Two buses, fifty strip malls, and a three-minute walk later, Carly stood at the staff entrance to the High Rollers' stadium. The domed structure with its clear roof and silver and black exterior looked as if a sleek alien spaceship had touched down on the south end of the Strip. The curtain-like side windows were closed this early on a Tuesday morning, but come game day, they'd retract to create a gorgeous open-air entrance that framed the Las Vegas Strip and was the envy of the entire league.

Never in her whole life did she think she'd be standing outside a two-billion-dollar stadium and actually belong there. Carly had fought hard for everything that had come her way, and at times disappointment had rung more loudly than success. But there was no denying it. Her gambles had paid off. She was a High Roller.

The guard at the door put down his ratty coffee cup and held up his hand to stop Carly. "The girlfriend entrance is through the Welcome Center." He pointed to the massive glass-and-steel structure to his left.

"Oh no. Sorry. I'm the new assistant AT...um...athletic trainer." Carly tried to infuse her voice with an authority she didn't feel while she dug around in her backpack to find her stadium ID. Her fingers curled around plastic, and she held the badge out to him. "See?"

"Nice try. That's a bus pass."

"Oh. Sorry. They're both sort of silver."

Her stomach churned as she pulled the real ID out. She couldn't even get in the front door without a snafu. What made her think she could pull off the rest of the day?

She glanced at the front of the real badge before she showed him. The picture of her under the Rollers logo was a good one. Her hair was behaving, and the complementary shades of golden brown of her hair, eyes, and skin looked as if they had been coordinated by a stylist. No wonder the guard had thought her a groupie. All her life she had looked more like arm candy than the knowledgeable professional.

The guard took the ID and carefully looked back and forth between the picture and her. "All right, Carolina Lee—"

"Carly. The Car of Carolina with Lee added on. Just Carly."

"You should go by Carolina Lee. There's heft to it." He returned the badge to her. "Have a good first day."

"Thank you." She took a step but then swiveled back with her arm outstretched. "You know, I really do belong here."

"It's not me you have to convince." He clasped her hand in a solid shake and then pointed to the steel door on the side of the building.

Carly walked into the rarified air of the training complex that butted up against the stadium. She was inside a giant glass football. The steel trusses supporting the glass looked like the stitching on a ball. No expense had been spared when the center had been built. The press had instantly dubbed it the Gamblers' Den, and the name had stuck.

She wound her way through the labyrinth of treatment, rehabilitation, and recovery rooms and past a ten-thousand-square-foot weight room, a cafeteria, and the hallowed locker room. Every door had a Rollers logo—a silver skull with two neon-green dice for eyes.

The head trainer's office was at the end of a hallway with no natural light.

Even this early in the morning, Buck was already hunched at his desk, shuffling through paperwork with one hand and holding an oversized iPad with the other. He was such a big man that the desk looked as if it had been made for a child.

Carly knocked on the open door.

Buck glanced up, his burly shoulders tensing. "Well, you're here early. I'll say that for you." His voice sounded resigned, but she wasn't fooled.

"I know how busy it can be even on the players' day off."

Buck grunted his assent. "Look, let's get one thing straight, right away. Marina strong-armed me into hiring you. I've got a hundred resumes in this desk drawer that are more qualified. But she's got this crazy idea about staffing the organization with more women. And she wants a local female. You've apparently got both the anatomy and the UNLV pedigree. So, I am stuck with you."

"I understand." Carly rolled her neck. She had been here before with men who thought women did not belong in the training rooms of male sports teams. Actually, she had been here a lot in other ways too. People had looked at her gender, the color of her skin, as well as the fact that she came from a low-income household, and they promptly decided that she was not quite enough like them to be embraced. "I get it," she said again, hoping to put Buck at ease.

"I'm not sure you do. We're fully staffed, and even though we're in the middle of this miserable season, my trainers are a well-oiled machine. I can't afford anyone to muck with my system. You'll start as a glorified intern, maybe not even glorified, and we'll see how long you last."

Carly knew what that meant, too. She would spend long hours in the stockroom and make gallons of Gatorade from powder until it tasted as if it came straight from the bottle. Fair enough. All she was asking for was a chance. The irony was, if Marina wanted a rabble rouser, she had chosen badly. She wasn't here to make waves or stand up for women's rights or whatever the hell Marina required. "Thank you for this opportunity. I'll make the most of it."

"That's what I'm afraid of." His eyes narrowed as he stared at her. "What exactly is your game here?"

"Huh?" Carly's brow furrowed. "To help the players and learn as much as I—"

"Why did you leave the UNLV training room? From all accounts, you had a good thing going there and a job that might actually last beyond this season."

She ran a hand through her hair. The real truth—creating a less stressful life for her grandmother—wasn't what he wanted to hear. The lesser truth might work, though. "It's the NFL. Every trainer dreams about going pro, and I—"

"You married? Got kids?"

"No." Carly was pretty sure that she knew where he was going with all this. "I can assure you I'm a work-centered employee. The Rollers will be my top priority—"

"That's not it." Buck slapped the top of his desk with an open palm, not hard, but the sound reverberated loudly in the tight space. "I expect all my trainers to be completely aboveboard."

"Excuse me?" She rocked back on her heels.

"And, in your case, that means absolutely no fraternizing with the players. Is that clear?"

She sighed deeply. He had taken, what, two minutes to get here? Why did most men think she had become a trainer to land a rich husband? Why could no one believe that she actually enjoyed smoothing out aches and pains and putting athletes back on the field better than ever? Sometimes she even felt medicine was in her DNA.

Buck was clearly waiting for her answer. When none came, his mouth puffed up as if that cartoon steam actually was swirling inside. "You think I'm kidding?"

Carly shook her head. She couldn't ever imagine the hulking man in front of her making a joke. She should just tell him that dating a male player would never be a possibility. But coming out to her boss on the first day probably wasn't the best idea. She hadn't even come out to her family.

"I don't like drama. Especially right now." Buck continued as if he hadn't heard her. Clearly, he was only interested in his own agenda, whatever it was. "These players are inventing excuses for the way they're playing. Shit. You're just going to be another distraction." He blew out a puff of breath. No steam, but air whistled in the room. "Go to HR if you want. Claim sexual harassment if that's how you want to play this meeting, but the plain fact is you're way too pretty for this job. They'll come in the room for all the wrong reasons. Honestly, I don't know what Marina was thinking bringing you into the organization."

Carly swallowed hard. Not this nonsense again. People always seized on her looks, focusing on her golden eyes or her wavy hair instead of her skills as an athletic trainer. News alert: the way she looked had nothing to do with her ability to do her job—and do it very well. "You'll find that I'm a professional, Buck. I'm here to work hard. Nothing more."

"Look, if I get even one whiff of you and a player crossing the line, you're flat-out fired. And Marina and her cockamamie ideas won't be able to save you. You're here for only one purpose. To support the players on the field, and that's it."

"I understand." She reverted back to her go-to line.

"Good." He picked up the paperwork. "Allen's in the hydrotherapy room. Report to him, and he'll tell you what to do."

"Thank you."

"Don't thank me. I wouldn't wish the rest of this miserable season on anyone. Lose your quarterback and everything goes to shit. Like it or not, you're part of the Rollovers, as the press has so kindly dubbed us." He focused fully on the iPad. In the one second it took him to pull up the electronic health records of the injured players, he had clearly forgotten she ever existed.

Well, that was better than being in his crosshairs. If she kept her head down and did her job well, maybe she could last all the way to January—with a lot of luck maybe even into the off-season, and Teddy and her grandmother could have breakfast on a bar that wasn't falling apart.

⊷⊸⊷

Parker's eyes popped open a full minute before her cell phone alarm chimed. Even as a child, she could wake up exactly when she wanted. Her father had called it a parlor trick. She announced that as a true athlete, she could control her body, even down to her circadian rhythms. Her father had laughed. But that was far better than her mother's response. She, as usual, was off *meditating* alone or worse yet, at the center, and had never weighed in one way or the other.

Parker stretched like a cat rising from a nap, first rolling out her head and then her behind. She slid toward the bedside table and dialed room service. "I would like egg whites, scrambled, with spinach and onions. Turkey bacon and whole wheat toast, unbuttered, on the side."

"Anything to drink?" the man at the other end asked, his voice tired and bored.

"Please. Coffee and a large, fresh orange juice. That's room 1623."

"Okay. That will be thirty minutes." Clicking on a keyboard filled the silence as he was probably punching in the room number on a computer.

Parker sighed as she waited for what always came next.

"Ms. Sherbourne?" The man's voice quickened. "Oh my God, I'm sorry. I didn't realize... We can get it to you sooner, of course, if you—"

"No, no. Thirty is perfect. Thank you." She hung up so the man could stop falling all over himself.

The knock came fifteen minutes later. He had pushed the order anyway. They always did when they realized who she was. She opened the door, expecting to see someone in the deep blue of the hotel uniform and a pushcart with a shiny bell-shaped cover. "Excellent. I'm starving…" Parker froze.

"A little late for breakfast, isn't it?" Her father filled the frame of the doorway. For such a tall man, he stood casually, his lips curved in a laconic smile. "Late night?"

"Dad, how'd you find me?" The urge to shut the door nearly overwhelmed her. "The reservation was through the Rollers."

"It *is* my hotel, you know. May I come in?"

Parker backed up, and her father took possession of the room. Energy flowed off his six-foot-five frame, rushing off into all four corners. He glanced around but made no move to take her in his arms or kiss her hello.

"I thought you were in France," Parker said softly, not knowing whether to make the move herself.

"I will be, but I had a meeting in Vegas, and so do you, I hear." He pulled at a wilting flower in a nearby vase and crumpled it in his hand.

"Come to wish me luck?" She looked at her father sideways as he dropped the flower into the trash. She tried to tamp down the wisps of hope rising in her chest. "It's not a wasted trip. You've always liked football."

"True. But I'm not so sure you and the NFL are a good match."

Of course, he's not here to support me. Their conversation had gone south even faster than it usually did. She rocked back on her heels, waiting for his agenda, whatever it was, to bubble to the surface.

"What happened to soccer and the Fire?" he finally asked. "I thought you were making a home up there."

"Nothing. It's the off-season in Portland. I wouldn't be there anyway."

"So, you're going back?"

Parker looked down. Just a simple question, but he always made her feel like a teenager explaining why she had missed curfew. "Maybe. I don't know. I wanted to take a stab at something different before I decide for sure."

Her father pointed to the plush couch in a corner. "May I sit?"

Parker nodded, and her stress level rose as his behind hit the cushions.

On the couch, her father ran his hand through hair as blond and thick as hers. "I'm wondering if coming down here and trying out for the Rollers is just another one of these leaps you make when you get so restless and wound up, you can't think straight."

And here they were. The complete opposite of supporting her. "I don't do that. Besides, I love football, even more than soccer."

"Funny, when you joined the Fire, you told us that soccer was your life."

"I'm a better kicker than a goalie," Parker said, fully aware that she now actually sounded, as well as felt, like that teenager.

"That's not the point. We both know you can kick for the Rollers if you really want to. The point is: Are you ready to embrace the responsibility that comes with this job?"

"I'm going to do something that no woman has ever done before."

"Exactly. The first woman in the NFL? It's going to come with a lot of baggage."

"I'm pretty strong." Parker crossed her arms and met her father's stare.

"I wasn't going to tell you this, but Marina Fisher is one hell of a businesswoman. When the NFL lifted the ban on events in casinos, she contacted me about a partnership with the Rollers a while back. And I said no."

Parker yanked on the end of her ponytail. "And you think this is her way of getting to you?"

"Don't fidget, honey."

Parker dropped her ponytail as if it had erupted in flames. She opened her mouth and closed it just as quickly. On any field her voice called out commands, but here with her father, it was barely audible.

"Honestly, I don't know what Marina is up to. She's booked the hotel for an event later this week. But whatever her game plan is, I certainly don't want her toying with you."

"I'm a big girl, Dad." Parker rocked up on her toes to prove it. Fully extended, she was well over six feet herself. "I can take care of myself."

"Yes. And that's also what I came here to talk about."

"There's more?" A chill ran down her back.

He sighed and ran a hand down the tight crease in his pants. "I think I've been enabling you to jump from one thing to the next. It's time for you to stick around and truly finish what you start. Your mother and I have talked—"

"Really?"

"Well, I talked and she listened. Look, it doesn't matter. We both agree that it's time you found out what is truly important to you."

"And?"

"And we're cutting off your allowance."

The words pierced her like tiny daggers. Parker let the sharp edges settle before she answered, "You can't be serious."

"This hurts me more than it hurts you; believe me."

She didn't.

"You should have enough to last you for a while. And we think if we take away your cushion, you'll be forced to find out what really matters to you. Maybe it's this caper with the Rollers. Maybe it's soccer and the Fire. Or maybe it's something else completely."

"For how long?"

"Until you come up with a solid plan for your future."

"I'm not going to work for you like Jem does. If that's what you're after." Her fingernails dug into her palms. Had that been his goal all along?

"Nothing would make me happier than if you would join me in a business venture. You do have a business degree, after all." He waved his hand around the room. "But if hotels aren't your passion, I can live with that. I just want you to find—"

"Okay, Dad." Parker moved to the door. She didn't have it in her to listen to another lecture. "You've made your point loud and clear. Thank you for coming. If you don't mind, I've got a tryout to prepare for."

"True, but all I'm asking you to do is examine your motives." Her father rose from the couch and with two long strides, finally took her in his arms.

Parker stiffened. Was he hugging or suffocating her? Who could tell?

"I know all this seems harsh," he said. "But it's for the best. It really is."

Clutched to his chest, Parker bit her lip so hard she tasted blood. Maybe he believed his own rhetoric, but this was her life. She wasn't fourteen, and he wasn't choosing her classes at Calmont Prep anymore.

She wriggled out of his hold and swung the door open.

A bellboy with a curled fist raised his hand to knock. When he saw them both crowded by the doorway, he took in a quick breath. "Mr. Sherbourne?" His eyes went wide. "I'm...I'm just delivering breakfast."

Her father squeezed around her to straighten first the boy's name tag and then his collar. "Harold, we always need to look our best at the Sherbourne." He nodded once to make his point, and without a backward glance at either of them, he strode down the hallway.

"Shit," Harold said under his breath. He clapped his hand across his mouth as he looked at Parker. "God, I'm sorry, Ms. Sherbourne."

"Don't worry." Parker patted his arm and pulled the cart in herself. "He never sticks around to see the damage he causes."

Harold let out a long sigh.

"Believe me, I'm right there with you."

Not for the first time, she shut the door on her father.

CHAPTER 2

CARLY PULLED OUT THE LAST drawer in the long line of taping tables in the training room and forced her eyes to focus. She had been restocking all morning, and the colored pre-wrap and tape in the drawer swam in her vision as if she were looking through a giant kaleidoscope. A better analogy would be an abstract oil painting. For Carly, rolling tape on an injured athlete was an art form; finding the delicate balance between comfort and support, sending an injured athlete onto the field with the confidence that he could make the game-changing play. Even the ripping noise when she pulled tape off the roll was music to her ears.

Standing there, with tape in her hand, she wondered if she would ever get a chance to show her skill. Players were superstitious, usually going back to the same taper again and again. Even if they weren't, they usually didn't want a female athletic trainer. Something about small fingers and weak hands. She dropped several silver PowerFlex rolls into empty spaces in the drawer. There. Done.

What next? Sanitizing the hydrotherapy pool? That's what she would suggest if she were trying to get an unwanted hire to quit. *No matter, I'll beat them at their own game.*

"Hey, Allen?" She crossed to the doorway of her colleague's windowed office at the back of the facility.

Allen raised his head. He had such a baby face Carly wondered if he had grown a beard to look older.

"I'm done," she said. "I could take a stab at cleaning the whirlpools, unless you had something else in mind."

"That would be great." He gave her a real smile and lifted a *football is my life* mug as a thanks. "They're on today's schedule."

Carly smiled back. Allen seemed like a good guy. He had looked her straight in the eyes and given her a firm handshake when she had introduced herself that morning. What's more, he had been professional, cordial even, as he had shown her around the Rollers' kingdom.

"Okay. Point me in the direction of the—"

"Allen!" A man wearing a yellow security shirt stuck his head through the training room front door. "That kicker's here. You coming?"

"You bet." Allen jumped up, exited his office, and then turned to Carly in the main room. "We've got a new kicker trying out. You want to come watch before you tackle the whirlpools?"

Carly nodded. "Sure."

"Then come on. This should be especially interesting since—"

Allen backed right into Buck, who was waiting for them outside in the hallway. Allen ricocheted around. "Oh, sorry, Buck."

Buck stood like a mountain in the middle of the hall, his hands knotted up into tight balls at his side. "The travesty continues." He didn't give Carly a glance.

"Now wait a second." Allen gave all his attention to their boss. "Let's give Marina a chance. She may have something up her sleeve. And I don't see how things can get much worse this season." He patted Buck on the back before they moved around the corner and out of Carly's earshot.

Carly smiled. With his sunny nature, Allen seemed like the pony that a racing track kept with the thoroughbred to calm its nerves.

She didn't need to hear the rest of the conversation to know that Buck was grumbling about something. It *was* odd that the Rollers were scouting a new kicker this far into the season. The kicker already on the roster wasn't a superstar, but he was decent; actually, the special teams were regularly outperforming the other units. Buck might actually have something to gripe about this time.

Carly watched the men disappear. She was still invited, right? Allen hadn't looked back after the initial invitation, but neither of them had told her not to come. She trotted after them.

Stepping onto the field from the players' entrance, even with the stadium empty, sent chills down Carly's spine. No expense had been spared, from the natural warm-weather Bermuda grass on the ground to the silver and green banners flapping in the breeze at the very top. An eighty-foot jumbotron towered over the far end, and yet the stadium was still intimate. The seats rolled almost down to the field, putting the first-row fans so close they could practically touch the players as they moved around the field. The hulking bodies, the blazing speed, the hurtling passes, and the loud thuds and grunts—the stadium brought the game to the fans in full HD.

A small group of people stood on the sideline near the end zone. Other people from the organization—players, coaches, the security guard who had grabbed Allen—dotted the stadium on and off the field.

Carly swiveled to take them all in. Why would so many people show up to see a kicker try out? A lot of people considered kickers and punters an inferior subspecies of football players. She wasn't one of them, of course. She had respect for any athlete, but something unusual must be going on here.

Allen and Buck, with Carly on their heels, stopped twenty yards out, giving the group at the end zone its privacy. Three players dressed in helmets and full pads trotted out to the field. Carly recognized the center and the holder by the numbers on their practice uniforms, but the third player, face shrouded under the helmet, remained a mystery.

Carly sucked in a breath. The way the kicker moved was… was… She searched for a word.

Exquisite.

Her mouth went dry. There was absolutely no extraneous or wasted motion. The player's feet struck the ground in a straight line, and by extension, his body appeared to float effortlessly across the field. He personified grace and agility. Goose bumps ran up her arms. What the hell? This was a guy!

She quickly averted her gaze. Had Buck noticed? She hadn't been on the job for a full day, and already she was proving him right. She stole a glance at the head trainer.

Luckily, he had eyes only for the field, and the way he rocked back on his heels told Carly he did not approve of what he was watching.

She swallowed hard, willed herself not to react, and returned her gaze to the field. He was just another athlete. Her line of work was creating smooth movement. She was just reacting to him as a five-star example, right?

※

Adrenaline coursed through Parker's body. Now that she was finally active and moving, everything felt right. Her father's visit to her hotel room had been distressing. The car ride over from the hotel had been awkward, to say the least. Tanya, at first, had tried to make small talk, but the memory of rolling around in twisted sheets loomed too large between them. In the end, her agent had pulled out her cell phone even before they cleared the hotel's long driveway.

Jogging onto the field with the soft grass under her cleats and her helmet fitting snuggly on her head, she was in her element for the first time in a while. The rhythm of movement had always called to her. Had filled the empty places in her heart. There was something primal in physical activity that stilled her mind and opened up pathways to her soul. She was moving, and it didn't matter that almost everyone on the sideline was against her. Or that other people in her life had walked away.

This contest was only about her and a ball and if she could send it through the uprights. She rarely lost this kind of battle.

She quickly assessed the conditions on the unfamiliar field. The playing surface was dry; her plant foot would stick. No wind, thank God. The air temperature was a little cooler than she would've preferred, but it wouldn't affect her length.

The long snapper set up, and the holder dropped to one knee, waiting for the ball.

Parker pulled a breath deep into her lungs and let muscle memory of the kick she had perfected in high school take over.

She dropped three paces behind the ball and two to the left. Centering her body weight over her hips, she bounced lightly on the balls of her feet. She was ready.

She would have to trust that she would get a good snap and that the holder would align the ball correctly. Kicking a point after was an exercise in true faith. Everyone started moving at the same time, praying that the others were in sync.

These men were professionals, right? They'd do their job.

"Ready. Ready," the snapper called out, and the holder stretched out his hand to receive the ball.

Here goes nothing.

As she had done a thousand times before, Parker strode toward the ball in a diagonal line. First, the jab step, then the drive step, and then finally, a solid plant by the ball with her left foot. The ball, which had arrived right on time, was leaning, laces out, slightly into the holder. She squared her torso and met the sweet spot on the football with the top of her foot.

BAM!

Her speed and consistency were textbook-perfect; the ball sailed smack right through the center of the uprights.

"Again!" Hill, the special teams coach, smoothed a hand over his receding hairline and waved her back without giving her even a second to celebrate.

When she made that one too, he called for a dozen more, all from different angles on the field.

"Back to the twenty."

Parker moved back five yards and sent the ball through the uprights—not quite as high, but her aim was still true. The coach kept pushing her back, way past the distance she would ever have to cover after a touchdown, but the coach must have wanted to see where the end of her leg was. She finally missed at the thirty-yard line.

A shrill whistle echoed through the stadium, and the players in front of her leaped up. Hekekia, the long snapper from Hawaii, probably resentful that he had been called in on his day off, stomped off the turf, but the holder, Veris, a five-year, five-team veteran, turned to Parker with an outstretched hand.

"I thought the Internet had it wrong."

"Had what wrong?" Parker lifted her hand slowly to meet his. She might be sliding into a trap.

"Your excellent percentage in college. But no, you got game."

Parker took his hand gratefully and held it for a beat. "That was basically a publicity stunt as well. My father donated a lot of money to the school. They had to play me."

"Then it was a win-win for everyone. You can kick." He raised a hand in farewell. "Maybe we'll see you around, Parker Sherbourne. I'll happily play on the right side of history with you."

"Thanks." She watched his back as he trotted off the field. *I still have to make the team.* Her mind whirled. How was she going to play this? As if she were already a High Roller? As if she didn't care? As if Marina needed her more than she wanted to kick? No, she should come at it honestly. She loved football, and she wanted this job. Actually, for the first time in her life, she needed this job—both for the paycheck and to prove her father wrong.

She spun to the group on the sidelines. Every type of reaction possible greeted her. The scowl on Hill's face deeply creased his forehead. Marina, in her elegant suit, clapped her hands softly and nodded repeatedly. A man to whom she had not been introduced stared at her with an open mouth. Tanya's face, however, was the most interesting. Her lips slid into an easy smile, and her eyes popped wide, pushed up and out, no doubt, by the dollar signs she saw.

Parker shuddered. Strangely with everything they had done the night before, right now was the first time their relationship felt a little dirty.

Marina separated herself from the group and bobbed her head to the left to avoid the helmet as she met Parker with a friendly hug. "Well done, young lady," she whispered as she held Parker as close as she could with all the padding. A familiar floral smell swirled around them. What were the odds? Marina wore the same expensive perfume as Parker's mother.

"Thank you, Mrs. Fisher. I—"

The words caught in Parker's throat as if all the air had been squeezed from her body.

Over Marina's shoulder, she spotted another spectator. A shapely woman, curvy but not at all soft, stood on the sidelines. Silky, brown waves framed an angelic face. Parker had grown up in the land of sculptured movie stars, but this woman's beauty was artless and fresh and spoke of cool breezes on sunny days. She dug her cleats into the field to prevent herself from floating over.

"None of this Mrs. Fisher business." Marina released Parker from the hug.

Parker forced herself to take a breath and refocus on the woman in front of her.

"Don't make me feel any older than I am. Call me Marina."

"Oh. Okay." Parker barely found her voice again. Her gaze drifted back to the sidelines.

Wait a sec. The woman was staring at her too—although not in the way Parker would have liked. She was looking at her with all sorts of questions, as if her favorite food had mysteriously gone bad. Heat crept up her neck and across her cheeks.

Marina peered into the helmet. "Oh, no need to be embarrassed, dear. I'm old. That's a fact. I just don't like to be reminded of it."

"It's not that…" Parker wrenched her gaze from the woman and fumbled with the chin strap on her helmet. "I… I…" She glanced back. Who was she? A girlfriend? A reporter?

Shit, she had to get her libido in check. She couldn't fuck this up. She slid around Marina to literally put her back to temptation. "I… I'm the right one for this job." Her voice gained strength since she was now looking only at Marina. "I've been kicking field goals since I was ten in the Pop Warner youth leagues." She grabbed her helmet by the face mask and slid it off her head so she could give her full attention to, if luck would have it, her future employer.

Freed from the helmet, her hair tumbled down her back. She shook her head to get some air under it. She had totally forgotten how sweaty the helmets were.

———— ✦ ————

"She's female?" Carly blurted out and then clamped a hand over her mouth.

No. that was a bad assumption. Long, blonde hair meant nothing these days. It was so shiny and lovely, and the sun was hitting it just right as it spread out over his or her back. The tiniest tingle fluttered beneath Carly's stomach.

"Oh, that's right. I didn't get a chance to tell you." Allen laughed. "You thought we'd race out here for any kicker?"

Carly blew out a long breath. Of course, she could see it now: the curve at the kicker's hips. The uniform had been just baggy enough to reinforce all of Carly's prejudices about what gender the kicker had been. Her bad.

"You're not the only experiment on this team." Allen nodded at her.

As usual, Carly said nothing and let the situation play out around her. Frankly, she didn't know how to react. Sure, she felt a little stupid that she had made the assumption that the kicker was male. Especially since the flutters in her stomach had been telling her the truth from the beginning. Guys had never made her quiver like this. She pressed a palm to her chest. She still liked women.

Out on the field, the kicker couldn't keep still. She bounced on her toes and waved one arm as she talked to Marina. In anyone else, the constant movement would have been annoying, but for her, it seemed right. Motion was this woman's language, and the call came loud and clear: she was very comfortable with herself and her place in the world.

Must be nice.

"Come on," Buck said, breaking the spell. "Show's over. Back to work." He turned and lumbered down the field.

"You have to admit, boss, she was pretty good." Allen followed closely on his heels.

"For a sideshow, maybe." Buck glanced back at Carly. "I'm beginning to feel that's all there is lately. Put a big top on the stadium, and it could be *Circus, Circus.*"

Allen chuckled. "Sure going to be an interesting rest of the season."

Buck only grunted in response as he led the way into the players' tunnel.

Carly followed and forced down the desire to turn around and take another look at the kicker.

She barely remembered sanitizing the whirlpools. Muscle memory from her previous job with the Runnin' Rebels took over as she scrubbed the stainless steel with the chemicals. She tried to pay attention. She didn't want to make a stupid mistake on the first day of a new job, but the image of long, blonde hair, shimmering in the sun and tumbling down a Rollers uniform, kept popping into her mind. No matter how many times she tried to push it away, it played in her head like a Hollywood blockbuster in slow motion, complete with dramatic music.

On a bathroom break, Carly leaned against the cool tiled wall and made sure she was connected to the stadium Wi-Fi—she, Minnie Lee, and Teddy shared the lowest data plan imaginable—and typed *female + kicker + High Rollers* into Google on her phone.

What am I doing?

The blue line was only halfway across the search bar when she tapped the phone back to the home screen. Even if Buck hadn't banned any off-the-field activities, thinking about this woman was the very definition of idiotic—it was unlikely they would ever cross paths again. This had to be a stunt. There were no women in the NFL. Besides, a relationship, or even a friendship with anyone, at the moment was counterproductive to her long-term goals. There would be plenty of time for a life later, when her career and bank account were solid. She slipped the phone back into her pocket and, with the single-minded focus that had gotten her to the NFL in the first place, banished the kicker from her mind.

Long after the sun had set, she slid her key into the door of her family's apartment to find her grandmother sitting where

Carly had left her that morning—on the same stool, in the same bathrobe. Her legs were even crossed at the ankles just as before. If Carly hadn't known better, she would have guessed that Minnie Lee had only gotten up to get the out-of-date *People* magazine that she was leafing through.

In reality, Minnie Lee had had the fullest day of any of them, starting with banana pudding for two and a long shift at the diner and ending with a healthful meal and homework help for Teddy. But for a moment, Carly stood at the door, smiling at the only real mother she had ever known, and imagined a day when Minnie Lee could laze around, reading about current Hollywood celebrities and European royalty.

"Oh, sweetheart. You're home!" Minnie Lee dropped the magazine on the counter with a plop. "Tell me all about your day. Did you like it?"

"It's going to be good, I think. I hope." She walked over and kissed her grandmother on the temple. "Buck Johnson didn't give me the warmest welcome. No surprise there. But his assistant seems okay with me being around, and tomorrow the players show up and I'll get a real feel for the job."

"See, I told you."

"It's only the first day. A hundred things could still go wrong." The kicker bouncing lightly on her toes slipped into her mind. Son of a gun, she had lost her focus. Carly pushed her right back out again.

"It's just as easy to be positive about things, you know? Try it." Minnie Lee rolled stiffly out of her chair and moved to the fridge. "You hungry?"

"No. I ate at the stadium. Oh my goodness, Grandma, they've got this unbelievable cafeteria. Well, actually, it's more like an upscale buffet. A lot like that casino where we splurged when I got the UNLV job. The place with a million choices. Remember?"

"Of course."

"You know, we should do that again. Celebrate somewhere if I last the week."

"You will. This cafeteria of yours. How are the desserts?" Minnie Lee wrapped her bathrobe around her. The cool desert air seeped in through the thin walls of the apartment.

"Don't worry. Not even close to yours. Even on your worst day."

"I beg your pardon." Minnie Lee tipped her head at Carly. "I don't have a worst day."

Carly laughed and met her grandmother's gaze. "It looks like I'm going to get all my meals for free when I'm working."

"Really?"

Carly nodded. They were probably both thinking the same thing. The weekly food bill would be a little less. The extra money would quickly get eaten up by other expenses—they both knew that—but maybe if a few more of these freebies dropped into their laps…

Carly pushed that thought out as well. She didn't want to jinx their future. There was a dangerous line between being relentlessly positive, as her grandmother called it, and living in a fantasy world.

"Hey?" She glanced at the empty spot in front of the TV. "Where's Teddy?"

"In his room." Her grandmother inclined her head to the back of the apartment. "He said he had a lot of homework, but I think it's something else. I tried to get whatever it was out of him at dinner but got nowhere. There's something, though. He passed on another helping of the banana pudding."

"That's not good."

"I know. Too tired to take a shot?"

"Never." Carly grabbed her backpack off the sofa, made her way to Teddy's room, and knocked softly on the door. "Can I come in?"

"I have homework." The muffled reply came through the closed door.

"Can you take a break? I have something for you." Carly slid a Rollers baseball cap out of the front pocket of her backpack and opened the door.

Teddy sat at his desk with an open math book, plotting out the problems on graph paper. He glanced at her. "What's up?"

"For you." She held the hat out and was about to drop it playfully on his head but set it on the desk at the last moment.

He fingered the skeleton's eyes. "Thanks."

"It's a special edition. Only players have silver on the brim."

"Cool."

One-word responses. No bad jokes. Her grandmother was right. Something was definitely wrong.

"How was school today?" Carly sat on Teddy's single bed, smoothing down the frayed edge of the Batman comforter that he had outgrown ages ago.

"Fine."

"And your science lab? How'd that go?"

Teddy rotated his wrist until the joint popped. Had she really gotten lucky on the first guess? He only cracked his wrist when he was nervous about something.

"Fine." But this time he didn't sound so fine.

Carly bit her lip. She would have to move slowly. "Did you get to finish?"

She remembered Mrs. Shantley, the honors IPS teacher, all too well—already ancient and stuck in her ways when Carly had attended Cannon Junior High. Teddy said the labs had gotten even harder. No one could finish them in one period.

"No."

"Does she still let you come in at lunch?"

"Yeah, but…"

Carly waited.

Teddy dropped his head.

"But what?" she asked gently.

After a moment, he met her gaze. "My lab partner's a jerk."

Right. He probably wanted Teddy to do all the work. She had certainly been in that position. She could run with this. "What do you mean jerk?"

"He doesn't know anything." Anger crept into Teddy's voice.

"Okay." She didn't want to scare him off. "What did he say or do that pissed you off so much?"

Teddy turned around but kept his head down. "He told me that…" He paused and opened his mouth, but no words came out.

This was more than an unfinished lab. "What did he say, sweet pea?" Carly used her grandmother's pet name for him. Minnie Lee always voiced it with such love, and Teddy clearly needed some.

"First he said I was lazy." The words finally tumbled out in a rush.

"Lazy? You?" Carly couldn't hold back the surprise in her voice. No one was more industrious than Teddy. He had straight As in science thanks to an inward focus that CEOs of Fortune 500 companies would envy.

"Yeah, that's what he said. Loud and clear for everyone to hear." Teddy squeezed his hand into a fist. "He's an asshole." He glanced up, guilt flashing in his eyes. Their grandmother had a strict no-swearing policy.

Carly met his gaze and let the asshole part go. "Why? Why would he say that you're lazy?"

"Well, no one likes working with Justin. He gets Cs on his tests, and when Mrs. Shantley paired us up, he said he didn't want to work with me."

"Because?"

"He said that my father was probably a stupid janitor or cook or both and that I was a dumb Mexican too, and he didn't want to end up doing all the work." Once he began, the words tumbled out, and his eyes flooded with tears. He bit his upper lip in an obvious attempt to fight them back.

Her stomach clenched. She longed to reach out and take Teddy in her arms. To tell him that everything was going to be okay. But she knew from her own experience that it wasn't. For her, the name-calling had started in middle school too with the viciousness of twelve-year-old girls. It had only stopped when she started managing the high school football team and became one of the football pack.

"Did Mrs. Shantley hear him? What did she say?" She tried to keep her voice calm.

"She just told us to stop arguing and get back to work."

"She didn't ask what you were arguing about?"

"No. She only talks. She never listens."

Carly nodded. She remembered how Mrs. Shantley ran her class. She never moved out from behind her desk and rarely interacted with the kids. "You're right. Justin is a complete asshole."

Teddy's eyes widened.

"Don't tell Grandma." Carly widened her eyes as well.

His lips curved up just a bit.

"So, what do you think about what he said?" she asked.

"Well, it's not true. I work really hard. And I get As on all my tests. I'm not lazy."

"I know. And probably everyone, including Justin, knows that too. So, I'm thinking maybe this is not about you. If he gets Cs, he's probably worried that a straight-A student won't want to partner up with him, and if he attacks you first, then maybe he won't have to feel bad about himself."

Teddy dropped the pencil and clutched his hand shut. "That doesn't make it right."

"No, it doesn't, but it says more about Justin than it does about you. Does this make any sense?"

Teddy took a deep breath and nodded.

"What about the other part?" Carly started up again. "What about him calling you a dumb Mexican?"

"That made me really mad." Teddy opened his hand. Little red marks from his nails rose angrily on his palms. "I don't even know if I am Mexican. I mean, I look a lot like Oscar, and his family's from Puerto Rico. How can I tell Justin off if I don't even know who I am?"

Carly sighed and reached out for Teddy's hand. "I don't know. Honestly, T, I haven't figured out how to deal with it myself."

"You haven't?"

"No. I wonder who my father might be all the time. I wonder where this crazy eye color comes from or this hair." She tugged on thick waves that were just shy of curls. "Neither you nor Grandma has this."

"I wish at least we had the same dad."

"Me too." Carly moved in and rubbed his palm with her thumb to smooth out the angry half-moons in the center.

"Do you think our mother will ever come back? She could give us answers."

"Maybe, but I wouldn't get your hopes up. Truly, I don't know." What she did know was that they were both better off if their mother didn't return. From the little Carly remembered about their mom, she was big trouble. Teddy, on the other hand, had no memory of her whatsoever. Sitting there, Carly couldn't decide which reality was worse.

They stared at each other in silence for a beat as their personal truths swirled around them.

Finally, Carly squeezed Teddy's hand and released it. "So, you go in tomorrow and get the lab done whether Justin's there or not, and if he is and starts up again, tell him that you're already done. That he can finish the lab on his own. Just threaten to walk out. That's what he's really scared of. That you'll dump him, and he won't be able to finish it."

"You think?"

"I do, but can you talk to Mrs. Shantley if that doesn't work?" Carly asked, although she already knew the answer.

"Not really. She doesn't listen to us."

"Okay. We'll figure out a plan B later if we need one."

Teddy nodded, his eyes clear.

Carly smiled. And if plan B didn't work, they'd find plan C and D and make their way down the alphabet if they had to. They were in this together. "I bet if we go out and ask Grandma nicely, there might be a little more of that banana pudding for both of us."

"But what about my math?"

"You can finish it later."

"Okay." Teddy jumped up, his mood seemingly rebounding. "A person can't turn down dessert when it comes his way, right, sis?"

"Those are words to live by if I ever heard any. Come on."

"Hey, you know why it takes longer in baseball to run from second base to third than it does to run from first to second base?" Teddy's brown eyes already sparkled with the answer.

Humor. That had always been Teddy's coping mechanism.

"No. Why?" Carly played along.

"Because there is a short stop between second and third."

"Ha." Carly punched him gently on the shoulder. "Good one."

Teddy smiled. His teeth, never straightened, slanted here and there and only added to his silly grin.

Carly opened the door to find two plates had already been set on the breakfast bar. Each had a dollop of banana pudding and a full serving of their grandmother's love.

<hr />

"Here you go, ladies. Drinks for two." The waitress dropped two flower-shaped coasters onto the table. *Tulip,* the name of the Sherbourne's most exclusive cocktail bar, ran across the center in a light purple squiggle.

"Excellent." Tanya rose halfway out of her chair to inspect the signature cocktail before the waitress set it down. "Heavenly Tulip?"

"Yes. Made by our best mixologist." The waitress pointed to the red Angostura Bitters shaped like a tulip floating in clouds of frothy egg white. "And for you, miss, mineral water bottled at the height of springtime."

"Really?" Parker asked.

The waitress leaned in, her long, dark hair almost brushing Parker's shoulder. "I wouldn't know. My boss makes me say that."

Parker shuddered. Which boss? At the end of that line of bosses was, of course, her father. Had he personally written that script? She wouldn't put it past him.

The waitress slid the bubbling water across the table to Parker. "May I get you anything else?" She straightened to show off her curves in the tight uniform. Two pink tulip petals rose from her lace skirt to push up her breasts.

Was she flirting or just angling for a bigger tip? If Parker was being honest, the view was nice in either scenario.

"I'll let you know." Parker smiled at the waitress to keep the door open. She wasn't sure she was really interested, but some habits died hard.

"Sure. I'm April, if you need anything else."

Parker studied the waitress as she walked away.

"Are you going to let every cute behind distract you?" Tanya peered at her over the rim of the overpriced cocktail. "Or are you ready to get to business?"

Parker shrugged. "You got the contract?"

"I got a copy, yes." She pulled a document from an expensive leather work bag by her side and handed it to Parker. "There are one or two addendums that I would like to include, but basically, it's boilerplate, and if you like what you see, Marina would like to hold a conference and have you sign in front of the press."

"I can do that." She flipped the coaster off the table and caught it one-handed.

"Good. Right after another tryout tomorrow." Tanya held up her hand as Parker opened her mouth to protest. "I know. I know. This one is public, for the media."

"Seriously?" Parker's eyebrows pulled together.

"You do know that a PAT specialist isn't a real position, right?" Tanya's tone turned patronizing.

"Of course. But it could be, if I play well."

"No. It never will be. If you're interested in playing well and often, you should head back to the Fire. Maybe win another championship as the number-one goalie. I might even be able to represent you. Gridiron's looking to expand."

Parker shook her head. "Been there, done that. I need something new."

Tanya met her gaze. Her eyes narrowed, and for a second she wore the exact same expression as her father had that morning. "Marina wanted you to be especially aware of the fourth paragraph."

Parker picked up the contract and scanned the page.

"This one? The one that says *a player will cooperate with the media and will participate upon request in reasonable activities to promote the club and the league?*"

"Yes, and note the part about publicity rights and you granting the Rollers the authority to use your likeness and name and basically every known fact about you for their own purposes."

"Okay. I signed something like that with the Fire."

"I'm sure you did. But there, Parker, they wanted you as a player as I've said. Here, with the Rollers, it's more about what you can do for them off the field. The first woman in the NFL and all that."

Parker sighed deeply.

"Don't worry. You'll get on the field sooner rather than later, if that makes you feel any better. Fisher won't have anything to publicize if you sit on the sidelines for the rest of the season. But let's be really clear on this. You're not there to take the team to the Super Bowl or anything."

Parker eyed her agent. Tanya was only ten or so years older than her own twenty-seven years, and yet she was treating her as if she were a child coming in off the playground from a game of kickball. She flipped the coaster higher and again caught it with ease. "Yes, I get it."

"Good. Because..." Tanya jabbed the contract with a short, manicured fingernail. "I won't let you sign unless we can immediately enter into a group license with the NFL Players Association for profit sharing on official merchandise and the okay to go out and get individual endorsement deals with whoever we want. We could really clean up in that last area. I hear Under Armour is looking for a female spokesperson. There's just one question. Do you really think you can put the ball through the uprights in a live game?"

"I know I can." Parker bristled at Tanya's question.

"Well then, we might all make a pretty penny before this stunt plays out. We should celebrate." Tanya raised her nearly empty glass for a toast and smiled hungrily at Parker.

Again, Parker shivered. Take off all their clothes, exchange the cocktail table for a bed, and this was exactly how Tanya had looked at her last night. Parker blew out a breath and raised her drink. She should be dancing in the end zone. Why then did the clinking glasses sound like tiny alarm bells?

Tanya moved the festivities around the lake to Harvest. The Sherbourne's steak house, of course, had a celebrity chef's name emblazoned above the door. When the maître d' told them that they would have to wait two hours for a table, Tanya threw Parker's last name out, and they were ushered past an elderly couple, all gussied up, and seated immediately.

"Don't do that." Parker slid into the big booth right on the edge of the huge lake in the center of the hotel's complex.

"Why not?"

"Because it's not right." She rolled her shoulders back into the soft seat. "We took this table away from that couple. What if they are celebrating their fiftieth wedding anniversary and they wanted something special?"

"If they've survived fifty years, they'll get through this minor disappointment too."

Every time a Sherbourne employee heard Parker's last name, they went all bootlicker on her. Nothing she could say ever made any difference. Her father's shadow loomed too large. Instead, she called over the maître d' and leaned in so no one else, especially Tanya, could hear. "Please charge that couple's meal to my family's account. And add a bottle of nice champagne to whatever they order."

"What did you do?" Tanya asked as she scanned the menu.

"Nothing. Just made sure they had a good table too."

Tanya glanced around the luxurious room of red brocade and sparkling crystal chandeliers. "Every table's a winner. This place rocks. Your dad—"

Parker held up her hand. "Yeah, I know. You don't have to say it."

But apparently, there were plenty of things that Tanya felt she did need to say. She talked nonstop over dinner, drawing up at least a dozen different plans of attack for the next few months. Nike, Gatorade, Red Bull, even Avon were all sniffing around with endorsement deals, and according to Tanya, a simple kick through the uprights could bring in a ton of money. It was all business until, after dinner, the elevator doors slid open on the sixteenth floor. Tanya eyed Parker up and down.

"Right now, I kind of wish there wasn't a potential contract burning a hole in my briefcase." Tanya moved out into the hall. "Then we could play another sort of game." She ran a hand down Parker's chest, lingering for a heartbeat between her breasts.

The heat of lust swirled in the hallway, and despite the quiet unrest that had plagued Parker all day, she remembered the magic Tanya's tongue had created the night before. It could again if she just stopped talking.

Tanya's phone rang. A huge iPhone was in her hand lightning-fast. "Oh, fuck, it's my boss." Her words cut through the desire like a knife.

She turned her back on Parker. "Hello?... Tonight?... Yes, I'll write it up and get it to you before your commute in the morning... No, you're not interrupting anything."

Tanya ended the call. "Something's come up." She reached up to kiss Parker fully on the mouth. "The car will pick us up at noon."

She was leaving? One second ago, Parker hadn't been sure Tanya's annoying personality was worth an orgasm or two. She still wasn't sure, but she wanted to be the one to make that call. Not Tanya.

Surprising even herself, Parker reached out for Tanya's arm and pulled her back around. "You're not up for a rematch?"

"I've got to play a different game tonight." Tanya's fingers were already on the phone, pulling up whatever her boss wanted. "Sleep tight."

Parker winced. Tanya's was the second backside she had seen in less than twelve hours.

Once Tanya had disappeared into her room, Parker reached for her own cell. "Dad cut me off," she blurted out the minute her brother picked up.

Silence.

In the background, his teenage son pounded on a big bass drum, one of many overindulgent birthday gifts through the years.

"Oh my God, Jem. You knew?" She tapped her foot on the dark carpet of the hallway.

"Dad might have mentioned something in passing before he left for Paris."

"And you couldn't pick up a phone to warn me?" She jammed her key card into the door lock. It flashed red.

"He made me promise that I wouldn't. Parker, he said you—"

"I know what he said. I was there." She took a deep breath and slid the key into the lock—this time slowly. The lights went green, and she slipped into her room. The perfume of fresh flowers greeted her. "Can I ask a favor?"

"What?" The hesitation in his voice boomed louder than his son's bass drum.

"You know I'm in Vegas, trying out for the Rollers. I'll probably sign a contract with them tomorrow. But who knows how long it'll last. I was wondering if you could lend me the family suite here while I ride it out. Seems silly to get my own place for what could be only a few weeks."

46

This time the silence lasted far longer.

"You don't have to tell Dad." She was fully aware that she sounded as if she were a teenager sneaking out of the house and asking her goodie-two-shoes brother to cover for her.

"He'll find out, Parker. He always does. And then it's on me as well."

"Yeah, but by that time this whole dog-and-pony show will be over. And if it isn't, I'll have time and money to find a long-term rental or an apartment or something."

"Parker, I—"

"You're the only one I can really count on."

Jem's sigh was almost loud enough to travel the three hundred miles from Malibu without a series of cell towers.

"Okay." He drew the word out into its full two syllables. "I'll place the call right now. Starting tomorrow?"

"Thanks, oh and Jem?"

"There's more?"

"Not really. There's going to be a bill from Harvest. Let me know how much it is, and I'll Square Cash it to you."

"You don't want Dad to comp that too?"

"Nope. That one's on me."

He hung up without further comment.

Parker dropped her cell on the bedside table and studied her reflection in the mirror over the chest of drawers. A faint worry line rode across the middle of her forehead. Her brother had been her go-to guy when they had been kids. Now there were as many pauses as words in their phone calls. She ran a finger across the wrinkle, trying to smooth it back into her forehead.

That's why she had always gravitated to sports. Her body and not her mind was in action. Tomorrow, she'd be the one to walk away from Tanya, her father, and even Jem to kick a bunch of balls through the goalposts. She stretched out her skin between her thumb and forefinger. The wrinkle disappeared. Sports were far safer than people.

And yet the thought popped into her head like a rainbow on a rainy day.

I have to find out who that woman on the field was.

———— ✦ ————

I have to stop thinking about that woman on the field.

Carly forced herself to lie still as a statue. Her grandmother snored softly across the room, and the last thing Carly wanted was to wake her up. Why she wasn't sound asleep as well was a complete mystery. She had been so tired earlier, she had almost dropped headfirst into her banana pudding, and her grandmother had convinced her to climb into her own bed rather than make up the couch in the living room.

Now her mind raced with a thousand worries. Her only chance was to unpack the day, unravel her problems until they seemed manageable. Teddy's dilemma loomed large. He had mentioned his father, or lack of one, at least three times in as many weeks. Not for the first time, Carly wished her mother had left some information about Teddy's father—or hers—before she had taken off all those years ago. It would really help Teddy if he knew a little bit more about who he was.

Her mind slipped over to Teddy's school problems. She could go talk to Mrs. Shantley. The old biddy might actually think Teddy and that little creep were arguing over who got to pour the base into the acid. But she could hardly ask for an afternoon off from work practically before she had started. She imagined standing before Buck, explaining that her brother needed her. He would pull ten of those resumes from his drawer and throw them on the desk. Besides, it was better if Teddy learned to fight his own battles. This wouldn't be the last of them.

And then there was the Rollers. She had survived the first day pretty well—without the players. Tomorrow could be a whole new ball game.

The kicker slipped back into Carly's mind. She had popped up during the banana pudding, when she brushed her teeth, and now. Surely, she wasn't the reason sleep evaded her. Okay, the woman moved around the field like a finely tuned sports car with a deep, sensual rumble. But they hadn't even exchanged a hello.

With a little luck, she would never see the kicker again, and this problem would fade of its own accord. There would be plenty of time for thoughts like these once she proved herself to Buck and moved her family into a nice, new life. Then she could relax, find someone special, and finally broach the subject of her sexuality with her family.

Besides, it wasn't as if the kicker knew she even existed.

CHAPTER 3

"Told you the new AT was fine as hell," said a man with a deep voice as he entered the training room.

"Yeah, you said she was fine, but not a dime piece." The second voice was even lower.

"Her eyes are gold, like a lion."

"Man, quit playing."

"Just look at her."

Her back to the door, Carly froze with the first *fine*. This had to be some sort of record. Fewer than twenty-four hours on the job, and the players were already talking about her as if she wasn't even there.

The morning's team meeting had just ended, which could not have been fun for anyone. The Rollers had lost on Sunday, 28–6, to the Cougars, a team with a losing record almost as bad as theirs, and the head coach's yelling had reached the training room. But a lousy meeting was no excuse. Carly had met this kind of harassment at UNLV. It was everywhere. There, however, she had a head AT who didn't put up with any unprofessional behavior. Here, who knew?

She turned to face them and instantly recognized the stocky man whose chiseled muscles filled out a Rollers sweat-wicking T-shirt. J.J. Ocean, the future Hall of Famer who was riding out the end of his career with the Rollers. He was chasing an eighth straight year with one thousand rushing yards and was the only one who had benefited when the Rollers' quarterback went down early in the season. Since then, the team's strategy had turned to the running game.

She approached J.J. with an outstretched hand. "Carly Bartlet. I just started yesterday."

"Nice to meet you, Carly." He took her hand, raised it to his lips, and looked at her as if she had just won the lottery.

Carly tamped down the urge to jerk her hand back. Instead, she tried to slide it out of his grasp as soon as the kiss ended. J.J. held tight before he finally let go.

She hid her hand behind her back and rubbed it against her shirt. "Nice to meet you, too," Carly said although he hadn't introduced himself. "Can I help you? Do you have an injury?"

J.J. looked her up and down, cocking his head and glancing at his friend, whom Carly didn't recognize.

"I think I pulled something. I felt a tweak during the game right about here." J.J. slowly rubbed the inside of his thigh near the pubic bone. "Didn't think much of it. But I woke up today, and it was as sore as my girlfriend on a Monday morning. I think it needs some attention."

J.J.'s companion snickered and raised his eyebrows at Carly, leaving no doubt in her mind that the treatment they were seeking had nothing to do with a football injury.

She rubbed the back of her neck to give herself a minute to think. Crap, she was in a real pickle. Ogling her across a training room was one thing, but thanks to the girlfriend comment and probably a fake groin injury, they had opened the door to a hostile work environment with her very first patient.

She couldn't let J.J. Ocean silence her, but she also had to fit into the male athletic culture where proving you could take it was key. It was a fine line, and Carly's toes were bruised from walking it for so long even in her short career. Carly took in a deep breath, shook out the hand that J.J. had kissed, and opened her mouth. "I…um…I…"

"No need to say anything. Let's just get to the treatment."

"Seriously, J.J.?" Allen ambled over from the other side of the room. "If you really have a groin pull, come here. I'll slap some ice packs on you myself and give you a rubdown on the back table. If you don't, get out of my training room and stop wasting my trainer's time."

J.J. laughed and raised both palms toward Allen. "I'm good. I'm good."

"Then take off." He glanced at the schedule posted on the whiteboard. "The O-line walk-through is starting."

"I'm cool on her. I'll be coming round." J.J. dug an elbow into his friend's ribs as they backed out of the room.

Carly stared at the empty doorway and kept her head up. She didn't want to look at Allen.

"Hey." He forced the point.

Carly closed her eyes for a few beats of her heart and then pivoted.

Allen's eyes were soft; he looked at her almost as a father would. "Sorry about those boneheads."

"It's okay." Allen had meant well; he didn't know that his interference had only made it worse. She was now fair game if J.J. came back when he wasn't there to stop him.

"Don't worry. I got your back." He clearly thought the problem was over.

"Thanks." Carly forced a smiled to her lips. It died the instant Allen swung around to a young cornerback with a grade-two ankle sprain.

Maybe, in hindsight, Allen had done her a real favor. She had been making a mess of the conversation and for sure wasn't going to call J.J. out. If Allen hadn't come over, she would probably still be standing there, stammering or, worse, rubbing J.J.'s groin. Allen, however, couldn't fight her battles for the rest of the season. And she couldn't complain to Buck—that would pretty much be ringing her own death knell. *What am I going to do?*

"Hey, Allen." The young cornerback swiped a screen on his phone while Allen pulled out the pads to an EMS machine. "Did you know we're trying out a girl kicker?"

Carly's ears perked up. She would've welcomed any diversion to pull her away from the J.J. dilemma. She glanced at the whiteboard. There was nothing on the schedule.

"Another one?" Allen smoothed out the pads on the cornerback's ankle.

"No. The same one as yesterday. Today's tryout is public. Parker Sherbourne, right? It's all over Pro Football Weekly. Says here she plays professional soccer, played football in high school and college, and, oh, she does well with the ladies." He swung around his phone to show them pictures of Parker with several hot women—looking into a blonde's eyes, dropping a kiss on a redhead's lips.

A whooshing sensation rolled through Carly's head, and she looked away. *She's gay?* The pictures said yes. And they also said that she was a player on and off the field.

"Holy shit, did you know she's the daughter of Keaton Sherbourne? Why is she doing this? She must have money coming out of her ass—" He glanced at Carly. A flush crept over his cheeks. "I mean her behind… I…I mean, no one would want to be a kicker if they could do anything else."

"Who knows why anyone does anything?" Allen flattened down a pad that hadn't adhered to the cornerback's skin.

"When? Does it say when she'll be trying out?" Carly surprised herself by drifting over.

The cornerback ran a finger across his cell. "Doesn't say. But you could find out. I mean we're at the place where it is happening."

Allen glanced at her, his eyebrows forming a V-shape.

"Whatever. I'm not that interested." Jesus, she was making Buck's point for him. She was the most unprofessional employee in the room. Carly turned back to her work and wrapped herself in all the resolutions from the night before to not think about the kicker.

But her skin tingled as if someone had just run a finger down her spine. Parker. Parker Sherbourne. The name rolled silently off her tongue.

The kicker was back.

Once again Marina, Hill, and Tanya stood on the sidelines of the Rollers' field. Not the main one, but a smaller practice field that butted up against the stadium. A small John Deere tractor had pulled portable goalposts to the far end and was parked at an angle to pull them right out again when Parker was done.

The press snapped pictures as Parker trotted out onto the field in full pads and a Rollers practice jersey. The fake turf of this field felt like a slab of moon rock under her cleats. Like most professionals, she preferred natural grass, but it wouldn't put her off her game. The tryout, this time staged for the press, marched along with almost soldier-like efficiency. Hidden behind mirrored sunglasses, Hill barked out orders, and Parker, like the highly trained athlete she was, hopped to.

A shrill whistle cut through the air, and the spectacle was over. Marina, all smiles, rushed out to Parker with a Rollers jersey, her name and number already emblazoned in big green letters on the back.

A thrill of excitement ran through Parker when she saw number eight, her number in high school. Wow. Marina had gone to a lot of trouble to make her feel at home.

Only as the extravaganza wound down did Parker scan the field. She scoured the crowd, looking for wavy hair and the face of an angel.

Damn, not here. She must be a girlfriend after all.

After the tryout, they bustled her straight into the press room and plunked her down at a table. She picked up the black and green pen and scrawled her name on the contract. And just like that, Parker Sherbourne became the first female player in the NFL.

Afterward, the questions from the press came at her fast and furious. "Hey, Sherbourne, are you for real?" She threw the answers back in quick volleys. "You saw me kick out there. What do you think?" A snicker in the back made her hackles rise. "Look, most NFL pros have won the genetic lottery. They're strong, agile, incredibly athletic. Kickers are different. They're not born; they're built. If they really commit, listen to their coaches, and practice hard, a lot of people could become good kickers. I've kicked since I was ten. I've perfected my form. I may not have the length, but I've got the accuracy. And I never get rattled." The snickers stopped. "I'm absolutely for real."

"How does it feel to be the first woman playing in the NFL?" another reporter shouted.

"I can't tell you quite yet." She glanced at Hill, off to the side. He had declined to sit at the table with her, and his face read like stone behind the mirrored sunglasses he hadn't taken off. "I certainly hope to get on the field during a game. But I'll tell you this. Gender doesn't play football. Athletes do."

A third reporter flung his hand into the air. "What do you think about the Rollers' chances for the rest of the season?"

"The Rollers are so much more than their win–loss record. I can't tell you how excited I am to be part of this incredible organization. Marina Fisher is a true visionary, and I couldn't be prouder that she believes in me."

Perfect. Professional. No drama. Let her father put that in his pipe and smoke it.

When the press and the Rollers' front office filed out—Hill left without one word of encouragement or any word at all—she finally stood up. A band of tightness squeezed the back of her thigh. She had kicked more field goals in the last two days than she had in years, and her hamstring cried out in protest.

"What's the matter?" Tanya eyed her critically.

"Nothing." Boy, she was observant. Parker filed that tidbit away. "I'm just a little stiff. To be expected."

"You should see a trainer before you head back to the hotel." Her brows drew together in concern.

Not for me. It's her bottom line she's worried about. Parker put some weight on her leg. Just tight, not strained. "It's not that bad."

"Go see the trainer. We need to be seen celebrating this momentous event tonight, and you can't be hobbling around."

"Seriously, I'm okay."

"Why risk it? We can't jeopardize this before it's even begun," Tanya said as if it had already been decided. "I've called in a few photographers to Tulip at eight. Don't worry. We've worked together before. They won't be obtrusive, and you'll get the kind of publicity that'll do us good."

"Do I have a choice in this?"

"No. And can you wear something a little more feminine? Like a dress or a frilly top or something?"

"I didn't bring anything like that with me."

"Okay. I'll get something sent up to your room."

"Tanya, I need to be completely myself when I'm not in front of the press or proving myself to the team."

"I know you're out and proud with the Fire, and believe me, no one is happier about that than I am." That hungry smile again. "But let's not lead with your sexuality tonight. We're looking for personal endorsements from men and women."

Parker pursed her lips. "The way I dress has nothing to do with my sexuality."

"Well, it has plenty to do with commercial promotion and cash in both our pockets."

The wake-up call came loud and clear. Since her dad had cut her off, she needed to think about these things as well. "Fine. Just send something up. But not too girly."

"Gotcha. Call the hotel and give me access to your room. And I'll send the car back. It'll be waiting for you at the main exit." She strode from the room, her phone already out, probably reeling in the next client.

Parker wandered the halls, looking for the training room around every corner. A wrong turn brought her to the players' lounge, where most of the starting defense sat in huge movie theater chairs, clutching Xbox controllers and screaming at a large flat-screen TV. Guns blazing, soldiers in WWI uniforms ran around virtual-reality France. Another turn led her into an indoor practice field that stretched out over an acre and was far more beautiful than anything at the Fire stadium.

The sign for the training room popped up all of a sudden. She paused outside the door. Did she really want to announce herself as the rookie who needed treatment after only two tryouts?

All that walking had loosened up her hamstring, and the ice in her hotel room was just as cold as the ice inside. Maybe she should get a taxi and head back to the Sherbourne.

"They don't bite." A massive, square-shouldered man had materialized in the hall beside her. "You're the new kicker, right?" His soft voice did not match his bulk, and his brown eyes were kind and fringed with long, dark lashes.

Parker introduced herself with a smile.

"Denarius Brown. Right defensive end. Come on in. I'll show you around."

Shrugging, Parker let herself be led into the room. The training room was bright and active. Two men rode stationary bikes in the center. Other players rested on custom treatment tables surrounded by state-of-the-art equipment. Rock music circled down from speakers in the ceiling and signaled a whole new monetary universe compared to women's sports.

"Allen. This is Parker Sherbourne, the new kicker."

Everyone in the room froze at the announcement. Sure, they were all professionals, as she had said at the press conference, but no one was really happy about her being there. First, she was a woman, and second, she had taken a roster spot away from one of their own. Parker didn't know which one was worse in their eyes.

Either way, they stared at her as if she had turned up naked at a church social. A little nudity had never bothered her, so she smiled at the trainer with the baby face who was on his way over.

"You need treatment, or you just taking a tour?" he asked.

She dropped a hand to the back of her thigh. "My hamstring's a little sore." Guess she was staying after all.

"Then you're in the right place." He glanced at the open door that led to the storeroom and called out, "Carly."

Parker followed his gaze, waiting for this Carly—what kind of nickname was that for a male trainer?

—————◆❦◆—————

Carly dropped the drink cooler Allen had sent her in to retrieve. What now? A Gatorade emergency? Maybe the ice bags weren't quite full enough?

She stuck her head out the door and found Allen standing in the middle of the room, blocking her view of the people he was chatting with.

She tried to wipe her growing frustration from her face before she spoke. "Yeah? How can I help?"

"You got a customer," he called.

Right, another player with a fake injury high up on the thigh?

He stepped to one side to reveal—

Holy moly.

Carly's heart flip-flopped. Parker Sherbourne—that was her name, right?—stood not fifteen feet away from her. This close and in light pads, she looked like an Amazon. Energy, almost electric in origin, swirled around her. The buzz tugged at her from all the way across the room.

"Hi." Parker raised a hand. Her gaze met Carly's and held on, her hazel eyes smoldering with intensity.

Denarius cocked his head and glanced back and forth between them. "You two know each other?"

"No." Parker shook her head. "Parker Sherbourne. Just dropping in for a little treatment."

"Carly Bartlet." The space between them crackled with a static charge. "What's…what's troubling you?"

"My hamstring. It's not that bad." Before anyone could reply, Parker quickly added, "Maybe a quick exam. You can never be too careful. Right?"

"Right." Carly swallowed hard. "Come on. Let's check you out." She moved to a free table, slid the backrest down, and tapped the padded bench.

Like an Olympic gymnast, Parker hopped up and flipped over on her stomach with such agility that Carly almost went weak at the knees. There was no wasted energy or fumbling gestures. Carly, who was trained to study movement, marveled how efficient Parker's body was…and, as she could see, so firm and tight as she twisted on the table.

Lying flat, Parker shook her right thigh. "What's the prognosis? Am I going to make it?"

Carly filled her lungs and dropped her hand onto Parker's leg. A blue spark jumped between them. Carly jerked her hand up.

"Whoa," Parker said. "What was that?"

"Static electricity?" Carly glanced at her hand. There was nothing there now. "Sorry."

Parker wriggled on the table. "No. It's all good. I just wasn't expecting it."

Neither was I.

"Should we try this again?" Swallowing, Carly gingerly placed one finger on the back of Parker's knee. Thank goodness. Nothing this time. With a long, slow stroke, she slid her right hand up the ropey muscle of the hamstring. *You've got to be kidding me.*

Of course, her skin was soft and warm and made for touching. She pushed all the way up to the top of the thigh. Tightness was there, but nothing to be too concerned about. An ice bath, rest, and light compression, and she should be good to go.

Just like any other client.

Carly dug in slightly with her thumb on her second pass, and a warm electric current jumped to meet her touch. For the first time in her career, she was all too aware if she drifted just a little, her hands would be all over Parker's shapely behind. She pulled away from the table as if she had been stung, shaking out her hands as she moved back.

"You're right." Her voice was breathless. "Not too bad at all. Let's get you into the ice pool."

Rapidly putting space between them, she led the way into the hydrotherapy room, separated from the treatment room by a glass wall. The six-by-ten cold plunge sat in between two other dips: a hot whirlpool and another, larger tub with an underwater treadmill. An injured running back sidestepped in the second one. Water frothed around his waist as he gritted his teeth in obvious pain.

Carly glanced at the screen on the wall, where an underwater camera recorded his movements. "You okay, Stephon?"

"Fuck, no. This shit hurts."

"Take shorter steps. It'll hurt less and put you back on the field faster."

The player made the adjustment. "Yeah. That's better."

The short conversation centered her. "You know the drill?" Carly turned back to Parker and pointed to the cold plunge. "To your waist for fifteen minutes."

"Yep. Sadly, I've been here before." Parker slipped off her sneakers and socks, made a neat pile on the tile, and dropped her Rollers practice shorts and jersey on top.

Carly tried to focus on the growing pile to give her some privacy. With each piece of clothing, however, her gaze darted back to Parker's body to see the slow reveal. "You want gloves or a hat?" she asked when Parker had completed undressing.

"No, I'm good." She gave Carly a lopsided grin.

Parker stood at the entrance to the pool in tight compression shorts that cupped her shapely behind. She reached out with one foot to test the water. Her legs were smooth, with long, lean muscles, and clearly created for stretching.

Stop! She's a client.

Frowning, Parker gingerly dropped one foot into the pool. "Son of a mother trucker, this is cold."

Despite herself, Carly smiled at Parker's choice of swear words. Refreshing, since in her line of work, four-letter words were king.

"Okay. Here goes nothing." Parker shrugged off her top and tossed it onto the nearby pile. The Nike swoosh on her black sports bra matched the compression shorts, and her state of undress revealed a flat stomach complete with a six-pack and the soft curve of each breast.

Carly barely had time to appreciate the view before Parker slipped into the pool to her waist.

"This can't be above freezing." Parker held her arms above her head so they didn't touch the water and swiveled to face Carly.

"Forty-seven degrees." Carly choked the words out. Standing in the near-freezing water, Parker's body tightened. Especially her breasts. They rounded into perfect half spheres, and the nipples swiftly hardened underneath the bra. Carly jerked her head away, but again her gaze drifted back almost of its own accord. Parker's body, especially with her hands still above her head, was one long, delicious line. Carly dropped a hand below her navel. Something began to twist in her stomach.

This wasn't like her. She never ogled women. Usually, she had to get to know someone really, really well before she got physical. Two times, if anyone was counting.

"Remind me why I'm doing this?" Parker danced around in the water.

Carly forced her gaze up to Parker's eyes. Were they sparkling? With what? The cold? Something else?

"Immersion in water this cold causes the blood vessels in your hamstring to constrict. When you get out, the blood shoots into your muscles and speeds up repair."

"Promise?" Parker gave her a lopsided grin.

"Promise." The huskiness in her reply surprised her, as if she were committing to more than medical treatment.

I've got to get out of here. She stumbled back until her hand was on the handle of the glass door. "Fifteen minutes. The clock's over there." She waved to a digital wall clock beneath yet another Rollers logo. "Come find me when you're done. I'll get you a compression sleeve for later."

Without waiting for a response, she opened the glass door to the training room. Tom Petty's drawl dropped out of the speakers in the ceiling. He was singing about good girls and bad boys and free falls that never ended.

Yep, Tom. That's how it works. The door closed behind her with a soft whoosh and put an end to whatever possibilities were swirling in the waters of the plunge pool.

I'm losing my touch.

Parker had done everything she could think of to keep Carly in the room. She had stripped down to almost nothing; she had blurted out the cutest expletive she had heard her nephew say, and she had faced her when her body had reacted to the cold. That last one alone should have sealed the deal. Her face was pleasant enough, nothing special, especially now that she had seen Carly's, but her body had never, ever let her down.

While her gaydar was still pinging all over the place, maybe it was wrong. Maybe only she had felt that zing of excitement when Carly had walked out of the storage room and Parker had seen those gorgeous eyes. Were they gold or brown? Shit, she would take a five-yard penalty on every kick to be able to stare into their depths and figure the color out.

Beyond the glass wall, Carly moved around the training room. Allen called her over, handed her a chart, saying something that brought a shy smile to her lips and eased the tension in her face. Even a room away, Parker marveled at the transformation. How her normally serious expression softened, making her even more stunning.

I can do that. Talk to her like that. She could totally be my next diversion.

Warmth flooded her core. Fantasizing about a night with Carly was certainly one way to stay warm in water only a polar bear could enjoy.

The clock finally measured out fifteen minutes, and Parker quickly slid out. Her teeth chattered as she grabbed a couple of towels and dried off as best she could. After pulling her shorts and shirt off the pile, she headed to the nearest bathroom to change. When she returned, a black compression brace was neatly draped over her shoes. She looked for Carly in the hydrotherapy room and beyond the glass doors but couldn't find her anywhere. She must have snuck in and left the brace while Parker had been gone.

Damn. Her first real miss of the day.

———◆◇◆———

"Did anything exciting happen at work today?" Minnie Lee stood behind the breakfast bar, stirring honey into a cup of mint tea. The honey, which dripped out of a plastic straw, had been *liberated,* as Minnie Lee liked to call it, from the diner. In truth, she only took things they were about to throw out, but Carly knew it made her feel daring to imply otherwise.

"No. Nothing." Carly shook her head. Home was a safe space. She had left J.J., the kicker, and everything else outside the door when she came in.

Minnie raised her eyebrows and slid the cup of tea to Carly, who swooped it up gratefully. "Well, actually, I met some of the players."

"Who?" Splayed out on the couch, Teddy peered at her over a paperback with a decomposing zombie on the cover.

"Denarius Brown, for one."

"Seriously?" Teddy's eyes widened, and he dropped his graphic novel on the coffee table.

"Yes. And I think I'll be able to get you to a game at some point soon, and you can meet him if you'd like."

"That would be awesome."

Teddy, clearly, was in a better mood, so she decided to risk the question she had wanted to ask the moment she had walked in. "How's the lab going?"

"Good. Almost done."

"What about…?" She turned and with her back to Minnie Lee silently mouthed the word *a-hole* at him and added out loud, "Justin?"

Teddy bit his lip so he wouldn't laugh. "I did what you said. Told him that we could do the procedures at lunch and then we could each do the math at home by ourselves. That way he wouldn't have to do my work."

"And he said?" Minnie asked, pouring herself a cup of tea.

Carly handed her the half-used honey stick from the counter.

"Grandma, you should have seen his face. He was so mad his eyes kind of bulged out. He told me that I should give him the math so he could check my work. I told him I was good and walked away. Sweet Luck totally came through. It just took a while."

"Oh, Teddy. I'm really proud of you." Carly smiled at her little brother. If only she could handle J.J. half as well.

"You know." Teddy got up from the couch. "I think I'll finish so I can turn it in during class tomorrow, and he won't be able to get his hands on it."

"He might just learn his lesson. And if he does," Carly hurriedly added, "and he apologizes or isn't rude to you anymore, you have to be gracious."

"I do?"

"Theodore." Minnie Lee shook her head. "Two wrongs don't make a right."

Teddy trudged the rest of the way to his room. He rarely had the upper hand in anything, and Carly knew in his mind they were asking him to give away what little power he had. "Hey, what was the lab about anyway?" she asked.

"Static electricity and conductivity. Did you know that when two materials or objects have different charges, electricity can build between them?" Excitement took hold, and he didn't wait for an answer. "And when you place them next to each other, electrons that would normally repel each other can jump from one to the other to create a more perfect current. It's like an electron dance."

"Really? I don't remember that lab."

"Well, it's pretty cool. It's not just rubbing a balloon and watching your hair stand up. It's all about movement and attraction. It can even happen with people."

Carly almost choked on her tea.

Her brother gave one final nod and disappeared into his room.

"What's that all about?" Minnie Lee eyed her carefully.

"What?"

"That look on your face."

Carly shrugged. "There's no look on my face."

"You'll tell me when you're ready." Minnie Lee wrapped her fingers around her mug. "Well, I'm glad that lab problem resolved itself as well as it did."

"Me too, but the other thing I didn't tell you about last night was that Teddy was asking about our mother and his father."

Minnie Lee sighed. "That's not the first time."

"I know. It's come up more than once lately. What are we going to tell him?"

"The truth. Teddy's a bright boy. He'll be able to spot an evasion a mile away."

"Yeah, but can you imagine what it'll do to him if we tell him our mother just dropped him off on your doorstep, with barely a word, when he was three days old? Just a 'here you go' and 'his name is Theodore'?"

Minnie Lee reached out to take Carly's hand in hers. "Maybe we can soften the blow with a cup of cocoa and tell him that she couldn't even take care of herself, and she loved him enough to make sure that he was in a good place."

"That's a better spin on it." Carly bit the inside of her cheek. "Grandma, why do you think she never came back?"

Minnie Lee looked down at her tea for a long time before she finally answered. "Because she doesn't know where we are."

Carly's forehead furrowed. "Of course, she does. You left a forwarding address at our last apartment." She stared at her grandmother across the bar when she didn't respond. "I saw you do it."

Minnie Lee shook her head. "It was a fake address."

Carly wasn't sure that she had heard her right. "You gave them a fake address?"

Her grandmother nodded.

Carly's mouth dropped open. She had willfully separated her and Teddy from their mother? It made no sense. A great pressure descended on her as if she were sinking to the bottom of the ocean.

"Breathe, sweetheart. Breathe."

Carly took a raspy breath. "Why?" Her voice was shaky. "Why would you do that?"

"Well…" Minnie Lee released Carly's hand and let out a deep breath herself. "Harsh truth? I was being selfish." She pursed her lips and nodded several times before she continued. "I was sixty when your mother showed up with Teddy. I had already turned my life upside down for you. Don't get me wrong. I love you and Teddy more than I ever thought possible. You make my life complete, and I wouldn't change anything, not one thing, but…" Her voice dropped to barely a whisper. "I just didn't have it in me to raise a third grandchild."

The silence spread out between them, almost pushing them apart.

Finally, Minnie Lee looked up and met Carly's gaze. Her blue eyes, so like those of Carly's mother, swirled with pain and regret…and something else that Carly couldn't pinpoint.

Resilience.

Don't judge me, they said.

How could she not? Her mother might have come back if she had known where to find them. Sometimes, all people had to do was get a lucky break or grow up a little bit to realize that past decisions were wrong. Her grandmother had robbed her mother and Teddy—and her—of a second chance. A lump formed in Carly's throat. She couldn't even look at Minnie Lee.

Instead, she glanced around the tiny, broken apartment—the cracked sink, the ratty couch from Goodwill, the cabinets that looked as if they were made out of plywood. It was a dump. The three of them were just making ends meet in this place.

Her grandmother was still working at an age when most had been retired for years. And she was doing that for Teddy and her, not for herself. And she had been doing it with a positive mindset that had continued to shine no matter what life threw at her.

Minnie Lee rarely talked about her life in Alabama before she had come to Las Vegas to rescue Carly when her mother had abandoned her at six. But when she did, Carly gathered her days had been full of friends and laughter. Las Vegas had only been filled with hardship—two kids and no money.

The truth hit Carly hard. Her grandmother had sacrificed everything for them. She had always known that in the abstract, of course, but she had accepted it with a naiveté and the selfishness of a child. There was a limit. And Minnie Lee had to protect herself.

She bobbed back to the top of the ocean.

"I get it." Carly finally turned her gaze to her grandmother.

"You do?" Minnie Lee's shoulders dropped half a foot, and she sagged against the breakfast bar.

"Yeah, I do." Carly slipped around the counter to embrace her. "My mother made mistakes and expected you to clean them up. She had no intention of helping at all. She never came back between leaving me and bringing Teddy, did she?"

Minnie Lee shook her head.

"She clearly knew where we lived. Good heavens, I probably would have run too."

They clung to each other, saying nothing, although the fact that she would never see her mother again banged up against her skull and a dull ache spread through her body. Finally, Minnie Lee pushed Carly away and rocked back and forth on her heels, giving her the once-over.

"Now, what're you going to wear to that party thing, on Friday?" Minnie Lee tried to infuse a brightness she clearly didn't feel into a new topic.

"I don't know." Carly rubbed her hands over her face, suddenly exhausted. The Rollers' party-slash-command appearance tomorrow was yet another stress on her plate. Any more and she might break into hives. "Oh, I liberated some of the peach cobbler from the cafeteria today. Taste it, and you'll see it's got nothing on yours."

"Ha. I knew it." Minnie Lee grinned and then swiveled to get a fork while Carly pulled out of her backpack the neatly wrapped cobbler that her new friend in the cafeteria had given her.

Parker glared at the two identical blouses draped over the sofa in the Sherbourne family suite—two tops, different sizes, same huge flowers. Flowers? Seriously? She would be a walking advertisement for her father's hotel if she showed up to Tanya's photo op in this blouse. Coincidence or was Tanya just that good? Parker flipped the absurdly expensive price tag over. Yep, *Springtime.* Her father's high-end clothing store downstairs. Of course, Tanya knew that Parker was worth a lot more to Gridiron Sports with her father's businesses behind her.

Parker stood in the center room of the two-bedroom family suite near the top of the main tower. The hotel reserved the very top for the real high rollers and big spenders. Nonetheless, no expense had been spared. The huge living room, full of plush furniture, and a small game room opened up to a wrap-around balcony complete with a Jacuzzi, a fire pit, and an outdoor wet bar. The view, though, was the main attraction. Las Vegas in all its neon glory spread out in both directions, and when it got too much, a swipe on the hotel's smartphone sent curtains down over the floor-to-ceiling windows. On either side of the great room, two master bedroom suites flowed off the living room—each with four hundred square feet, huge flat-screen TVs, and walk-in closets. Even the ensuite spa bathrooms had views of the Strip from the soaker tubs.

The panorama and the luxury were lost on Parker. She knew the suite like the back of her hand. She and Jem had spent a lot of time here when they had been kids. They used to call their trips here *camping* since they had to share a room. Her father had used the hotel as a hub for some of his biggest deals—he said Las Vegas put people in a spending mood—and he had brought Jem and Parker along to give their mother a break.

"A break from what?" she had asked Jem once when their father had left them alone for a meeting. Even then, she had seen a trip to the hotel as more punishment than fun.

"I don't know," he answered.

"From us, you think?"

"No." Jem sounded unsure, though. "Maybe from too much yoga or meditation."

"You need breaks from those things?" she had asked. Even at a young age, she knew something was up. "I think those are the breaks."

"Guess not." Jem had shrugged, and a pained look had slipped across her face.

Her phone quacked and brought her back. Her nephew had changed her email notification setting the last time she visited their Malibu estate, and she had never bothered to change it back.

Tanya's text read, *Where are you? LATE.*

B right there, Parker typed. She tossed the phone to the couch and grabbed the larger of the tops. Oh my God. It had frilly sleeves. She was definitely going to have to send for her own clothes now that it looked as if she would be here for a while.

CHAPTER 4

THE NEXT DAY AFTER TEAM meetings, film study, and conditioning, Parker stood with the field goal unit at the far end of the practice field. On a shrill whistle, they dropped down into a group stretch and then straight into a series of reverse crunches and push-ups.

Happy to finally be in motion, Parker reveled in the conditioning. She always had. It was the only time the chaos of her mind stilled. As a kid, she had turned to sports to quiet the growing unrest from her mother's absence and her budding sexuality, and had found a home. Her thoughts and worries ground to a halt, and she entered the Zen of the moment to become a better version of herself—the athlete, the one who connected wholly to something, the one who couldn't disappoint.

As always, the run calmed her, and she jumped into the following drills with ease. They perfected prancing ponies and ball drops in which they walked the width of the field, releasing balls to practice hand-eye coordination. They did snapping drills and other set plays.

Eventually, Hill gathered them all together. "Sherbourne, Veris will hold and Hekekia will snap for you."

Across the circle, the two men she had met at her tryouts perked up. Veris, the holder, sauntered over and gave her a quick thumbs-up. "On the way to making history here."

Just as sullen as at the tryouts, Hekekia was tight-lipped.

"Don't mind him." Veris shrugged. "He takes a while to come around."

They settled into short field goal kicks, trying to find a rhythm between snap, hold, and kick. Hill threw some advice at them but mostly let them work things out on their own. All in all a good first day, until Hill blew the final whistle and called them to the team meeting at the end of practice.

"Get the equipment and the duffels, rookie." Hekekia headed over to the other side of the field.

Parker quickly packed the footballs, tees, and holders into the bags and, hitching one on each shoulder, ran after the long snapper. "What's your problem?" she called out to his back. When he didn't turn around, she started trotting. "Hey, I'm talking to you."

"My problem?" Hekekia picked up the pace. "The guy they placed on injured reserve for you was a good friend. And when you score, or rather *if* you score, you, not us, will get face time with the press. Nobody'll give me the time of day. This isn't just about you. I'm one of the best snappers in the league. I got over one hundred thousand views on my YouTube channel."

He strode on, leaving Parker struggling with the bags.

"Here come the grass killers." A strapping tight end sneered as the kicking unit joined the main practice.

Parker shook her head. Although integral to the team— often a win rested on their feet alone—kickers got little respect. The rest of the team thought they just stood around on the sidelines on game day, literally killing grass.

"Up your ass, Zennel," the first-string kicker said.

"You wish, Koch."

An air horn rang in the stadium, ending the conversation.

"Let's go. Bring it up. Bring it up." The head coach called them in.

The team formed a circle around Rhodes. Some, Parker included, took a knee.

"Fellas, we're in fucking slow motion here," Rhodes shouted. "This is bullshit. This isn't how we practice. You think the other teams are practicing like this?"

"No, sir," came a couple of half-hearted shouts from the players.

"That's right. I tell you, they're not. This is the adversity part where we push through the losses and come out on the other side. Come on. Let's stop feeling sorry for ourselves and drive through this season. We're not going to do it with this slow-motion bullshit."

Rhodes continued, four-letter words popping up every couple of seconds. This kind of coaching style—the yelling, the swearing, the tearing-down of egos—had never worked for Parker. Fidgeting, she pulled out a tuft of grass by her knee as her mind drifted back to an earlier kick when her foot had hit the ball a little low. She mentally replayed the kick, this time hitting it straight on.

"Sherbourne!" Rhodes yanked her back into the huddle.

"Yes, coach," she shouted back.

"Get up here. You're going to kick. Show the team what you can do."

Adrenaline whooshed through her veins. This was the moment Parker lived for—when everything on a sports field boiled down to one crucial moment. Live or die.

"You make it, we'll call it a day. You don't, there's some gassers calling our names."

A whoop of protest rose from the team. "Come on, coach." A big linebacker who clearly struggled with conditioning whined like a toddler. "Not this shit again."

Parker got up slowly. Not what shit? Was he setting her up? "From where?" she asked.

"The fifteen. Just like a regular point after. Show us you can do it here first."

Okay. Fifteen she could do. She could make that kick in her sleep, and the team could hit the showers early, patting her on the back the whole time. Maybe Rhodes was setting her up in a good way.

"Hekekia. Veris. Take the field."

An assistant coach tossed Hekekia a ball as he trotted out to the ten-yard line.

Jogging out herself, Parker could feel the men's gazes boring a hole in her back as the grumbling continued.

"Come on. We've got this." Parker patted Veris on his helmet and took her three steps back.

"Right through the middle. Like clockwork." Veris gave her another thumbs-up.

Hekekia grunted as he bent down into position.

"Hit that shit," someone called out.

"Don't choke," came another shout.

Parker shook off the insult, and the players around her faded away. The moment right before physical execution, the stillness before the explosion of movement, had always been a special place for her. The second where everything slowed down and what she had to do spread out around her, sweeping her up into a momentum far bigger than she.

"Ready. Ready," she called out and began her forward movement.

Hekekia snapped the ball.

Fuck! No!

It was...high. Reaching up, Veris brought it down, but he struggled with the tilt.

Instantly, Parker could see the position of the ball was off and tried to adjust. It was no good. She was already in motion. Her plant foot slipped, and her kicking foot skimmed the grass before connecting with the leather. The ball soared into the air.

"To the left! To the left!" someone from the sidelines yelled out.

Parker dropped her head as her stomach lurched. It wasn't going in.

"No. No. No." Now the cries were a chorus.

At the last moment, Parker jerked her head up to watch the ball fly high and far enough but sail just to the right of the goalposts. Son of a bitch.

"Ahhhhh." The sideline groaned as one.

Several thumps of helmets hitting the grass in anger and then the commentary erupted.

"Way to go, Sherbourne."

"That's what you get when you hire a girl for a man's job."

Parker rolled her eyes. But the fact was she hadn't made the kick. The reason almost didn't matter. The miss was on her.

"Motherfucker. I ain't doing no gassers."

Another air horn echoed across the field, and Rhodes called, "Line up!"

Parker yanked on her face mask as she jogged to the sideline to join the rest of the team.

"Sorry about that." Veris was at her shoulder.

"It wasn't your fault." Parker's voice was thin. She jogged ahead to poke Hekekia in the back of one shoulder. "Hey. Did you snap high on purpose?"

He turned and looked her straight in the eyes. "Why would I? I don't want to run." He cocked his head and raised his eyebrows in what could've been a challenge before he ran away.

Parker almost leaped after him—this time grabbing him by the shoulder to spin him around. If she had been on the soccer pitch and still the captain of the team, she would have. But here, on the football field, and as just a rookie, she couldn't make a big deal out of one stupid snap. If she did, she would look like the biggest loser possible, as if she were dumping her mistake on someone else. Not one person looked her way as she jogged to the sideline and took her place by her teammates.

The whistle sounded, and Parker dug her cleats into the grass, getting a jump on the first of many sprints to the other side of the field, which, thanks to her, was a group activity.

No matter, she could take whatever the Rollers physically threw at her. It was the mental game she wasn't so sure about. She had to find a way to reach Hekekia, or her tenure with the Rollers was going to be a complete disaster.

As the public bus inched up the Strip, Carly glanced out at the neon lights and the wandering tourists, only to drop her head on the hard plastic headrest. After her crazy day at work, she was exhausted, like barely-keep-your-eyes-open exhausted, and the muscles in her lower back were starting to seize up.

Her grandmother had taught her never to give in to discomfort, so she got up to stretch and then impulsively jumped off the bus when it stopped in front of the Bellagio

Hotel. She would walk to her next connection and maybe loosen up her back.

She had taken only two steps when the first lyrical notes of "Time to Say Goodbye" echoed around her. She glanced across Las Vegas Boulevard to the huge lake in front of the Bellagio Hotel. Already water from the fountains gyrated high into the air. The streams, illuminated from within, danced to the pulse of the Andrea Bocelli song.

I shouldn't. I need to get home.

And yet her tired feet crossed the street almost of their own accord.

Like a reward, a white jet of water mixed with light shot up over four hundred sixty feet into the night sky to the crescendoing music. So much of Vegas seemed tacky to Carly in a rhinestone and sequin kind of way, but the fountains at the Bellagio were real diamonds in that equation. The large crowd jammed into several balustrades that jutted over the water.

Hurrying to join them, she squeezed around a cooing couple, eyes wide with amazement as they stared out across the lake. Their hands gripped two huge sippy cups—one, a giant red and blue Eiffel Tower, the other, a big plastic guitar slung around the man's neck. A long straw ran out of its fretboard, and he sucked noisily on something bright red and frozen. Who needed that much alcohol? And how much did something like that cost?

Only in Vegas.

"Only in Vegas, right?" a soft voice echoed her exact thought.

Carly whirled around. What the hell? The kicker, of all people, leaned her hip against the stucco of the balustrade and regarded her with tired eyes. Even so, she took ownership of the space around her.

Carly furrowed her brow. What were the odds that they would run into each other out in the wild like this? Was this Teddy's electron dance?

"Parker." The kicker tapped her chest. "Don't you remember? You helped me yesterday with my hamstring."

"Yeah, I know who you are." She had to stop thinking of her as *the kicker* since she was clearly going to pop up everywhere now—in her head, at the stadium, at the Bellagio fountains. "What are you doing here?"

"Same as you. Watching the show. I need to relax after the day I had…" She let her words trail off into the music.

Carly studied the ki—Parker's body. Always in motion, she tapped the nails of one hand with the fingers of the other. She wasn't favoring her hamstring, which was good, but her shoulders rode a little high. She was clearly stressed.

"What happened?" Carly already knew the players' side of the story. They had stumbled into the training room with nothing but complaints on their lips. About the gassers, about strained muscles, about the *fucking woman* on their team who couldn't even kick straight. Babies.

Parker balled her hands into fists and shrugged. "I missed a field goal."

Carly waited for more. A few players, not defending her, of course, had mentioned that the snap had seemed off.

Parker pursed her lips and added nothing.

Carly stifled her surprise. She had expected Parker to throw her teammates under the bus. Women like her, with family money and not a day of adversity in their lives, usually took the easy way out.

"You didn't hear?" Parker swallowed. "I would've thought—"

"I heard." Carly jumped in so Parker wouldn't have to relive the embarrassment of the afternoon. Here was the second surprise: she was more than a little sorry for her. "I just wanted your side of it."

"There's just one side. I couldn't get my foot on the ball right, so I missed." Parker raised her chin defiantly. But Carly guessed it was just for show. Her shoulders still hadn't relaxed.

Carly reached out and cupped Parker's arm. Her skin was as smooth and warm and just as alive as it had been the day before. Only when Parker looked down at the fingers curled around her arm did Carly fully realize what she had done. She quickly pulled away.

"Sorry!"

"Shhh!" The man with the guitar drink stomped his foot and shook the fretboard at them like a little kid. "I'm trying to listen here."

Carly rolled her eyes at Parker, who bit back a laugh. Thank goodness for guitar guy; the whole mood of their conversation shifted for the better.

In an unspoken invitation, Parker scooted over, and Carly squeezed into the small space against the railing. The dense crowd jostled around them, forcing them even closer. Her shoulder bumped against Parker's upper arm several times until eventually Carly just gave up and leaned against Parker to watch the end of the show.

She tried to concentrate on the music, but Parker was so close, too close. The refreshing scent of ginger and mint, maybe from Parker's shampoo, tickled Carly's nose. The soft fabric from Parker's expensive sweatshirt brushed her face. She almost didn't notice the water jumping and spinning until the delicate spray fell back into the lake with the last note.

The crowd around them instantly thinned. Tourists raced off to find their next adventure, and Carly reluctantly shifted so they were no longer touching.

"I love these fountains," Parker murmured, clearly lost in the moment.

"Me too." Carly rubbed her shoulder, missing Parker's heat in the cool night air. "I'd forgotten how much. When I was a kid, we used to come down here in the summer. We would stand up there," she pointed to a point closer to the hotel's entrance. "Sometimes the water would spray on us, and for half a second we'd forget how ungodly hot it was. It was like magic."

"I came here as a kid too." Parker stretched her arms out over the railing and studied the calm lake. "With my dad and brother. When we were building our hotel, we'd stay here. They have a channel on TV that plays the fountain music. I would stare out the window and watch show after show after show."

Go figure. They had had the exact same experience as kids, even though how they had gotten there was vastly different.

"My father would never admit it." Parker shrugged. "But he always wanted his show to outshine this one."

"Does it? I've heard about the one at the Sherbourne, but I've never seen it."

"Oh, you should. The story changes with the season. As for outdoing the Bellagio..." She cocked her head back and forth. "I don't know. The Sherbourne's got all the bells and whistles, and then some. But for pure emotion, this has him beat...hands down." Parker turned to her with a lopsided smile and added, "Don't tell him I said so."

She couldn't help smiling back. "When am I ever going to meet your father?"

"You never know. But now you got me. You should give me something on you so we're even."

"That's not how it works." Carly's smile turned into a chuckle. Third surprise: Parker made her laugh. She was a lot different than she had thought she would be, but Carly wasn't about to start giving up all her secrets to a woman she had just met. Especially one who, according to the Internet, was a player in all definitions of the word. A no-go in so many ways.

"Sure, I can take a rain check on that." Parker bounced on her toes. "Hey, have you eaten? You want to grab a bite?" She leaned in, her lips slightly parted, and waited for the answer.

Carly shook her head slowly. "I already ate at the stadium." She glanced at her knockoff Fitbit. "Oh crud, I've got to get home. My family's waiting for me."

"Okay." Parker nodded and bit her bottom lip.

Something in her tone almost made Carly want to reconsider. Parker clearly needed a friend, and Carly had a weakness for vulnerability. Buck, however, did not. "Stop by the training room tomorrow," she said instead. "I'll stretch your hamstring out before practice."

That was the best she could offer.

———◦⋄◦———

"Thanks, I will." Parker's chest tightened. Another conversation that had disintegrated into only awkward pauses. It had been moving along perfectly. They had laughed together, even shared confidences—personal, but not too confessional. And yet, in two seconds, Carly would be another person walking away from her, her dark waves swinging around the back of her head.

Just to prove her right, Carly slipped into the stream of tourists and was quickly swept away.

Parker followed her bobbing head but lost her behind a large tree that canopied over the sidewalk. Still searching, Parker stared into the sea of people and saw only strangers.

— ◄ ◈ ► —

"Carly? You free for a taping?" Denarius stood in the doorway of the training room, his bulk blocking the entire entrance.

Morning meetings had just ended, and the defensive line had a little bit of time before they were due on the field. Denarius was one of many to show up asking for treatment, but he was the only one who had asked for her.

"I am." Carly's heart leaped in joy, and she patted the table nearest to her.

For such a big man, he plopped down lightly on the padded bench and stuck his right foot out at a ninety-degree angle.

"This foot?" Carly ran a hand down the back of the ankle to feel for any tender spots.

"Yeah. It feels fine," he said sheepishly. "But I hurt it bad in college, and ever since then, it feels better to tape it. I know it's silly. But I'm kind of superstitious." He rolled his eyes and shrugged one shoulder. The movement was full of self-deprecation. Rare for a football player in Carly's experience.

She laughed, grabbed a can of quick-drying adhesive, and held it out to Denarius. "Yes or no?"

"No. I get a rash sometimes."

"Good to know." She filed that tidbit away so she could later write it down in a little notebook in which she kept the players' likes and dislikes.

She quickly positioned the heel and lace pads on his ankle and settled into pre-wrapping, rolling the thin foam material from his mid-foot to the bottom of his calf muscle. "So, you played your college ball at Alabama?" she asked, falling happily into the communal role she so often found herself in as a female trainer.

"Roll Tide."

"My grandmother's from Alabama. From outside Birmingham, though, not Tuscaloosa."

"She still live there?"

"No. She's out here with me and my little brother, who's a big fan, by the way. I think she misses it sometimes, though."

"Me too. I haven't found good barbecue here at all. There are days I would kill for some decent collard greens. How'd y'all end up out here?"

Carly glanced up at Denarius. His eyes were shining, and he seemed genuinely interested in her and not in the J.J. Ocean way—another rarity in football. "My mother moved out here right after high school. I think she wanted to be a Vegas showgirl or something. And when that didn't work out, my grandmother moved out to take care of me." She marveled at how detached she sounded. Inside, her heart constricted, as it always did when she spoke about her mother. Today, the tightness spread throughout her entire chest, thanks to last night's revelation.

She concentrated on two anchor strips at the top of the pre-wrap. "Good? Not too tight?"

"No. Really comfortable, in fact. You got the touch."

"Thanks. You got people back in Alabama?"

"My whole family still lives there. Parents, two brothers, and a little sister. In a little town called Magnolia Springs. Ever hear of it?"

Carly shook her head and started with the u-shaped stirrup straps that ran over the bottom of the heel.

"It's about an hour southeast from Mobile. The Magnolia River runs through town. Bought my parents a house right on its banks. We used to live over by the Family Dollar store. Now they get their mail delivered by boat to a mailbox right on their dock." His voice blossomed with pride. "It's the only place in America where they do that year-round."

For the first time at the Rollers' facility, the tension in her shoulder muscles eased. This camaraderie between player and trainer—sharing a moment of relaxation in an otherwise grueling day—was another thing that she loved about her job. Sure, there might be jerks like J.J. on the team, but as long as there were some truly good guys like Denarius, she'd be fine.

And girls… That conversation with Parker the night before had been good too. Surprise number four.

As she finished up the foot, Denarius waxed poetically about tree-lined streets, swimming holes, and other places he had frequented as a kid. Finally, he tested the foot by flexing it against the floor. "Very nice. Thanks for letting me reminisce."

"Anytime. And I'll work up a strengthening program to wean you off the tape if you want."

Denarius threw her a half salute as he walked out.

With both the offense and defense in walk-throughs, the room was clearing out. Only special teams had no activities scheduled. She picked up the order forms that Allen had handed her at the same time as a large mug of coffee that morning. She would put hard money on the fact that in just four days, she knew the storeroom better than anyone. Just as she pivoted toward the windowless room, she heard her name again.

"Carly?"

She didn't have to even turn around to know who it was. She recognized the voice, of course, but in surprise number five, the goose bumps running up her arms had announced Parker's arrival just as clearly. Carly took a deep breath before spinning slowly on her heel to face Parker, who stood in the doorway.

She wore another pair of tight compression shorts and a formfitting Nike T-shirt that left little to the imagination. Her hair was pulled back into the high ponytail of soccer players everywhere, and her eyes were wide with a question she had yet to ask.

A slight smile touched the edges of Carly's lips. Parker stood tall and strong, and Carly realized that without knowing it, she had been on the lookout for her all morning.

"Do you still have time to stretch out my hamstring?" Parker asked. The tightness around her eyes from the night before was still there.

Carly nodded and cocked her head to the empty table to her side. "Face up, please."

Parker slid onto the table with her usual grace.

Carly's breath caught with the movement. She couldn't meet Parker's gaze, so she studied her ankle instead. It was slender and pale against the black plastic of the table. *Okay, I can do this.* She reached out to pull the leg into the stretch and froze.

What if I can't? Stretching anyone on the table involved lots of touching and close body contact. Normally, the whole experience was clinical, like a doctor's examination. But the last time she had treated Parker, Teddy's electron dance had happened, and who knew what the next science experiment would be when she circled her fingers around Parker's ankle? And she was beginning to wonder if she had suggested that Parker drop by for non-medical reasons. What kind of professional was she?

"Everything okay?" Parker raised her head to look at her.

A flush crept across her face. How long had she been just standing there?

"Yes. Of course." Carly swallowed and cleared her mind. *Just don't think about it.* She moved to the side of the table, grabbed Parker's leg, keeping it nice and straight, and placed it gently on her shoulder. *Nothing. Thank God. Just another leg.* She walked it back, pushing against Parker's body until she felt tension in the muscle. Ever so gently, she continued to press forward, monitoring the hamstring and Parker's body for resistance. Almost at the breaking point, she cupped the back of Parker's shoe. "Push your heel back into my hand."

Parker did, and Carly counted to five out loud. Turning her head to the side, so she only had a view of the training room, she once again leaned her body into Parker's leg to deepen the stretch. Another count of five and Carly felt the muscle lengthen.

"You're pretty flexible." She kept her mind clear of any other thoughts.

With those words, Parker's whole body tensed up under her.

"Relax." Parker's body softened underneath her hands, and Carly grabbed the top of the table to complete the stretch. Perfect! Calm, professional, effective... And that was when she made her mistake.

Lost in self-congratulations, she swung her head back toward the table, only to realize just how tight she was to Parker's torso.

So close, she could feel Parker's warm breath curling up over her own cheeks.

So close, she saw Parker's eyes flutter open, revealing flecks of green in the sea of hazel.

So close, she heard the soft pop of air when Parker parted her lips.

"God. I'm sorry." She leaped back and then jumped in again so Parker's leg wouldn't crash to the table.

"No. That was…ah…um…really good." Parker sat up and slid back against the wall. A wave of color rushed up her neck.

Shit, I did embarrass her.

"I'm due on the field." Parker slid from the table and, without a backward glance, strode from the room.

So much for keeping it professional.

Only a few feet down the empty hall, Parker stopped and dropped the back of her head against the wall. She curled both hands into tight fists and tapped them against the cool drywall behind her. She had been completely lost the moment Carly had pulled her leg up against her. Most of the weight had been on Carly's shoulder, but then as she had pushed, Parker could feel the roundness of Carly's breast against her calf. That brief touch, so unexpected, had sent shivers down her spine and had forced her eyes to flutter shut. When she had opened them, those golden eyes had looked at her from just a few feet away. Those eyes—shining like precious jewels. They drew you in until you were caught.

She paused. Caught? Nope, no one caught Parker Sherbourne first. And no woman ever put her so off balance. She never had trouble talking to women. A few well-chosen words and she was typing contact numbers into her phone. With Carly, all she could drum up was "ahs" and "ums." When she was around her, she became a tongue-tied middle schooler.

"You lost, rookie?" A player in a practice jersey trotted past her, his cleats clicking on the floor. "You need to go that way." He pointed away from the field to the players' parking lot. "Back to where you belong. Playing with girls."

"Really?" Parker pulled herself away from the wall and readied herself for what he might dish out next.

The player didn't even slow down to see her reaction.

She tamped down the impulse to race after him, grab his arm, and give him a piece of her mind. That stunt wouldn't get her anywhere with the team.

"Oh, I've been looking all over for you." A young man with a bushy beard and trendy jogger pants stood at the other end of the hall. "I'm Sam. They sent me down from the front office to take you to your locker." He headed in the opposite direction of the field.

"Come on. We've set you up in a place near the main locker room. It's got its own door and running water. So, it's private for changing and all that, and you'll be able to head into the locker room for meetings."

"Thanks."

"No problem. You know, Kevin Fisher, when he built this place, didn't really prepare for this kind of scenario. If you stick around, we'll make it work better."

If she stuck around? Was there dissent in the front office as well?

"Mr. Fisher thought of everything else, though. Have you had a tour of the complex?"

"Some of it."

Sam was off and running, detailing the specs of the stadium as if he were talking about his first new car. Finally, he pulled up at a closed door and waved a hand as if she had just won a grand prize on a game show. "Here we are!"

She glanced at the sign at the door. "A maintenance closet?"

"Like I said, we'll upgrade if you end up staying." His voice didn't even carry a hint of embarrassment. "We—"

"I just want to play. It doesn't matter where I get dressed to do that."

"Great, then. I'll leave you to it." He turned to immediately swivel back. "Oh, I almost forgot. The pass to the party tonight." He handed her a ticket with the skull-and-dice logo and was gone.

She swung the door open. Inside the hastily cleaned room sat a lone locker, a dirty sink, and a mop in the corner.

The locker, if not the room, was the real thing. Tall and made of maple, it contained several built-in shelves, drawers, and cubbyholes. A white home uniform draped over game-day pads perched on the top shelf. *Sherbourne* and the number eight rode the back in big, green letters. Underneath, her helmet—a new one that looked as if it was specially fitted for her, with extra pads inside—was stuffed into one of two cubbyholes. A black away-game uniform and several practice jerseys hung on a garment rod below the cubbyholes. At the bottom of the hutch, kicking cleats in Parker's size rested next to a padded stool turned upside down. Hats, water bottles, and other team swag, all with the Nike swoosh, lay neatly in boxes on the floor.

Parker pulled out the stool and flipped it over in one fluid motion. She sat down and started the process of getting dressed in light pads.

Home, sweet home...for now.

CHAPTER 5

"OH WOW, CAR, YOU LOOK great." Teddy sat at the breakfast bar, dipping a grilled cheese in a bowl of tomato soup.

"Do I?" Carly glanced at her reflection in the mirror on the coatrack. She had found the black rayon pants and the shirt with the white zigzags online for only twelve dollars each and free shipping the month before.

"Do you want something to eat before you go?" Minnie Lee held up a spatula as an invitation to a golden cheesy delight.

"No, thanks." She was too nervous to eat. As soon as Sam had handed her the VIP pass after lunch, her stomach had started to roll. The party was scary enough, but she had hoped to have at least twenty-four hours before she had to face Parker again.

Dropping the spatula on the counter, Minnie Lee joined her and smoothed an errant curl behind her ear. "Don't worry. You're going to be great," she said as if Carly had announced her troubles out loud.

"I've no idea what I'm supposed to do tonight."

"Be a High Rolling woman, it sounds like."

"Yeah, but what does that mean? I don't want to be on stage or schmooze. God, I'm so bad at both those things. I've really nothing to add to the scorecard here."

"Sure you do."

"What? I'm not front end or a player. I don't have an Ivy League education or a father who owns hotels around the world."

"Thank goodness, because then you wouldn't be you. Just be yourself, and you'll be fine. Mrs. Fisher knew what she was getting with you. You're exactly what she wants." Minnie Lee folded a thick roll of one-dollar bills into her hand.

"Grandma, what's this?"

"A safe trip there and back."

"No, I—"

"I don't want you taking the bus. Please, take a taxi. Sometimes, when I have to, I use Desert Cab." She pulled a flyer from her apron's pocket.

Carly pushed the money back at her grandmother. The wad was probably all her tips for the entire week. "No, seriously. I'll be fine."

"Yes, but I won't be. I don't like worrying about you out late at night on the bus. Who knows what time you'll be home? Do this for me."

"Okay." Carly finally circled her hand around the roll of bills. "I'll take a Lyft. Thank you."

When Carly rode up fifteen minutes later, the nightlife was in full swing on the Strip. Neon reflected in the car's windows; casino after casino overflowed with tourists and gamblers, all spilling out to Las Vegas Boulevard to create one massive party. Scantily clad women with tassels swinging from their nipples mingled with polo-clad cowboys from the Midwest and hipsters from both coasts. Just another night on the Strip.

When the Lyft driver pulled up to the glitzy entrance of the Sherbourne Hotel and the smiling doorman helped her out,

Carly realized why Minnie Lee had insisted she take a cab. The area outside the grand double doors was teaming with people. Women and men in elaborate costumes, most likely there for an early Halloween party, gathered by the enormous potted palms, while on the other side, couples in ball gowns and tuxedos congregated. Carly would have melted onto the pavement if she'd had to navigate this show by walking in from the street. Her grandmother, as usual, had known what she needed before she did.

"Welcome to the Sherbourne, miss." The doorman looked at her as if she mattered. "Which event are you attending tonight?"

She flashed the VIP pass. The time on the invitation read 7:00 pm. Her watch had just ticked over to 8:00. Her strategy was to slip in while the party was in full swing, to mill around with the crowd, and to fulfill her duty without calling any real attention to herself. "The High Rollers' party."

"Yes, of course. That's on the Holly Deck. May I give you directions, or are you familiar with our hotel?" His voice somehow cut through the crowd's commotion.

"No." Carly shook her head. "I've never been here before."

"Well, in that case, I can show you how to get there, if you want." He waved his hand to the gilded doors. "The layout can be a little confusing."

"Great." Her shoulders dropped as she began to relax into the evening. *Thanks, Grandma.*

The doorman led the way, and like magic, the huge doors swung inward, revealing an enchanted inner atrium and a brave, new world. Under enormous skylights, two lines of professionally sculpted ficus trees ran the length of the lobby. White fairy lights sparkled in their branches, which stretched up into a canopy above their heads. Hanging flower balls of red and green dropped down and peppered the lobby with flashes of energy and color. Carly didn't know where to look first. She and her family rarely came to the Strip, and even when they did, they never ventured into the luxury hotels. She realized that she was staring with an open mouth and quickly pressed her lips together.

"You ain't seen nothing yet." The doorman smiled and walked across the flower mosaics in the tiled floor.

At the far end, the atrium opened up onto a vast three-acre lake. Flanked by a grove of real pine trees, a waterfall cascaded down a small mountain and eventually ran into a stream that babbled happily past their feet. The continuous murmur was clearly designed to drown out the horns and sirens from the Strip beyond the lobby doors.

"This is beautiful." Carly breathed a little deeper.

"It really is, isn't it?" He pointed across the lake to a wooden deck that jutted out over the water. Huge planters of red flowers graced each corner, and people already crowded around stand-up tables and a bar at one end. "That's where you're headed."

Carly stared at the throng of people on the deck. "That's a lot of people," she said almost under her breath.

The doorman touched her lightly on the elbow. "Just keep to the path around the lake, and you'll see the sign for the Holly Deck eventually. You good?"

"Yes, thanks." Carly nodded to herself long after the doorman had left.

Winding her way around the lake was quite the adventure. She could hear the ringing of the slots and the cheers of big winners, but she couldn't see the actual casino. The nature vistas had a way of taking Vegas out of the equation. She passed a Halloween exhibit where pumpkins, carved into scary frogs, sat on lily pads, and then a fountain where one topiary hand threw water to another.

Carly paused outside the party's entrance. Sam, the front office assistant, stood outside, checking names off a long list attached to a clipboard. Glancing up, he caught sight of Carly and waved her over with rapid circles of his hand.

"Finally. You're here," Sam called out over the line of people waiting to enter. "Come along. Marina's been waiting for you."

"Sorry." Carly glanced at her watch. Her strategy to fly under the radar was backfiring.

He handed her over to another assistant who thrust a Rollers windbreaker into her hands. "Here, put this on." The woman dragged her onto the deck before she could slip a hand into one sleeve.

The deck, like everything else in the hotel, was breathtaking. Jutting out over the lake, it rode just barely above the water, and the dark wood was so highly polished, Carly slid her foot along one slat to see if she were actually walking on the water. A decorated guardrail ran along the perimeter. Real holly branches wrapped around both the posts and the handrails and red berry-shaped lights twinkled in the night. Simple and elegant, the space was a testimony to the principles of restraint.

As they moved to the center of the deck, Carly glanced around, looking for Parker. Just to apologize for the morning stretch, she told herself.

Across the deck, Allen raised his hand in a greeting. Beside him was Buck, his frown etched into his forehead and as impassive here as he was at the stadium. Great. How was she supposed to enjoy the party if every single one of her bosses was here?

Besides the training staff, the deck was crowded with women of all sorts. Some in corporate dress, others in cocktail attire, and a few by the bar looked as if they had just stepped off a Vegas stage. One even had a small set of feathered wings, like a cupid, fluttering in the evening breeze above her shoulders.

"Oh good, you're here." Marina strode over to Carly and echoed Sam's words but with a friendly tone. As she walked, her silk wrap-around dress with chevron stripes in Rollers green, of course, swung around her and showed off her curves. Carly marveled that at sixty-something, Marina was still a very striking woman. She gathered Carly into a quick, but real hug that was more than just the customary pat on the back.

Carly flinched at first; she didn't normally hug her bosses, but the contact felt more motherly than anything else.

"You look very nice. Lucky you. You wear clothes well." Marina then tapped the jacket in Carly's grasp. "Put this on, and we'll get this party started." She waved two fingers in the air, and the Sherbourne staff at the bar circulated with trays of golden champagne.

As Carly slipped into the jacket, she spied Parker in the crowd, heading her way. She wore an ornate flowered blouse with puffy cuffs. Strange. She would have bet her last dime that billowy tops with flowers were not Parker's style.

Parker swiped two flutes of champagne off a passing waiter's tray and leaned in to Carly.

"I know, I know. The shirt's ridiculous. My—"

"Shh. Marina's going to start." Sam cut her off with a glare.

Parker twisted her mouth shut and threw away the pretend key. "Here," she whispered and handed Carly one of the glasses. Their fingers brushed in the exchange.

Carly's belly betrayed her by quivering. *Not again.*

"Welcome. Welcome." Marina's voice came at them from hidden speakers in each corner.

Carly forced her attention back to her boss. Someone had given Marina a wireless mic, and she stood in the center of the deck, calling her guests to her like a mother hen. As the crowd drifted closer and grabbed flutes of champagne, she met their eager gazes with a nod or a smile before she continued.

"Thank you so much for coming out on a night so close to Halloween. I hope I didn't drag you away from any other exciting engagements. But with our newest roll of the dice..." She pulled Parker even with her. "I thought it high time to remind everyone that there is always a method behind my madness."

The crowd chuckled. With only two sentences, Marina had them eating out of her hand.

Carly stood in awe.

"A lot of us have been friends for a long time and some of us," Marina patted Parker's shoulder, "are brand-new to this hand of cards. But I'm proud to say that we've all been fighting for the same thing. Bringing women to the forefront to change the dynamic and reshape the conversation so that everyone can have an equal voice. Some would say that football is not the place to make this gamble. But guess what? I own a football team. So why not?"

The crowd laughed, and one of the few men near the front raised his flute in an early toast.

"Now, I'm lucky. I know. I've been put in this position by a pair of very sexy legs and my late husband's money, but I am more than the sum of these parts, and so is every other woman. One thing I've learned in this life: you can waste your time drawing lines in the sand, or you can just walk over them." She clinked glasses with the nearby man before lifting hers high. "Join me in a world where there is no scrimmage line, just an end zone. Meet the women of the High Rollers who will help us all over the goal line."

Several people called out, "Hear, hear," while others cheered and clinked glasses.

Carly clicked glasses with Parker, who, she noticed, didn't drink.

Marina took a sip and then another. "Any excuse to drink good champagne." She handed their flutes to an assistant and gathered Parker, Carly, and the community director for a photograph. "Smile, ladies."

Several flashes strobed in their faces.

The photographer studied the camera's screen. "Thanks. I've got what I need here. I'll just take more pictures of the party." He melted into the crowd, snapping candids as he went.

Marina pulled the three women into a tight circle. "I'm sure you already know this," she began softly so only they could hear, "but your role on the Rollers is also more than the sum of the parts of your contracts. I want to thank you for being part of something very special tonight and even more so as we move into the future." She called the waiter back over and passed out more drinks.

Parker held up her hand in refusal. The woman in the suit clinked glasses with Marina and then knocked back a third of her drink.

Carly looked at her own flute. Tiny bubbles rose in the pale golden liquid like a string of pearls. She'd had cheap sparkling wine in college, but never real champagne. She took another sip, and the bubbles exploded in her mouth with intensity and hints of citrus.

"Good, yes?" Marina laughed, but not unkindly.

Carly shifted her weight. Was it that obvious she was inexperienced? "Very." She nodded and pulled up the windbreaker's collar to hide the color creeping up her neck.

Marina smiled and reached out a friendly hand to Carly's shoulder. "Relax. Tonight is about being seen and heard. Chat up a few CEOs or not, but make sure you enjoy the party." She turned to meet each of their gazes. "Not too much. Tomorrow is still a workday, after all." With one last smile, she drifted into the crowd to take her own advice.

"Oh. Marina? May I run something by you?" The woman in the suit jumped to her side, leaving Parker and Carly alone in the midst of the crowd, facing each other awkwardly.

Silence stretched out between them. Parker glanced at a black and rose gold watch that must have cost the world, then to the waterfall beyond the deck, and eventually back to her watch.

She's embarrassed to be around me after the stretch.

"Do you need to go somewhere?" Carly decided to give her an easy out.

"No." Parker finally met her gaze and grinned broadly. "But you do."

"Come on." Parker grabbed Carly by the elbow and pulled her through the crowd to the waterside edge of the deck. She positioned Carly, as if she were an actor hitting her mark on stage, over a white letter H two inches long that was laid into the darker material of the deck. Her elbow was slender and warm under the thin material of her shirt. Parker longed to run her hand up her arm and into those dark curls, but there was no reason to hold on to her anymore, so Parker pointed across to the waterfall instead. "Look."

"I don't see anything."

"Hang on a sec. You will. We're less than a minute away."

As if on cue, mist surged from the top of the mountain, creating the optical illusion that the waterfall was tumbling up and down at the same time. Then, projected on the screen that the mist created, a luminous moon rose slowly from behind the mountain. A lone wolf howled over the speakers on the deck and completed the picture.

"Oh. Your dad's show." Carly turned to her with a smile that lit up her entire face.

She gave Carly a smile and a nod. *So pretty. Yep. I'm totally going to ask her out.*

She liked having someone around to cut the tension of playing professional sports. And the energy between them was undeniable. But she wasn't asking for the world. Just a bit of fun and a quick fling while she kicked for the Rollers.

Oohs and aahs erupted from the crowd as everyone swung to face the mountain. Projected bats flew across the full moon and moved off the mist screen as if heading straight to the deck. A beat later, flapping noises rushed out of the overhead speakers, and puffs of air that felt like wings darted through the air.

Carly ducked as the wind blew her hair.

With little screams of laughter, the crowd followed suit.

"It's not real." Parker pointed to a header over the end of the deck studded with tiny holes. "The air's coming from the back."

"That's fantastic. It totally felt as if the bats were flying over my head." Carly laughed again and smoothed her hair back into place.

"Just wait. The Halloween show is my favorite one." Parker directed her attention back to the mist screen above the mountain.

A silhouetted witch on a broomstick soared over the mountain and stopped dead in the center of the moon. The witch slowly rotated until she was facing the deck and the crowd.

Carly took a quick step back. "It's like she's looking right at me."

Almost as an answer, the witch threw her head back with a cackle that echoed all around them, and cast a gnarled wand into the air. A spark leaped from the tip and fell in great bounds down the waterfall. With each drop down the boulders, the spark grew in intensity until it was a ball of fire. Then it plunged into the lake and set the whole thing ablaze.

"Oh my God." Carly sidled closer to Parker.

Parker closed her eyes to appreciate Carly's proximity. Heat hummed through her body as she remembered how Carly's touch had felt earlier. Her nerve endings began to tingle.

On the lake, the flames rolled over the water toward them, stopping only a few feet shy of the deck. As they petered out, a giant animated jack-o'-lantern rose from the center of the lake.

"How?" Carly's question was barely a breath.

"Projection mapping on a solid surface."

"What?"

"Just watch."

Out on the lake, dark pupils popped into the pumpkin's fiery eyes, and its toothy grin widened. "A long time ago, I was human. Like you." A deep male voice boomed all around them as the pumpkin's mouth moved in sync.

"That voice is...um... He's that movie star, right?"

Parker nodded. Her father, as usual, had spared no expense.

"I was Jack, then, a boy up to no good." The recognizable voice rang out as the silhouette of a young man climbed across the boulders on the mist screen.

The story played as a movie above the mountain as the animated jack-o'-lantern in the lake recounted how his human self had stolen and swindled his whole life, and upon his death, he'd cheated the devil out of taking his soul. Not able to go to heaven, he was doomed to roam the earth forever in the darkness of night and his own sin. He begged the devil to take pity on him. Eventually, the devil tossed him an ember from hell.

At this point, a lone firework shot across the deck and the lake and landed in the hand of the projected man still on top of the waterfall.

"I carved my own face into a turnip, my favorite food, and now this is how I travel," the pumpkin on the lake said. Another spark flew from the mountain to the pumpkin. A thundering laugh dropped from the speakers, and the pumpkin glowed from within as flames once again rolled across the lake.

"Soon I'll be on almost every porch and windowsill. Beware when you meet the face of Jack on Halloween night." The music soared to a crescendo. "Because I'm still up to no good!"

With one last evil laugh, the jack-o'-lantern fell back into the waters. A whoosh of wind sped by Carly and Parker as if the pumpkin was taking them with it into the fiery depths.

Parker glanced at Carly. Her face was aglow with the pyrotechnics, and the dying flames dancing in her pupils brought out the gold even more. "That was...amazing." She shook her head. "I've never seen anything like it."

"Different than the Bellagio, right?" Parker asked.

"Yeah, but equally as good."

Parker nodded and studied her. A band of light freckles ran across her nose. They were really quite adorable. Carly's face was so classically beautiful with its high cheekbones, full lips, and gorgeous eyes that the freckles played against the model image and gave her a fresh, charming look. Parker tried to tear her gaze away, but she couldn't stop staring.

"You know," Carly began, "I felt as if it all was directed at me. Is that crazy?"

"No, not at all. You were on the H." Parker pointed to the white letter inlaid into the deck.

Carly's gaze followed her finger. "The H?"

"Here, H marks the spot. It's the best view for all the shows. All the spectacles play right to the H."

"Why H?"

"It's for my mom. Her name is Holly."

"Oh, like the deck, right?" When Carly's gaze met hers, Parker's heart missed a beat. "She must love it here."

"Actually," Parker bit her lip, "she's never seen it. My father built the deck for her, and she's never come. She's clinically depressed."

"Oh." Carly's eyes widened.

Parker's stomach churned. *Shit, shit, shit. How did that spill out?* Maybe she was too comfortable with Carly. She tried to backtrack and to infuse a lightness into her voice. "Hey, you want to see how they do it? I could get you into the control center."

Not giving Carly a chance to answer or even think, Parker grabbed her hand, gently wrapped it in her fingers, and dragged her through the tight crowd.

"Where are we going?" Carly pulled her hand from Parker's and skidded to a halt before they cleared the deck.

Parker pointed off into the distance. "Inside the mountain. It's hollow with the control center at its core. There's even a secret passageway to get inside."

Carly's gaze followed her finger to the mountain and then darted back to her face. "We're on the clock. We shouldn't leave the party."

"Are you kidding me? This is exactly what Marina told us to do. Mingle, make connections. Look," Parker waved her hand in the air as if the point was obvious, "I could totally use a friend at the Rollers right about now."

Carly cocked her head and zeroed in on Parker's eyes. "You? You want to be friends?"

The question was somehow loaded. With what, Parker hadn't a clue. The moment hung between them like a soap bubble in the air waiting to be popped. Here was her chance.

"Actually, I want to be more than friends. Nothing crazy. We can keep it light and see where the season takes us."

Carly said nothing.

Thanks to her father, silence always made Parker antsy. She tapped her foot until she couldn't take it anymore. "You know, if you're up for that kind of thing."

Carly lowered her head. "I... I..." she said to her feet.

Ah, shit! She's straight. Well, she wasn't the first straight woman to reject Parker's advances, and—since Parker didn't usually shy away from letting any woman, gay or straight or anywhere in between, know when she was interested—she probably wouldn't be the last.

Then why the hell couldn't she shrug off this rejection?

More than friends… Wow! This one sure didn't let the grass grow under her feet. They had shared, what, a couple of conversations in as many days? They hardly knew each other. And yet—her cheeks flushed—Parker thought of her in that way. As desirable and attractive and someone she wanted to be more than friends with.

No! Stop! Carly had to kill this fast. No matter how many times she had thought about sliding her hand up Parker's hamstring during the day, the bottom line was she wanted more from a relationship than to pop up on Parker's social media.

Something made her glance up. Not Parker, who was still waiting for a real answer, her foot tapping like a little Gatling gun. No, it was Buck, across the deck, staring straight at her. His scowl was the deepest it had been all week—and that was saying something. His gaze bore into her as if he had been standing inches away the exact moment Parker had asked her to be more than friends: the very definition of *fraternizing with the players.*

Carly swung her head over to Parker and took a step back. With the proposition, Parker had climbed into her personal space, probably breaking a dozen rules in Buck's book.

Parker's eyes widened as she nodded with encouragement.

"Actually," Carly pushed her words out fast, "I'm not up for it. Sorry."

A flash of hurt killed the hope in Parker's eyes.

Hurt pride, no doubt. How many available women said no to Parker Sherbourne? Carly would bet that she had just joined a small minority. "I think I should get back to the party and do my job."

Focusing on putting one foot ahead of the other, Carly advanced through the crowd. Her legs moved as if she had one-hundred-pound weights on them. Regret washed over her. That had been almost mean. She was the one to heal aches and pains, not cause them.

But there were all kinds of reasons to cut quick and deep. Buck had forbidden it. They were from completely different backgrounds. Parker probably wouldn't last long in Vegas or the league. She could go on and on. And yet, that vulnerability she had sensed at the fountains, it was here tonight too. What else was underneath Parker's bravado?

"What can I get you, miss?"

Distracted by her brooding, she had moved completely across the deck and was standing by the bar. "Um... A soda water with cranberry juice and a lime, please," she told the man behind the counter. The champagne was rolling around in her stomach, or that's what she told herself.

In a couple of well-practiced moves, he handed her the bright red drink. On its rim lay a skewer with two tiny green dice at the end.

She fingered them before squeezing the lime into the drink.

"She thinks of everything," a low voice to her right said.

Carly turned.

The woman with the angel wings, who had been bolstering up the bar since Carly had gotten there, was holding up tiny dice of her own. "Every little detail. She's already worked them all out before she puts any plan in motion. She's really that good."

Normally, Carly would quietly excuse herself from a conversation with a stranger at a party. She was too shy, and chatting with a scantily clad woman wearing a sparkly halo wasn't the type of mingling her boss had meant. But she was desperate to stop thinking about what she had done to Parker. "You mean Marina Fisher?"

"Yeah, who else?"

"Are you friends with her?" That word again. She took a large gulp from her drink to hide the shudder in her shoulders.

"Not really. But she never forgets her old show and us showgirls even though we never actually performed together. She almost always hires a couple of us to come to her events. She says we lend a Las Vegas panache, but we all think that she's just helping us out."

"With an extra paycheck?" Maybe the woman would carry the conversation herself if Carly threw her a bone.

"Yeah, the money's nice, but we make a good living. We're all classically trained dancers."

"I'm sorry. I didn't mean—"

"No. No worries. You see, Marina's giving us publicity, which is better. There's only one grand revue show left in Vegas these days. That's where Marina got her start, and she doesn't want to see it disappear. So, she pays us to come out here in full costume and talk it up."

"It's never about the bottom line with her, is it?"

The woman shook her head, and the halo shimmered like the real thing from the reflection of the party lights. Leaning in, she whispered, "I appreciate it. I really do, but this party's a bit of a dud. Mostly high-powered women. They don't want to be chatted up by a showgirl. We do better with men. Sexist as that is."

Carly glanced around the space. She was right. The guests, mostly women, were in tight groups, leaning in to each other, jabbing fingers in the air, probably talking about the next big deal.

"Although… There's a couple I might make some headway with." She gestured off to a far corner and chuckled. "No, wait a second. Doesn't look like there's room enough for three."

Carly followed her gaze across the deck to the second show of the night. A thin woman in an expensive pantsuit had her hand on another woman's hip. Carly couldn't see the other woman, lost in the shadows as she was, but pantsuit woman was in complete control and left no doubt that they were together.

Heat seared the tips of Carly's ears. She could never be so public, so obvious.

The couple rotated, and long, blonde hair fanned out. *Parker? Son of a gun!* Her hand flew to her chest. For a second, she couldn't breathe.

Okay. Okay. I said no. But she can't wait ten minutes before she moves on to her next more than friends?

"Sorry, sore subject?" the angel asked.

"Not at all." Carly took a deep breath and turned her back to whatever Parker was up to.

Then why was she still thinking about rolling the dice on that particular gamble?

———◇◇◇———

Parker jerked away from Tanya—or tried to. Tanya gripped her hip like a vice and was slowly maneuvering her into the back corner of the deck.

She had grabbed Parker as soon as she had rejoined the party. To be fair, she had been almost staggering in confusion. Her gaydar was legendary in three states. Obviously, it was jammed in Nevada. Tanya had reached a hand out to steady her, and somehow, while Parker's mind was reeling, they had ended up in a dark corner of the deck.

Tanya leaned in to whisper in her ear. "It's my last night here. One night. No strings. My bases are loaded. I know it's the wrong sport, but you could step up to the plate and… Are you listening to me?"

Parker wasn't. She was searching the deck for Carly and finally caught her at the bar, standing way too close to a tall, gorgeous showgirl.

Tanya followed her line of sight. "See, there are lots of games to be played here in Vegas. Look at them. Why not us?"

"No, she's not playing at all. She's straight." That's what Carly had announced loud and clear when she'd said she wasn't up for it.

"Okay. But happily, we're not." Tanya slid her hand around to Parker's behind.

Parker wrenched out of Tanya's grasp to study Carly better. From this distance, she couldn't tell what Carly was up to. The showgirl was pulling out long papers the size of bookmarks. From where? She couldn't have one pocket in that skimpy getup. She grabbed a pen from the bar and scribbled something on the back.

Wait a second. Was Carly giving the showgirl her phone number? And why did she care? Carly had walked away, making it clear that she was not interested.

Tanya stepped around in front of her, blocking off Parker's view of the bar. "I know you need to stay down here and do your job." She slid a room card into the back pocket of Parker's pants. "But when you are ready, come join me."

Still lost in her own thoughts, Parker transferred her gaze to Tanya only a second before Tanya reached up to kiss her.

Her tongue darted across Parker's bottom lip. It tasted heavily of vodka and expectations.

"Just a sample of what's to come." Tanya spun on a heel for a dramatic exit and strutted across the deck, her perfect behind swaying in her designer slacks.

Clarity didn't come often to Parker. Mostly she was moving, not thinking. But tonight, the truth crept in while she stood still: hooking up with Tanya was one of those leaps her father had been talking about. Different women in every city. Cutting out the second it got serious. He might have a point.

Dad, get out of my head or start paying rent!

She jostled her head as if he were really in there and then peered over to the bar. Her breath hitched in her throat.

Only the angel remained, sliding maraschino cherries off those cute dice skewers that were in all the drinks.

Carly was gone. Had she seen Tanya kiss her? Had the sight of two women together bothered her so much that she had to leave? She rubbed the back of her neck. Normally, she would have let her angst go. Just moved on to the next adventure, whatever it was, but tonight all she could think about was that she had run another conversation with Carly into the ground.

Parker headed straight for the Sherbourne party manager, who stood with a headset by the deck's entrance. "Hey." She slid the key card out of her pocket. "I found this over there. Can you take it back to the main desk?" She dropped it into his outstretched hand without a hint of regret.

See, Dad? Not jumping. Feet are on the ground.

CHAPTER 6

"What are these?" Minnie Lee stood at the breakfast bar the next morning, pointing to the two glossy tickets in front of her.

"Grandma, you don't have to get up with me every morning." Carly furrowed her brow and renewed her conviction to move out to the living room as soon as she got home.

"Don't flatter yourself, sweetheart." Minnie Lee smiled. "I just couldn't sleep. I was actually up before you were, and I thought you might want some coffee before you go."

"I do. Thank you." Carly gratefully took the cup that Minnie Lee offered. "Long night. Early morning."

"I know. How was the party?"

"Good." Carly kept to herself that she had stayed for only an hour and had taken the bus back so she wouldn't waste Minnie Lee's tips. "They took a lot of pictures. I think we might be in the paper."

"Really? My granddaughter's famous now?"

"Just the *Vegas Sentinel*. Not *USA Today* or anything. But if there's one left at the diner, can you get a copy? I might like to keep it."

"You betcha. Should I start a scrapbook?"

"Goodness, no. I'm just along for the ride, but the party was cool. The Sherbourne is breathtaking, and they had it on this deck that was right on the hotel's lake."

Crazy how easy it was to put a good spin on the night. She was almost ready to believe it herself. "And those," she pointed to the bar, "are tickets to the Las Vegas Revue. Right up front. You'll need to call the number on the back and reserve a date, but it's all free." Carly flipped the tickets over to reveal an 800 number written out in neat block print by the angel the night before. "I thought you could take Janice if she can get a night off from the diner. There's one show a week that's covered if them being topless troubles you."

"I'm not bothered by a few breasts." Her grandmother threw her a searching look. "Are you?"

"No." Carly felt the heat on her cheeks. "Promise me you'll ask Janice. And tell me what night. I'll try to get home for Teddy."

"I think I just might." Minnie Lee picked up the tickets and examined them. "I like this new job of yours. There are a lot of perks."

She pushed all thoughts of Parker in the arms of another woman out of her mind. "About time, right?"

"Right."

———— ✦❖✦ ————

The one perk that blew her away was the upcoming Monday night game in Buffalo, New York. She had assumed that the team wouldn't take her, the most junior of the AT staff and less than a week into her stint, but Allen surprised her the moment she stepped into the training room that morning.

"So, please check all the medical kits and fanny packs to make sure we are good to go. Oh, by the way, are you a fanny pack or a messenger bag kind of girl?"

Even this early in the morning, there were already two players on the exercise bikes. One wore white headphones and bounced to a beat only he could hear. The other held a book with a big blue cross on the cover and turned the pages slowly. Allen's workday had already started, and he was all business.

"Sorry?"

"For your supplies on the field."

Carly cocked her head. "For next weekend?"

"No. For the game. On Monday. Day after tomorrow. Which would you rather have? Fanny pack or messenger bag? We've got both."

"I'm going to Buffalo?" she asked, her mouth freezing in a perfect O at the end of the sentence.

"Yep. Joel, the operations manager, has you on his list. Look, it doesn't matter what you choose, just make one up for yourself."

A mile-long grin spread across her face.

Allen's expression softened. "It's a dream come true standing on the sidelines right in the thick of things come game day, isn't it?"

Carly nodded. "I never really thought I'd make it this far."

"Well, you have, and believe me, it won't disappoint. It's a total rush."

"I bet. I'll get right on those kits and the packing lists."

When she glided past him on the way to the supply closet, he dropped a fatherly hand on her shoulder. "You'll do great on Monday."

"Thanks, Allen." She drifted off to the supply closet.

"Oh, and don't forget to double-check for the mustard packs. The team has been cramping up a lot lately, and we've been a little lax about replacing them. Oh, and stuff a bunch in your pack. Tobias Smith likes to take a few squirts before the game. The acetic acid in the mustard helps produce more acetylcholine in the body, you know."

"I do," Carly happily listened to him mansplain. *I'm going to Buffalo!*

Her smile was still a mile wide when Denarius hopped on her table. He had just come from lifting weights and still had a green resistance band slung over his shoulder.

"I had a great practice yesterday, Carly." He slid back as far as he could onto the table. "Could just be coincidence, but tape me up exactly like you did yesterday." He raised both eyebrows and his right leg simultaneously.

"To tell you the truth, the taping job stretches out on the field. Your good day yesterday was all you. You know that, right?"

"Maybe, maybe not." He shrugged. "But why jinx it?"

"Okay." She laughed and reached into the nearby drawer to grab some tape. "Can't argue with that." And she couldn't. No one could talk an athlete out of a superstition once it took root. He pointed at the tape in Carly's hand. "I think I've found me the golden ticket. And it goes by the name of Carly Bartlet."

He turned to the player on the next table. "I'm giving all credit to Carly's taping ability. You should get some of this in Buffalo if you know what's good for you."

Carly tapped a loose fist against her chest in thanks. Sweet Luck was coming at her from all sorts of places. After only five days, she was finding her way in the maze that was the Rollers' organization. The Parker situation might not be an issue—she hadn't seen her all day. Her proposition had just been an impulsive lark and was hopefully long forgotten.

She pulled in a deep breath and let it out slowly. Good thing, too. She had no time for or interest in a fling. She would be working like a dog for the next twenty-four hours until she hit the hotel in Buffalo.

———— ⋆◈⋆ ————

The next day, Parker swung open the door to room 2016 in a hotel in Buffalo. Two beds, two burgundy club chairs by the window, and two stainless steel lamps. Nice, but uninspired. The modern pieces of art over the beds added a happy dash of color but were mass-produced. Her father would never have allowed such a thing.

A loud cheer from the room next door startled her. Veris and Hekekia were hosting a poker game but hadn't invited her.

She had a couple of hours to kill before dinner. She could go out for a run, but the churning gray clouds outside didn't bode well. The gym was an option, but did she really want to run into all the other players who wouldn't let go the missed field goal?

In the end, she pulled out her phone.

"Hey, Parker. What can I do for you?" Her brother's voice sounded tired and dull.

"Nothing." Maybe she should say she had butt-dialed him by mistake and hang up. "I'm in Buffalo. You know, for the game tomorrow. In a hotel that doesn't even come close to any of yours and Dad's." What was she doing? She and her brother didn't chat.

"There's a lot of crappy hotels out there."

Jem's beagle barked loudly in the background.

"Everything okay?"

"Yeah, Kristina's just coming home with sandwiches for lunch. She went to Malibu Kitchen. She likes their pulled pork and—"

"Shit." Kristina cut in. "They forgot Mateo's wrap. I'll go back."

"No. I'll go," Jem said. "He's got a question on that new editing program. He's been waiting for the expert. Can you help him? Look, Parker, I—"

"Yeah, of course, take off. Get your son's sandwich."

"Thanks. Bye. Hey, good luck tomorrow. We'll be watching."

"If I get on the field. I'm a little nervous." She took in a quick breath and held it, waiting for his answer. They didn't often share confidences. "Jem?"

Silence. Jem must have hung up.

She tossed the phone to the bed, crossed to the window, and plopped down in one of the club chairs. The view was the very definition of drab. Gray concrete buildings sat beneath an even grayer sky. The clouds churned at an alarming rate, growing darker almost by the second. She had never gotten to the real question with Jem. Could she pull this off? The kicking part was easy.

In Portland, however, she would have had the girls on the team to bolster her up on the field. Off the field in LA, there was usually the flavor of the moment. Vegas, on the other hand, had stripped her bare, and here in Buffalo, she was completely alone.

Maybe my dad is right. I should go back to the Fire.

Almost without thinking, she slid to the edge of the chair, dropped her hands by her behind and pushed her legs out until her entire body weight rested on her hands. *And what? Give up?* Slowly, she dipped down until her butt almost touched the ground. Then again and again until a welcome burning spread from her triceps to her back and chased all other thoughts away.

She almost didn't hear the click of the door. The gasp, however, got her full attention. Still leaning on the chair, she pivoted toward the sound.

Carly stood at the door with a spinner suitcase in her hand and her mouth wide open. "Oh my God. I'm sorry. I thought this was my room." She focused on Parker's plank position. "Are you okay?"

"Ah, yeah. Of course." Parker leaped up and was unable to meet her gaze. "You know, just working out a few kinks." She rubbed the back of one arm.

Carly studied the hotel envelope in her hand. "This has got to be a mistake, right?"

God, I hope not. I'm so glad to see you. She just didn't know how much until Carly appeared before her. "Sam didn't tell me I was sharing a room. But I think only superstars get their own rooms, and I'm certainly not a superstar."

Carly pulled on the collar of her Rollers sweatshirt as if it were suddenly a size too tight. Even so, she looked lovely. The gold of her eyes almost glowed in the darkening room, and her hair fell in soft curls around her shoulders. She was so put-together; she did not look as if she had just gotten off a cross-country flight.

"But I can call down just to make sure." Parker didn't want to scare her off. She had been down that path before at the party.

"We probably should, if you don't mind." Carly hadn't moved from the doorway and glanced around as if she were planning a quick escape.

"Okay." Parker picked up the phone by the bed and pushed a button. "Hi," she said when the front desk picked up. "This is Parker Sherbourne in…"

"2016."

"2016, and I was just wondering who was registered in this room."

If the front desk personnel thought it an odd question, he didn't let on. A few clicks on a keyboard drifted through the line. "Carly Bartlet and Parker Sherbourne. Is there a problem, miss?"

"Hang on." She put a hand over the bottom of the phone. "We're both registered in the room. He wants to know if that's a problem." She found she was holding her breath. The room felt a lot less empty with Carly in it.

Carly bit her lip and after a long beat shook her head.

"No, we're good. Thank you very much." Parker dropped the phone's headset into the cradle and bit back a smile. "I'm not sure what he could do about it anyway. These are the team's arrangements, not the hotel's."

"I know." Carly pulled her bag into the middle of the room and shifted uncomfortably. "Which bed do you want?"

"I don't care. You choose."

Carly placed her bag on the end of the bed closest to the door, opened the closet, and then transferred the suitcase to the luggage holder already set up inside.

Parker sat down on her bed, the one by the window, and watched as Carly moved around the room. "What's your schedule tonight?" Unlike Jem, Carly couldn't hang up on her.

Carly sat on her own bed, facing Parker, her back as stiff as a board. "Dinner and then curfew. We swung by the stadium before coming here to get everything in order. Buck apparently is a control freak when it comes to away games. I don't mind, though. I don't really like surprises either. Especially on game day."

Parker tapped her foot on the industrial carpet. She shouldn't ask, but she had to know where she stood. "You mean like this one?"

"Sorry?"

"Like sharing a room. I mean it looked like you were maybe a bit surprised…or something else when you came in."

"I… I…" Carly looked away.

"I hope this is not going to be weird."

"What?" Carly returned her gaze to Parker's.

"Us sleeping together. I mean, in the same room," she added quickly. "I hope you won't feel too weird about it."

Carly shook her head but said nothing.

"Look, I know it was awkward at the party when I asked you to be more than friends. I'm sorry. That wasn't my intention at all. Truth is, and I'm sure you already know, I only swim in the lady pond." Parker tapped her foot faster. "But, you know, it's totally cool if you don't. I mean, we should still be friends, right? Actually, it might even be better. It's crazy if the only two women on the front lines at the Rollers can't depend on each other."

Carly's gaze darted about the room, landing on the TV, the desk, and then the picture window at Parker's back.

Parker grimaced. She was pushing too hard.

"Or colleagues if that works better for you." Parker forced a smile to her lips and tried to catch Carly's gaze.

"No." Carly shook her head.

Parker's foot froze. No? What did that mean? No to colleagues even?

Carly took in a deep breath and then let it out as a sigh. "No. We should be friends, not just colleagues. Show a united front to the team and everyone else."

"Yes! That's exactly what I was saying."

"But that's all it can be," Carly added quickly.

"Okay." Parker nodded. "Honestly, I'm not sure why I went there at the party anyway. It wasn't the time or place. I got straight friends too, you know," she blurted out when an undefinable look passed across Carly's face.

"It doesn't matter. Let's just put that behind us."

"Okay," Parker said again. "That's good. It's all good."

And it was. Carly finally relaxed. She sank back on the bed and leaned on an elbow, no longer looking as if she had a two-by-four stuck up her sweatshirt. As she sat back, her hair fell in her face, and when she reached up with her free hand to brush her waves back, she struck a pose that could have been on the cover of a 1940s pin-up calendar. Unconscious and completely natural, it only lasted for a moment, but it sent a jolt to Parker's core for twice as long.

Slow down there, slugger, Parker told herself. *This is not what just friends feels like.*

Or maybe it was. There was something about Carly that reached out to her, seeped in and smoothed all her rough edges. Strange as it was, she just felt more whole, somehow, when Carly was around. Maybe that *was* what being friends felt like. Who knew? She really didn't have a lot of experience.

———⋆◈⋆———

As she walked into the dinner buffet with Parker at her shoulder, Carly swallowed several times. Why had she agreed to be friends? It was a colossally bad idea. She should have just mumbled something about professionalism in and out of the stadium. But when she had opened the door and seen Parker in that dip position—every muscle in her arms and legs tight and flexed—Carly's heart had fluttered in her chest like a flight of butterflies. Damn Teddy and his electrons. She should run as fast as she could from Parker.

"Carly!" Denarius called to her as soon as they turned to the tables with their trays.

They passed Hekekia, who looked at them sideways several times—what was that about?—and sat down with Denarius and two other defensive linebackers. "Carly, I need to be on your schedule tomorrow. Promise me you'll give me the first spot for my ankle."

"Sure." A wave of satisfaction rose in her. Whether it came from Denarius's show of confidence or from the fact that Parker had witnessed it, she wasn't sure.

The linebacker to the right of Denarius laughed out loud.

"I don't know what you're laughing at." Denarius pointed to the man's plate, filled high with only broiled chicken. "How many chicken recipes does Jeanie have? Five thousand? Ten thousand?" He circled a finger in the air at his temple. "You crazy as hell." And then to Carly. "He only eats chicken twenty-four hours before a game."

"My wife just got a connect with Trudy Mabel, from Food Network, on a chicken cookbook. You quiet now, huh?"

"Hey," a running back down the table tapped his plate with his fork, "you really go for girls, Parker?"

Carly nearly choked on a forkful of pasta. She glanced at Parker with the rest of the table and said nothing.

"No, I go for *women*. That an issue?" Parker didn't drop her gaze, and her tone remained even.

She had guts. Carly wished she could be so matter-of-fact about her sexuality. She wasn't even open about it with her family. Sure, Parker had her father's money behind her, but she wasn't apologizing for who she was. Impressive. Especially here at this table. Football was all about forced masculinity on so many levels.

"Step back, Teshawn." Denarius raised a finger. "Everyone here likes women except Carly. Parker fits in. No offense, Carly."

"None taken." A shiver ran up her spine, and it wasn't the good kind. She wished she could have said something. She had just agreed to be friends with Parker and then left her hanging in the wind at the first opportunity to prove herself.

Parker raised her fork with a piece of chicken on it. "I'm going to try it. Just chicken before a game? Seems to work for you, Kenny. You're an amazing outside linebacker."

Carly caught herself nodding. Maybe Parker didn't need her; she had bounced back quickly—tough for a rich girl.

"See, not so crazy after all." Kenny threw Denarius a playful glare. "You try it. You'd be faster in your get-off."

"What're you trying to say?" Denarius grinned. "My first step's a work of art. I get from my side of the ball to their side faster than anyone. My get-off clears the field for everyone."

Kenny slapped Denarius on the shoulder playfully. "You wreak havoc, man. Yes, you do."

"I played with a woman once," Parker said, "who would only turn right out of the locker room tunnel onto the field, and then she had to have three Swedish fish exactly three minutes before kickoff."

"Swedish fish?" the other linebacker asked. "Raw or cooked?"

"I think she's talking about the candy, Randall," Kenny said.

Parker nodded. "But next time I tell the story, I'm going with the raw fish. Much better." She met Carly's gaze, her eyes soft with a smile.

This time the shiver *was* the good kind. Nope. Parker totally had it handled. She was something. When her cheeks began to burn, she glanced away and prayed no one, especially Buck, was watching.

Carly sat back and listened to the players try to top each other with stories about crazy athlete superstitions. For the moment, she was happy to let the conversation flow around her.

They started with the football coach who ate a blade of grass from the field, even the synthetic ones, before every match—he said it made him one with the game. Then they branched out to other sports and mentioned a tennis pro who played entire tournaments in the same unwashed socks and the baseball player who peed on his own hands to toughen them up.

"That's nasty," Kenny said, sweeping the last piece of chicken into his mouth.

"Okay, what if I told you that you'd get fifteen tackles a game if you'd piss on your hands before kickoff?" Denarius said.

"Fifteen tackles. None of them assists?"

"Without doubt. Every game."

Kenny cocked his head back and forth.

"See?" Denarius said. "I know you're thinking about it. Everyone wants an advantage."

"At least he didn't tell you that you had to drink it." Parker jumped back into the conversation.

"That's right." Denarius pounded the table with one fist. "There is that one soccer guy who does that. Okay, I'll change it; you have to do that."

"Hell, no," Kenny said. "Even I have my limits."

The whole table laughed.

In the elevator after dinner, Parker turned to Carly with a bigger smile. "Thank you. That was fun."

"What are you thanking me for? I barely said a word all through dinner."

"But I did, and with a little luck, I may have put the whole gay thing to bed once and for all. No pun intended." She threw Carly a quick look. "Who knew being a woman would be worse than being gay?"

For you maybe. But what about me? Carly bent her head and scuffed a foot against the shiny floor of the elevator.

"I don't think they'd have sat with me if you weren't there." Parker touched her arm and then withdrew instantly. "Thanks to you, tonight, I was dealt a winning hand."

"Ha. Because we're the Rollers, right?" Teddy would have liked that joke.

"Yeah, that's what I was going for." Parker gave her a thumbs-up, stepped off the elevator first, and walked down the hall, passing the off-duty policeman on the players' floor.

Carly studied her gait to see if she was favoring her leg with the hamstring issue. She walked easily, gracefully even, and then Carly's glance drifted up to Parker's behind. The yoga pants she was wearing clung to her like a second skin. Funny and sexy. A deadly combination.

"How's your hamstring?" Carly caught up and tried to bring the professional back into the evening.

"Good." Parker glanced over her shoulder.

"I could get a few bags of ice to make sure. You might get to play tomorrow if all goes well, and why take a chance?"

"You've got your kit?"

"I do."

"Couldn't hurt." Parker dropped the key card decorated with the Rollers logo in the lock and pulled it out. It went green immediately.

Once inside, Carly grabbed a few plastic bags out of her kit and drifted back toward the door, waiting to see what Parker would do.

"I'll change while you're out," Parker announced and turned toward the bathroom with a small bundle—her pajamas and her toothbrush, Carly guessed. Parker had flipped off her top before the bathroom door had completely closed behind her, and the triple mirrors around the sink caught different angles of her body.

Despite every rational thought pushing Carly to the door, she froze and watched the show. The thin, black bra that covered and revealed everything all at once. The tight, tight stomach. The flowing blonde hair that swung around Parker like rays of sunshine or an angel's halo. *Oh my God! Did I just think of her hair as an angel's halo? Stop. Just stop.*

Didn't matter what corny similes popped into Carly's mind, they painted the same picture. Parker Sherbourne without her clothes, and even with her clothes on, was magical…and smoking hot. Thankfully, the bathroom door closed with a soft click before Carly went weak at the knees.

Outside in the hallway, Carly made her way to the ice machine around the corner. Heat rose from her chest to the tip of her ears. The situation was out of control. She had practically said, *Yes, I'm straight, and we can be friends,* but *I want to run my hands all over your body* flowed from a much lower place. She opened the ice bin and fanned her hot face with the cool air. When that didn't work, she dropped a neatly made ice bag on the back of her neck. *She's a player. She'll break my heart into a million pieces,* she added when the image of a half-naked Parker wouldn't fade from her mind.

When Carly returned, Parker was stretched out on her bed, ready for treatment, her sore leg bolstered by pillows. Dressed in a faded Fire T-shirt and soft-looking athletic shorts, she waved her large-screen phone at Carly. "Oh my God, you've got to see this!"

"What?" she asked, thankful for the diversion while she futzed around with the ice packs and Parker's very shapely leg.

"It's Hekekia. He's got this YouTube channel of him long snapping a football to all these crazy locations."

"Oh. Cool." Carly swung into the bathroom to add a little water to the ice bags and grab a towel to wrap them in.

"I can't believe it took me this long to look up his trick reel."

Carly glanced in the mirror. Her face still looked a little red under the bathroom lights. She needed to stall.

"No way," Parker called from the other room.

Carly shrugged at herself in the mirror. What did it matter if she didn't look her best? It wasn't as if she was on a date or anything. Although a date would have been much safer. A restaurant filled with people, both of them wearing plenty of clothes, and no touching…

Parker raised her leg before Carly was at her side, and Carly quickly slid the packs under her hamstring. She stepped away, but Parker patted the bed. "You got to see this one."

Carly sat on the edge of the bed and told herself that the wide space between them screamed platonic. When Parker handed her the phone and their fingers brushed, the flutter below her belly was definitely not. *For Christ's sake, this is what I would expect from her, not me.*

"Here." Parker scooted closer, ice and all, and pushed the play button.

Carly could barely concentrate on a tiny Hekekia in a red sleeveless T-shirt. A swirling black tattoo of the Pacific Islands rode one shoulder. He grinned from ear to ear and spun the football in his hand. "Second tier, Rollers' stadium, nothing but trash can."

The video cut to a tiny pedestrian pass-through high on the second level of the stadium. Hekekia bent and squatted, his body repositioning into a letter Z, before he slingshot the ball out into the open air. The camera zoomed back as the ball soared and rattled right into a trash can that must have been over one hundred yards away.

"That's amazing!" Carly said.

"Look, there's more."

The video continued. Hekekia snapped the ball into a basketball hoop from clear across the court, into the hands of a back-flipping gymnast, and through the front windows of a moving car.

They cheered as if it were live.

"He's really good. He's right; I never bothered to get to know him."

"Lift up your leg." Carly peeked at her hamstring to make sure the bags weren't too cold. Her skin was rosy and pink. "Roll around in them a little. Massage your leg with the ice and water so it gets to every part of what's left of your injury. Oh, play that one again. I didn't see it."

The video ended with Veris sitting in the locker room with a Gatorade bottle on his head. "Don't you miss," Veris shouted out to the camera.

Like a modern-day William Tell, Hekekia fired the ball through his legs and sent the bottle flying. Veris jumped up, and they bumped chests as they danced around in celebration.

Carly withdrew the ice and glanced at Parker's face. She should be cheering too, but her brows were furrowed and her lips pinched.

"It's not too late, you know?" Carly's heart went out to her.

"I know. My leg feels fine."

"No, I mean with Hekekia." Carly dumped the bags into the ice bucket.

"He's a tough nut to crack. You know, I should send this to my nephew. He's an influencer on the Internet. At the very least, he'll get a kick out of it." She chuckled at her own pun as her fingers flew across her phone.

Carly watched out of the corner of one eye. Crazy. Even this small movement was graceful.

"Want to watch a little TV?" Parker asked when she was done. Her voice was soft and unsure.

"Yeah." Carly retreated to her own bed and immediately felt safer.

Parker flipped on the TV. "What's your favorite show?"

"I don't have a lot of time to watch TV. But I guess if I've got control of the remote, which is almost never since my little brother rarely lets it out of his hands, I would watch...ah... *Adrenaline*."

"That makes sense. It's about a hospital. You're a medical professional."

"Hardly." But she loved that Parker thought of her as one.

Parker flipped around the channels and found an old repeat of the medical show. They chatted and watched until the credits rolled on the screen and Carly said, "Oh, wow. I had no idea it was so late. We should call it a night."

"Good idea."

Carly headed to the bathroom. Odd to be here, brushing her teeth and flossing, while Parker lay in a bed on the other side of the wall. Carly had had one crazy high school crush, which ended in long, slow kisses and not much else in the girl's bathroom for a month until Judy freaked out. There had been one woman in college and another in graduate school, but even though they had spent nights together, none of them felt this domestic. Those nights had all been about discovery and lust and realizing that women were her future. Although wrapped up in a lie, being with Parker tonight had felt remarkably easy, somehow. And that, ironically, made the muscles in her back tense up.

Trying not to look at Parker, she walked out in shorts and a Runnin' Rebels T-shirt and slipped into her bed. It didn't work. Two quick glances told her that Parker's gaze was on her the moment she stepped out of the bathroom and again when she was settled in bed.

"Sleep well." Parker reached over to turn off the light and the room dropped into darkness.

"You too." Carly plumped up the pillow under her head and pulled the covers up to her chin. Not so weird. She was used to sharing a room. She had done it every day of her life since she had been thirteen.

"You know," Parker spoke out of nowhere, startling Carly, "you kind of look like her. That woman on *Adrenaline.*"

"Which one?" Carly asked.

"The lead. The one from India. You're prettier, though." Parker's gaze rested on the ceiling above them, but her foot jiggled under the covers.

Pretty. The word traveled across the room and landed featherlight on Carly's skin. Prickles of delight traveled down her torso. "Thank you." She turned her head from Parker so she couldn't see the smile spreading across her face.

"Actually," Parker said after a while, "I think that woman, I can't remember her name, is part Scandinavian as well. I saw it on some e-news show."

Carly waited for the follow-up question. The one she hated more than anything. *Where are you from?* Which was immediately followed by judgment and *you must be…* People quickly put her in an ethnic box, so they could feel comfortable with whatever their own prejudices were.

The silence, however, stretched into the night and for once was a good thing. Parker hadn't asked. Carly could pick it up if she wanted to or not. Darn, she didn't want to like this woman.

"I think I'm something like that too. My grandmother's family is from Scotland originally. They all have freckles, pale blue eyes, and ice-blonde hair." She shrugged without looking at Parker. "I never met my father, so he could be anything."

Again silence fell, but it felt comfortable, as if Parker was really listening to her. She finally asked, "And your mother? What does she say?"

Her heart raced; she had been the one to open the door. And if they were really friends, she shouldn't close it. "Nothing."

More silence filled the room. Maybe it was the near darkness or the laughter they had shared earlier or how vulnerable Parker had looked at the Bellagio fountains when she had spoken about her own father, but Carly wanted to tell her story. "She left when I was young. She never mentioned my father before she took off. And now that I'm old enough to ask her point-blank, she's not around."

Carly squeezed her eyes shut. Would she get judgment from Parker—on her mom, on her life? Parker had said her own mom was clinically depressed, but sometimes people who were going through similar things were the harshest critics.

"That's tough. I'm sorry. She doesn't know what she's missing." And then, after a beat, Parker added, "I can imagine how hard it must be. How helpless you must feel."

Tears welled up behind Carly's eyelids. "You get it."

"I do. She's driving the situation. She's the one making the choice to not be there. And you're left out in the cold." Parker's voice was quiet, and she pulled her hair over her face like a shield.

"You sound like you know a thing or two about that as well."

"Strange as it seems, I'm in a similar position with my mother. I mean, she's there physically, but emotionally… Sometimes she's okay, sort of, but even then, she's usually so worried about slipping back into her funks, as she calls them, that she's off trying to prevent the next one. With meditations and yoga retreats and juice cleanses." She shook her head sadly. "That's the hardest part—seeing her actively make the choice to not be with us when she could be."

"Now I'm sorry. I don't know which situation is worse."

Carly turned her head and found Parker's outline under the covers. She was still staring up at the ceiling, not making eye contact, but this conversation was almost as intimate as if they were running their fingers up and down each other's bodies.

"The worst part is that we don't talk about it," Parker said. "It's the elephant in every room of our house."

Carly thought back to her recent conversation with her grandma and shifted in her bed, tucking the blanket around her shoulder with one hand. "Talking about it with your family is hard, but good, I think."

"I hope I'll know someday."

Carly had believed that Parker, who never had to worry about a dime, was carefree in all aspects of her life. Parker wasn't what she had expected at all.

"I know it's inconvenient, but I'm glad they put us in the same room." Parker's tone was soft and carried a vulnerability that reached out to Carly almost like a caress.

"Me too," Carly replied after a beat. "Good night."

"Night."

Carly closed her eyes. She found, to her surprise, that she was actually sleepy. She would have thought that nerves about her first game and the strangeness of sharing all sorts of personal things with Parker would have kept her up. But no. The conversation hadn't been easy, but strangely comfortable. Parker truly understood what she was going through.

Surprise number six was her last thought before sleep claimed her.

CHAPTER 7

New Era Stadium rang with a deafening cheer. A running back in red and blue stood in the end zone, thrusting the ball out to the crowd and celebrating his second touchdown of the day. Buffalo was up 21-6, late into the fourth quarter, and time clicked off the game clock fast. Four minutes and twenty-one seconds left. This game was almost history.

Parker hunkered down on the bench. She rubbed her hands together and blew on them for warmth. The temperature was unseasonably cold for the end of October in Buffalo, but it was more than that. She wasn't used to riding the bench for the whole game. In soccer, she was on the field for every second, directing the game from the goal, and even when she'd been kicking in college, she had warmed up on the sidelines and dashed onto the field for the point afters and the occasional field goal. But this experience was not like that. During the first quarter Hill had dropped a heavy hand on her shoulder and told her to sit tight until he called her up. Like a good soldier, she had followed orders, getting up only to trot into the locker room at halftime.

Now, it looked as if the clock would run out without her even putting a big toe on the field. Her leg jiggling, Parker glanced down the sidelines. She wasn't the only one having a bad game. The second-string quarterback had thrown two interceptions; receivers had dropped passes, and the only score had come from the field goal unit, which was two for two. Most of the Rollers hung their heads in silence.

Except for J.J. Ocean. He poked the player sitting next to him and said loudly for everyone to hear, "Don't try to smooth me out. No one's throwing a block for me out there. Shit." He drew the word out as if it had three syllables. "I'm not going to get my one thousand yards this year with these fucking little slant runs."

Parker shook her head. There might be no *i* in the spelling of *team*, but for J.J. there was certainly an *m* and *e*.

She scanned the bench in the other direction. Unbelievably, two people were actually smiling. One was Denarius Brown with a grin so big he could have been the model for half the emojis on the Internet. His play had been the only bright spot in the Rollers' game. He had put hard pressure on the quarterback and had already racked up two sacks. The last hit had been so hard that the ball had bounded down the field with a mind of its own before the Rollers recovered it. It wasn't Denarius's fault that the offense couldn't capitalize on the fumble.

And then there was Carly. Parker found her in the crowd as she darted here and there for the last three quarters. They hadn't said a word to each other since they both whispered "good luck" at the team pre-game meal, but Parker always knew where she was on the sidelines.

She had been practically shining all game long. Completely in her element, she moved about the sideline, keeping the players hydrated and constantly checking on the supplies. She handed Allen and the head AT materials even before they knew they needed them. Parker guessed at that last part because of the way the old bear—she didn't know the man's name—had looked at Carly with a combination of surprise and guarded appreciation. She was having the best game of any of them.

On the field, the official blew his whistle, and the game was over. The Rollovers had lost again.

Parker grabbed her helmet and rose stiffly from the bench. Despite Tanya's warning, this was not at all what she had signed up for. So much sitting was not in her nature. And she was getting up only to get on a bus and then a plane so she could sit some more. She bit her top lip and slapped the helmet against her leg. So much for the first time a woman suited up in the NFL.

Subdued, the team drifted into the players' tunnel in twos and threes.

Parker walked alone.

"Oh my goodness, it was…it was like… I don't even have the words." Carly's cheeks hurt, she had been smiling so much. "Being on the sidelines, right in the thick of things, was so awesome. I'm just sorry that we lost."

Late as it was, she, Minnie Lee, and Teddy crowded around the breakfast bar with three forks, picking at a chicken potpie that Minnie Lee had *liberated* from the diner. Carly wasn't eating much. She hadn't come down from the high of the game. At one point, she even glanced down at the barstool to see if she were actually floating on air.

"I wish it had been on basic cable." Teddy speared a carrot with his fork and popped it into his mouth. "I wanted to see you. You're kind of famous now, you know?"

Carly snorted.

"No, seriously." He jabbed his fork at the picture of Carly leaning up against the wall at the back of the bar. She looked cool and collected in the newspaper photo from the Rollers' party.

"I'm the least famous one in that picture, but thanks, T." Carly reached out to ruffle his hair, only to drop her hand midway when she remembered that he had told her he was too old for that kind of thing now.

"It was on the front page of the *Sentinel*. Everyone saw it. I say you're famous." Teddy nodded as if he knew a few things about life.

"What about that girl?" Minnie Lee asked out of nowhere.

"What girl?"

"That girl." She pointed to Parker in the photograph. "The kicker. Did she score?"

Carly flinched inwardly before shaking her head. Odd that her grandmother would bring up Parker. Carly had been involved with football since high school, and never once had she taken an interest in any of the players. "Not yet. The Rollers never got a touchdown, so she never got a chance. Actually, I heard in the training room afterward that the front office was relieved since they want her to score in front of a home crowd, and they don't want it to look like they planned it that way."

What she didn't repeat was that, apparently, Hill was royally pissed off. Rumor had it Hill was against playing Parker at all and turning the game into a profile raiser for some dinky soccer athlete.

She wondered if Parker knew. Even though they hadn't sat together on the plane home, she had tried to keep an eye on her. If their conversation the night before had taught her anything, Parker was more fragile than she looked.

"You've got a home game this weekend." Teddy brought her back to the present. He waved his fork in the air with excitement. "Do you think you can get me a ticket?"

Minnie Lee gave him the evil eye. "And do you think you can find the manners of a civilized person, young man?"

Teddy lowered his fork to his napkin. "Do you, sis?"

"Maybe. It might be too soon for me to ask. I'll see how the week goes. But I should be good for Tuesday night."

"I don't need a babysitter." Teddy rocked on his barstool and heaved a dramatic sigh. "I can take the neighborhood kids trick-or-treating myself. Raul will be there." He raised his eyebrows at Carly, and when she didn't say anything, he shifted his gaze to Minnie Lee.

"Maybe next year, Teddy." Their grandmother patted his head. "Besides, Mrs. Linsinger's grandson will be joining you, and from what I hear, he's a handful. Trust me. You'll be happy to have Carly with you."

"Fine." Teddy yanked his head away before piercing a hunk of pie crust.

Carly rubbed her sore cheek trying to hide another smile. Thirteen was such an odd mixture of man and little boy.

Parker's also full of contradictions.

Where the hell had that come from? The thought, uninvited, had just jumped into her mind. She let the impression of Parker unravel rather than shoving it back out. At first glance, Parker came off cool and more than a little entitled. But underneath…

Oh God, I have to find her tomorrow and tell her about what Hill said. That vote of no-confidence will bite her when she's not looking.

At the very least she could look after Parker. Buck had never said anything about that.

Tuesday, however, came and went without a Parker sighting. Carly looked around at meals. She and the other ATs were crazy busy tending to all the aches and pains that the players had brought home, like rubbish in their pockets, from Monday's game. This day, even though it was the players' day off, was no better. The day was gobbled up by one treatment after another, and when Carly finally tapped her fake Fitbit, the digital readout said four thirty.

"Wow, where did the time go?"

"You must be having fun." Allen looked at her in his fatherly way.

"I am. You know, I loved working at UNLV, but this… There's an energy here that takes everything to the next level." She swallowed. Was she giving too much away here?

"I know." Allen laughed softly. "But as much fun as you're having, I'm sure you want to go home and get ready for Halloween. I'm heading over to Buck to update him on Jonesey's ankle. Would you do a quick restock of the tables, and if no one else comes in, you can take off."

"Oh, Allen, that would be great. Thanks."

"Sure thing. Enjoy your night."

Once Allen left, she pulled out her cell and dialed her grandma. Minnie Lee had a cell phone but had never mastered texting. She said she just didn't want to be that available to people. True to her word, she almost never picked up either. Mostly, she preferred to listen to the messages on her own schedule. "Hey, Gran," Carly said after the beep. "Can you tell Teddy that I'll be home at about six? I'll text Raul and ask him to bring the van around at six thirty. Call me back if you see a problem with that plan."

She dropped the phone on the training table in the back as she started to restock its drawers. That way she could hear the buzz if Minnie Lee called back.

Twenty minutes later with no return call, she closed the last of the drawers, slung her backpack over her shoulder, and grabbed her phone. With her back to the door, she tapped the keyboard.

Raul, we'll meet you at the parking lot on Jeffreys St. at 6:30. C U soon.

"Ah-hem." Someone, probably a player wanting a late treatment, cleared his throat behind her.

Dang it. Men were often such babies where pain was concerned. Now she wouldn't get home in time. She tried to wipe her face of any annoyance and spun toward the door.

"Hi." Parker raised a hand in greeting; the other grabbed the door handle and jiggled it.

"Oh, it's you." Carly furrowed her brow.

Parker swallowed hard. She had hoped that Carly would wave her into the room and give her one of her wonderful smiles. "Sorry to disappoint you."

"No. No. That's not what I meant. I thought that you were… Never mind. Can I help you? Is it your hamstring?"

"No, actually that feels great. I came to get a real workout in without all the stupid comments from the guys and just thought I'd peek in to see if you were here."

"So, you're not hurt?"

"No."

This wasn't the conversation she had rehearsed in her head. Things had gone so well at the hotel in Buffalo. She had thought they would just pick up where they had left off, but this was back to square one. She was the client, and Carly was hiding behind the work. This friendship thing was way harder than a casual fling.

Parker stalled and glanced at Carly's backpack. "Sorry. You're on your way out. Big plans for Halloween?"

Lame. But at least they were still talking.

"Sort of. I'm going trick-or-treating. Well, I'm not really going trick-or-treating; I'm going with my brother. And he's thirteen, so he's not really going either. But we take some of the kids in our apartment complex out to another community every year, and I hide in the background. Teddy gets to feel like he's in control, and I make sure they're all okay." A light blush spread across her face, emphasizing her freckles.

She was rambling. Could she be nervous too? The tension flowed out of Parker's shoulders. Maybe they were in it together after all. "Do you wear a costume?"

"Yeah. Usually."

"Then you're going trick-or-treating."

The red color deepened on Carly's cheeks.

Parker's fingers slid off the door handle, and she took a step inside the room. "I think it's great. I love Halloween, as you know."

"Me too, actually." They smiled at each other. "You doing something at your dad's hotel?"

"No."

"I thought there might be a big party or something there."

143

"There probably is, but I'm not going. I like things lower-key." She shook her head. "I'm not sure what I'm doing." She peered over at Carly. Would she ask her to come?

Carly sighed.

That seemed like a clear no. She had totally flubbed asking Carly out at the party. She shouldn't go there again, and so, like a mental telepathist, she concentrated and willed Carly to throw out an invite. Nothing. Carly didn't even look up as she zipped closed the pockets on her backpack with an intense focus as if she were performing complex surgery.

Wait a sec. This isn't a date. Friends do stuff together all the time. I could ask.

"Do you think…? Maybe I could…?" Shit, she didn't know how to invite someone on a not-a-date date.

Carly finally met her gaze. "You could come with us, but…" Her voice was low and unsure.

"But…?" Parker's stomach churned. What was she doing? She was practically asking for rejection.

"It is a little complicated," Carly said.

Yep. Here came the brush-off.

"We're going to a gated community, and we obviously don't live there. Raul, this guy who lives in our apartment complex, is a gardener out there, and he has a pass. So, every year we gather up a bunch of kids, pile them into his van, and drive out there. The community's safe; the kids get a ton of candy, so it's a win-win. But there are a lot of kids, so…"

"You're full up?"

Carly nodded.

She could leave it at that. Carly hadn't rejected her. Not technically at least. But Parker found herself asking, "What if I can find my own way out there?"

Carly hesitated. "Okay."

A lukewarm okay? That was hardly a ringing endorsement of the plan. Parker's chest tightened. "You know what? I'm good. My father might actually appreciate it if I show up to the hotel's party." That was a bold-faced lie—her father couldn't care less—but if she let her off the hook, Carly wasn't officially brushing her off.

"No. No. It's not that I don't want you to come. It's... um..." Carly sighed deeply, then nodded as if answering her own silent question. "Buck told me not to fraternize with the players." She pushed the last words out quickly with almost no breath.

Parker couldn't quite identify her expression. "That's terrible, but I'm not one of the guys on the team, and you're straight. So we're good, right?"

Carly twisted the backpack with both hands. "Right."

Parker's chest expanded. *Great. It's a not-date.* She bit her tongue so she wouldn't say it out loud.

Carly sat in Raul's van and breathed in the pleasant smell of grass cuttings. She had read somewhere that the fresh green scent was a stress reducer. But it wasn't working for her. Guilt about Parker rolled in her gut. Letting her believe she was straight was not cool. Their friendship was grounded in a lie, and if she came clean, a true friendship or anything else was probably out of the question. Was that why she had made sure Minnie Lee was out of earshot when she'd told Teddy that Parker would join them?

"Cool," he said simply, but his attention had been on Eric Linsinger, who was at this very moment trying to pull the whiskers off Lily, the eight-year-old leopard in the row of seats behind them.

Teddy thrust his bloody zombie face around the headrest. "Eric." He raised his voice in a surprisingly good imitation of their grandmother at her strictest.

Vampire Eric dropped his hands immediately but tried to pinch Lily's side on the way down.

"Keep your hands to yourself, Dracula." Teddy gave him Minnie Lee's evil eye.

Eric exhaled roughly through his nose and sank back against the seat—for the moment.

A burst of pride spread in Carly's chest. Maybe Teddy was right. He was growing up and didn't need a babysitter. His costume was proof enough. Teddy had saved for months to purchase the latex and makeup to create his costume. He even had a fake bite mark on his arm, complete with blue veins to highlight the infection spreading into the rest of his body.

The warm feeling didn't last long, though. As the van approached the gate at the Desert Shores, Carly's heart began to thud.

"Where's your friend, Carly?" Raul called back from the driver's seat, voicing her own concern. She didn't want to hold up the group waiting if Parker turned out to be late or a flake.

"She should be here." Carly peered out the side window. The only person shuffling along the sidewalk was another zombie. This one was clothed in a tattered suit, splattered with moss, giving it that fresh-from-the-grave look. Oozing blood dripped down the creature's face from a bloody socket where one eye used to be, and it wore a blood-doused fedora with a bullet hole running straight through the center.

Hold on. Carly craned her head around in a double take.

A long, blonde ponytail snuck out of the hat and fell down the zombie's back.

"Stop. That's her, I think."

"Where?" Raul hit the brakes.

"That zombie over there." Carly pointed out the window.

In what could have been a scene from a horror show on cable TV, the van stopped, and Carly dove out the open door, moving right toward the zombie.

"Parker?"

Playing completely against type, the zombie gave her a huge grin. "Hey. I was just about to text you."

Carly grinned back. "Jump in." She got back in the van and scooted over as much as she could.

There wasn't a seat or a seat belt, but they were only going about three hundred yards. Parker perched on the armrest and took in the occupants of the van with one glance.

"Oh my God." Teddy's smile was a mile wide. "You're Hawker."

"No, Teddy, I said Parker, not Hawker."

Teddy laughed. "Hawker's a character from *Deadication*." When Carly shrugged, he added, "The TV show?"

"You really need to watch more than medical dramas." Parker swiveled back to Teddy. "Glad you got my zombie memo."

"Wow." He shook his head, almost in slow motion. "You got to tell me how you did your eye makeup."

"I didn't do it myself. Someone at the place I'm staying at did it for me."

That was one way of spinning it. Had a tribe of makeup artists from the spa or the beauty salon piled into her room and worked their magic?

"Yours is much cooler, though," Parker said. "You're Cooper Coons from *Whispers of the Dead*, right?"

Teddy's eyes widened. "You've read those books?"

"Of course. Who hasn't?"

Teddy pointed to Carly. "She hasn't. See, I told you." He poked Carly. "They're really good."

"I never doubted you, T." She glanced from her brother to Parker, who was nodding just as hard as Teddy. Her one good eye shone with excitement. Damn, she was hot even with gobs of fake blood oozing down her face.

"I like her," Teddy whispered to Carly as they got out of the van on the other side of the gate. Before Carly could answer, he jumped to grab Eric back from the curb as a car sped by. "You know you're not a real vampire. You need to stay alive to get your candy."

"Leave me alone." Eric stomped off.

Teddy trotted after him. "Hey, Eric, do you know why the vampire had no friends?"

Eric didn't turn around.

"Because he was a pain in the neck," Teddy called after him.

"Ha, good one." Parker appeared at Carly's elbow. "I like him."

"He said the same about you." Goose bumps rose on her arm. Parker and Teddy were a lot alike. "Well, then, on top of everything else, he has good taste, Dr. Bartlet." Parker tugged at the stethoscope around Carly's neck, pulling her sideways. Their shoulders bumped in a casual, friendly way. Parker's strides were long and smooth as they followed the pack of kids down the street.

Carly had to quicken her pace to keep up.

It was a gorgeous night. The warm desert breeze embraced them, running feathery-light over their skin. A man-made finger lake flowed to their right and gave the community the *shores* of its name and a hefty price tag for residency. Houses here had both water and mountain views and were far enough from the Strip to feel like a small town in the middle of the big, rambling city.

"Your costume works," Parker said. "Very realistic."

"It should be. I got the scrubs from a doctor at UNLV."

"Could use a hatchet and a bloody scar right about here, though." Parker stopped in the middle of the sidewalk and reached out for her cheek.

Carly's body went still, readying herself for the touch. Achingly, Parker stopped just inches from her face and withdrew her hand.

"I'll get Teddy on it for next year." The breathlessness in her voice surprised her. She glanced ahead. Teddy had rounded up the kids and was leading them through the ritzy neighborhood all decked out for the holiday. They strolled into a graveyard with figures who popped from the graves and then admired a tall tree at the next house with a transparent ghost swinging from the branches. More ghosts materialized in the upstairs windows of a huge corner estate.

"This is great." Parker scooted back from a robot spider that crawled down the front steps. Hanging over this particular door was a giant plywood clown's head whose teeth were so sharp and realistic, they looked as if they could drop at any second and bite off the heads of the screaming, laughing kids.

"I love how much this neighborhood gets into it." She had thought Parker might be bored trick-or-treating with a bunch of kids, but she seemed to really be enjoying herself. "Every year the neighbors try to outdo one another. And you wouldn't believe the haul. Teddy still has candy at Valentine's Day."

"I can see why." Parker motioned to the creepy clown handing out full-size candy bars to Teddy and his group.

Up on the porch, the clown sank to his knees in front of Lily. "And who are you supposed to be?" His soft voice—in fact, his entire demeanor—played against his terrifying costume.

"Just a leopard," Lilly answered and ducked her head.

"Well, Miss Leopard, which candy bar would you like?" He fanned out a Hershey's Bar and a KitKat as if they were a deck of cards.

Lily pulled the KitKat out of his fingers.

"Good choice." The clown dropped a plain Hershey's Bar into Eric's open pillow sack and turned to the rest of the kids crowding him.

"I want a KitKat." Eric snatched it out of Lily's hand.

"Whoa. Wait a sec." Teddy jumped between them lightning quick, missing his own turn at a supersized pack of Starbursts. "That's not your candy."

"It's not fair," Eric whined and clutched the KitKat more tightly. "I just got a stupid Hershey's."

"Life's hardly ever fair." Teddy echoed Minnie Lee. "Sometimes you need to realize that."

Carly bit back a smile; she couldn't wait to tell their grandmother how much Teddy was channeling her tonight.

"Give it back, buddy, and apologize." Teddy stood over him until Eric reluctantly passed the candy bar over.

"Sorry." He didn't sound sorry at all.

"How would you feel if someone took your candy?" Teddy tugged at his high collar. "Now, come on. You're with me."

Carly watched them hop off the porch and walk past her to the sidewalk. Calm, cool, and collected, Teddy was right on Eric's heels, explaining how might did not equal right in this world. Eric listened with only one ear, but he was listening. With a little luck, both of them might survive the evening, and Eric might actually learn a thing or two. The pride that had burst in Carly's chest earlier brimmed over, until she glanced back to the porch.

Lily hadn't moved; she was still staring at the KitKat, her mouth trembling as if she was fighting back tears.

Carly's cheeks burned. She had been so focused on congratulating Teddy that she hadn't noticed the real issue. Lily. And she should've. She'd been right where Lily was with her own Eric: J.J. Ocean.

But Parker had. She was at Lily's side in a flash and bent down. "What's wrong?"

"I just let him take it. I wanted the KitKat, but I just let him take it." Lily looked up at Parker and searched her face. "Why?"

"That's a really good question." Parker blew out a breath. "I don't know."

"I wish I could've told him that I wanted it. But I didn't. Teddy had to do it."

Just like Allen. Carly clutched the stethoscope around her neck as she waited for what Parker might say next.

"You know," Parker began, "sometimes girls think that they have to be nice all the time and are not allowed to say what's on their mind or what's right. But we don't. We can't be mean or say things that hurt people, but we should stand up for ourselves. Always."

Lily furrowed her brow as she clearly tried to digest Parker's advice.

Carly couldn't help shaking her head. *Could I have done that with J.J.? Maybe if I had started when I was eight. Maybe if I had someone in my corner, telling me I could.*

On the porch, Parker took off her hat and ran a hand through her hair.

"Oh," Lily said as soon as most of Parker's face was revealed. "You were in the paper. My mom showed it to me. She said," Lily's voice jumped up an octave, "that you were doing something that no other girl had done. She said that I could grow up to do things that no other girl could do too."

"Yes, you can. And you can start by believing in yourself and standing up to Dracula."

"Should I say something to him now?"

"I think so. We can't assume that people know how we feel. We need to speak up. Or at least try even when we don't know how." She stole a glance over her shoulder.

Carly's mouth went dry. Parker couldn't possibly have heard her thoughts.

"Practice with me first?" Parker pointed to her ear. "Sometimes we need to practice saying hard things out loud, so when the time comes, we can do it."

Lily thought for a minute, pulled her down, and whispered something too soft for Carly to hear. Immediately, the girl shook her head. "No. No. This is better." She tried again. "Yes?"

"Yes." Parker adjusted the cat ears on the top of Lily's head. "Go get him, tiger. I mean, leopard."

Lily set her mouth in a firm line and marched right to Eric, who was getting candy at the next house.

"Come on." Parker grabbed Carly by the arm and tugged her over.

"Eric." Lily stopped right in front of him as he exited the house. "You get what you get, and you don't get upset. Didn't you learn that in kindergarten?"

At first, Eric tried to scoot around her, but Teddy's hand dropped to his shoulder like an iron clamp.

"Fine." Eric's voice was thin.

A slow smile crept onto Lily's face as if all sorts of possibilities had opened up to her right then and there. She pivoted and gave Parker a thumbs-up.

Parker also threw her thumb into the air and grinned.

At her side, Carly clapped once in delight. Parker had orchestrated one of those quiet little moments that could bloom like a flower when it began to grow. She had run to Lily's side on instinct, not to be a role model, that wasn't her style, but she had been fierce and protective like a mother bear. Lily was lucky to have Parker at her side. Anyone would be. "That was wonderful," Carly said.

"Yeah, she did great."

"No, I mean, you." Her heart sped up as she shifted all her focus to Parker.

"Wonderful? That's going a little far."

"No, it isn't. It's hard for women to say what they think. What you said to Lily might make a real difference for the rest of her life."

Parker rolled her eyes.

"No, I'm serious." And she was. She might have had a louder voice in her own life if her mother had said something similar. By the time her grandmother had, she had been too hurt to hear it.

"You know," Parker cut into her thoughts. Her voice was soft and serious. "My dad told me that I needed to embrace the responsibility that came with my job at the Rollers. You think this is what he meant?"

"It could be."

Parker caught Carly's gaze. "That's a heavy mantle to wear."

"Your shoulders are broad enough." She ran a glance over Parker's shoulders. Literally they were. But not strong enough for betrayals from someone who was supposed to be on her team. "Look. I got to tell you something I heard at work."

"What?" In a habit that Carly was beginning to recognize, Parker began to fiddle with the brim of her hat again.

"I didn't hear it firsthand, but if it were me, I think I would want to know." She tamped down the desire to reach out for Parker's hand to ease the blow.

"Just tell me. I can take it."

"Okay." She would take Parker at her word and hope she was right. "I overheard a conversation between Buck and Allen. Apparently, Coach Hill told Buck that he didn't care what Marina wanted; he wasn't going to play you."

Parker crunched the hat's brim with both hands. A vein twitched in her neck. "Did he say why?"

"No." Carly couldn't stop herself and reached out to run a hand down her arm just the way she did when Teddy was upset about something. "Not that I could hear anyway."

Parker let out a heavy sigh. "Who else did Buck tell?"

"He wasn't gossiping, if that's what you're worried about." Odd that she was defending Buck, but that really had been her impression. "He's concerned. With Winslow going down early on and J.J. all about his one thousand yards, there's too much

154

bad energy floating around, and Buck doesn't want more drama brewing."

Parker pushed the hat back onto her head and tugged the brim down over her forehead. "Maybe that is exactly what the Rollers need. More drama. Someone to shake things up a bit."

Carly reached out again, but this time to pull Parker back toward her. They stood face to face. Carly swallowed hard against a sudden tightness in her throat, surprised once again how much she cared. "Parker, don't go looking for trouble."

The realization that she was giving her the exact opposite advice that Parker had just given Lily hit her hard. Wasn't she really telling Parker to be silent? Oh God, she was! It wasn't so easy when there was more than a KitKat at stake.

Parker pressed her lips together and curled her hands into fists. "I've heard that advice before."

"And do you ever take it?"

Parker gave her a smile that looked like a predatory animal showing its teeth. "Not usually."

Carly pressed a hand to her pounding heart. Going head-to-head with Coach Hill was trouble with a capital T. And yet... She took a deep breath and felt her lungs expand under her hand. Parker was standing up for herself and living her message. How many people actually did that?

Not her.

Not yet.

CHAPTER 8

Parker arrived at the stadium bright and early the next day. By the time the other players were suiting up, she had already run and hit the weight room. Endorphins buzzing, she strode into the locker room. She wasn't going to take any shit today.

Rumor had it that Hill was not happy with the way special teams had played in Buffalo. Parker didn't blame him. Missed opportunities and only six points weren't going to win any games. She'd be pissed too.

"Hey, Sherbourne! You responsible for this?" Hekekia held his phone out to her, daring her to come over.

She hadn't expected to be tested before practice, but she headed his way, head held high.

His phone held nothing but his trick-snapping video. "Responsible for what?" she asked. "You made that video."

"Yeah, but my views have doubled. Some influencer named Mateo Sherbourne got a hold of it and is directing traffic to my site. He related to you?"

"My nephew. But I didn't ask him to. I just sent him the video." She shrugged as if she didn't care that Mateo had run with it. "I thought he would like it."

Veris slapped him on his back. "Pakalani Hekekia. You're going to have to change your name if you're going to be a YouTube star."

"Never. My mother would kill me." But he smiled broadly as he pointed again to the number of hits.

Parker's eyebrows rose. Could this be a nut starting to crack? Of course, she couldn't buy his respect with followers; she knew that. But the videos were great. He deserved whatever he could get from them.

"Come on, you pansies. Quit standing around. Practice is starting." The punt returner strolled toward the door. "Yep. Just another day at the office."

——————◦✕◦———————

The assistant coach burst into the training room. "Hill's gone crazy!"

Carly swung toward him, her heart freezing. *Parker's out there* was her first thought.

"He's gone live on the practice field." The assistant coach could barely catch his breath.

"What?" Allen's brow furrowed. "Full contact this late in the season?"

What the heck? Carly glanced to the whiteboard on the wall of the training room. There was no live practice scheduled.

The assistant coach threw up both hands. "I told you. He's gone crazy. Said he's never seen playing as bad as Sunday. He's going to kill them to make his point. Can you send someone out?"

Allen inclined his head to Carly. "Good to go?"

"Absolutely." In fact, she had grabbed her kit the second Allen's head tilted toward her. This was what she lived for, but she didn't like the fact that Parker was on the other end of Hill's sudden insanity.

The assistant coach hadn't exaggerated. Fierce, almost desperate energy swirled on the practice field. Hill shouted instructions; players jumped to, and the clash of bodies reverberated in the smaller space. As Carly stepped on the turf, Koch limped off the field, favoring one ankle. Carly rushed out to help him off.

"Sherbourne!" Hill called out.

Parker jumped from the bench as if she had been shot out of a cannon and dashed onto the turf.

Carly immediately spotted the bounce in her step and admired her obvious sheer joy of being in motion. This was what Parker lived for too.

Offense and defense set up, and as Parker moved into the field goal formation, the defense surged. A linebacker got off the ball, slid through the gap, and jumped. High. His hand hit the ball with a hard slap, sending it back to the ground behind the line of scrimmage. Everyone went for the ball as if they were hitting bumpers in a pinball game.

"Holy shit." Koch jumped off the bench, clearly forgetting all about his ankle.

Carly did too, for a minute. Parker, despite her no-touch status as a kicker, was in the thick of the play, fighting just as hard as any of them to recover the ball. Carly sucked in a quick breath. *Be careful.*

Maybe it was all those years of being a soccer goalie at the highest level or just dumb luck, but Parker snatched the ball right out of the air.

"What's she doing?" Koch shouted into Carly's ear. "She could be pulverized if she makes a move."

Nonetheless, Parker zeroed in on the end zone and pumped her legs toward it.

Carly's heart froze and then started to pound. This was the real Parker. A woman who found the opening, now or with Lily, and went for it. She cut first to the left and then the right to avoid two defensive backs, hot in pursuit.

Carly brought a hand to her mouth. *Come on. Come on! You can make it.* Just as the thought formed in her head, a two-hundred-fifty-pound defender came out of nowhere and hit her with a ton of force. The thud traveled all the way across the field. Parker flattened like a pancake on the turf.

"Fuck me," Koch said.

Oh my God! Carly's stomach clenched. She raced onto the field. Hill held up a hand in her direction, but she didn't stop. Parker could be really hurt. She hadn't moved as far as Carly could tell.

Silence stretched out between players as they crowded around Parker on the ground. A no-touch player had been hit by a Mack truck. The defender rose from the ground and backed away with raised palms. Players had been released from teams for less. "Coach, I...I—"

"Relax, Watkins, she made her choice. She was fair game in my book." Hill moved to stand over Parker, hands on his hips. "You okay, rookie?"

Carly wove through the players to get to Parker's side and leaned in to hear her answer.

"Yep." She pushed up on her arms and then to her knees. "Just got the wind knocked out of me."

She sounded strong, but the true test was how she got up.

The players cleared; Hekekia was the only one to stay back. He stared at Parker for a while, and just when Carly thought he might offer her a hand, Parker rolled to her feet on her own, and the moment was lost.

As Parker walked back to the huddle, Carly studied her movement. She walked stiffly, but the tilt of her pelvis and her steady pace all said she really was okay. Even so, Carly longed to pull her to a concussion tent and stare deeply into her eyes to make sure.

As a professional, she told herself, not a worried friend.

But there was no blue tent set up on the sidelines for practice, and besides, she couldn't undermine Parker's big moment. A couple of players patted her on the shoulders as they huddled up, and one even called out, "Way to take it, rookie."

Carly blew out a long breath as she headed back to her place on the bench.

She would keep a close eye on her. That would be the professional thing to do, after all.

After practice, Parker raised a hand to Hill's office door and froze. She was sore all over, but that wasn't what was stopping her. She was afraid Carly was right. Was she looking for trouble by coming down here? No, something about Hill had always rubbed her the wrong way. That cold gleam in his eyes as he stood over her on the field that morning only confirmed her feelings. Besides, if she was going to be the person that Lily saw her as, she needed to confront him.

Tap. Tap. Tap. Her knuckles grazed the glass.

"Come in." Hill's deep voice seeped through the door.

When Parker stuck her head into the office, the phone was glued to his ear. "Do I sound like I give two shits?" His tone was soft and controlled, but he pounded his fist on the desk with each word. "He needs to quit arm wrestling with the defense and drive off his legs. In fact, tell him exactly that." The handset made a plastic popping noise as Hill pushed it back into the cradle.

"What do you want?" He didn't offer her a chair. Not that he really could have. Papers, several laptops, and plays drawn out in green ink spilled everywhere, even onto the two guest chairs in front of his desk.

"You got a second, coach?" Parker shuffled her feet.

"That was a dumb stunt, Sherbourne. Kickers have a red jersey for a reason."

"Yeah, I know. I just wanted to prove to you that I can play. To show you that you'd be smart to give me a chance at that extra point in a game sooner rather than later."

"The offense has to score. That's out of my control. Yours too, if I'm not mistaken."

"Yes, I know that too." Parker tried to beat down the exasperation rising in her voice. "But when they do, you'll play me, right?"

Pursing his lips, Hill hesitated—just long enough to announce, as if he had spoken out loud, that the rumors were true.

Parker crossed her arms over her chest to stifle the tightness spreading within. "If you don't, Marina's not going to be happy."

Hill's eyes widened and then almost instantly narrowed. A hard glint flashed. "Again. No shits given. My job is to make my best call, and that's what Marina will get regarding you. Who, if you haven't noticed, is hands-off where strategy is concerned. She leaves the coaching to the professionals."

Hill was intense, for sure. His tactics were sometimes questioned, but he was an excellent special teams coach. He should be jumping all over this opportunity to turn a soccer player into a football star. It would cement his name as a legend of the game.

"Coach." She licked her lips to give herself more time. "At least give this some consideration."

"I have. I plan to be on the right side of this."

"Which is?" Parker was pretty sure that she already stood on the right side of this equation.

"Football's side. It's a thinking man's game. It's ruthless and poetic all at the same time. Every play's a dogfight, and yet, there's more strategy in football than in a grandmaster chess game. You scoring will turn the game into a joke."

Parker's hackles rose. "It's going to happen, Coach. If not me, then some other woman."

"There shouldn't be girls on the field at all." He pursed his lips and shook his head slowly. "And if there has to be, you're not the girl to make it happen."

"Meaning what?" Parker stiffened, readying herself for a lecture on how a *girl* with as much money as she had didn't get how to work hard for anything. *Bring it on, little man. I've heard it before. I can take it.*

Hill's hard smile broke into an arrogant laugh. "Meaning that you shouldn't be a role model for anyone with your lifestyle choices."

"Excuse me?" Parker tipped her head and met his gaze head-on. Surely, she had misunderstood.

"You might be out and proud on the soccer field, and I know the Fire doesn't care. They hired that female coach. But even though the Rollers aren't having the best season, this is still Sunday's best down here. Or at least it should be."

"Let's be clear. You're not playing me because I'm gay?"

"I never said that in so many words." He leaned back in his desk chair.

A heaviness churned in her stomach. This couldn't be happening. "Hill, that's discrimination and illegal and... and..." Her breath hitched in her throat as the words and even her thoughts rammed up against each other. Her gaze darted all over the room, landing on everything but the man in front of her.

"Like I said. The team needs to score before any of this is a real issue." He pulled his playbook off the desk and flipped it open. "If you'll excuse me, I've got work to do."

Parker backed out of his office, her mouth set in a thin line, and by the time she turned the corner, her shoulders had tensed into one hard mass. She could take an attack on her skills, her training regime, even her choices on the field, but this wasn't about the game.

This was personal.

She banged open the door to her locker closet. The mop was still jammed into the corner. In over a week, no one had come to take it out. Throwing a locker into a janitor's closet didn't make a locker room. And putting a uniform on a lesbian soccer star apparently didn't create a football player in Hill's eyes either. She tore off her practice jersey, unbuckled the belts of her pads and yanked them off at the neck. She slammed them into the locker and missed. They dropped to the cement with a thud, and the mop clattered to the floor.

"Parker?" Carly knocked on the door. "You okay?"

Here Carly was. Just when she needed her. Like the hotel in Buffalo all over again. But this time Parker wasn't sure if she wanted her. She didn't want to be talked out of her anger. Carly was straight. She would understand in theory, but—

"Parker, I know you're in there. I can hear you. I need to check on you. It's protocol for a possible concussion."

"I'm fine. I never hit my head."

"Let me in. I'm not leaving until I know you're fine."

Sighing, Parker pulled at the door.

Carly pushed her way inside and immediately ran an assessing gaze up and down her body. "How are you feeling? No slurred speech? Confusion or nausea?"

"No."

Carly gently laid her hand on Parker's chin, tipped her face down, and looked deeply into her eyes. "No headache or blurred vision?"

"No. Seriously, I'm fine." She tried to wriggle out of her grasp, but Carly held firm.

"Well, there's something wrong. I can tell."

Could she? Did she know her well enough after such a short time? Carly's gaze drilled into her. However, there was kindness and caring in the golden depths of her eyes as well as professional concern. Parker couldn't remember the last time anyone had looked at her like that.

"I went to see Hill."

Carly dropped her hand. "And?"

"And what Buck said was true." She shook her head. "He doesn't want to play me. Because I'm gay."

Carly gasped. "Seriously?"

Parker nodded, unable to speak.

"You need to tell someone." Carly's words tumbled out. "Marina. Let's go tell her right now." She spun to the door.

Parker grabbed her arm. "I can't. If I go and report it, it will seem like a kid running to Mom when Dad said no, or, worse, it will turn into a he-said, she-said kind of deal. And the cardinal rule of team sports is you never *ask* a coach for playing time; you *show* them you deserve it."

"But you can't let him—"

"That's the other thing. There wasn't a chance to put me in on Monday. Technically, he's done nothing wrong."

Parker glanced down and winced. She was still holding Carly's arm long after she should have let go. After squeezing lightly in thanks, she released her hold.

"This sucks." Carly's voice was too loud for the small space. "It's not right."

Parker took in her first easy breath since Hill's office. Okay, she was glad Carly was there after all. Carly really cared. "You're telling me! I know this reeks of privilege, but I've never had anyone attack me for my sexuality. Not once. I came out in high school, kissed my girlfriend on the soccer field in front of everyone, and even then, in that conservative prep school, no one really cared. Or at least didn't care to my face. It's never been an issue with my family or the NWSL. Funny…I had to come all the way to Sin City to meet up with prejudice."

"It's not fun, right?"

Carly broke into her thoughts, and Parker focused on the woman in front of her. Carly's gaze had clouded over. Oh shit, how could she be so insensitive?

"I'm really sorry. You must see prejudice all the time too. I didn't mean to make this all about me." She had to stop talking before she dug a hole so deep, she couldn't climb out. She couldn't imagine what Carly must think of her now.

Silence spread out between them, long enough that more self-recrimination and another dozen ways to apologize popped into Parker's mind.

"That's not what I'm talking about." Carly's voice was flat and low. Her gaze darted about the room as if she was considering her next move very carefully.

Parker furrowed her brow. Whatever was going on here was beyond her but, clearly, was a big deal for Carly. At the very least, she could give her back the support that she had just soaked up. She reached out to lightly grasp her forearm again. Would Carly get the wrong impression? She truly meant the touch as only friendly and encouraging. Even so, she willed her fingers not to tremble. "So, what are you talking about?"

⚬⚬⚬

Carly looked down at Parker's hand. Her touch was warm and soft and sent a comforting tingle through her entire body.

Was she really going to do this? She couldn't take it back once she said it out loud. It also wasn't the best timing. Parker was already upset. This would make her only madder and rightly so.

But she hated lying to Parker, to anyone really, and the longer she waited, the harder it would get to tell the truth. Besides, seeing how confident Parker was in her own life made her want to be more visible in her own.

Squaring her shoulders, Carly took a deep breath and then another. "I…I like women too." When Parker threw her a questioning look, she added, "You know…as more than friends…"

Parker opened and closed her mouth a few times before she finally asked, "You do?"

Carly nodded and, as if giving proof, put her own hand over Parker's.

Frozen as still as statues, neither moved. And then Parker withdrew her hand. "Why didn't you tell me at the party or at the hotel? Jesus, I…"

"I'm sorry—" She stopped herself. No, she wasn't going to apologize, just explain. Parker could do with it what she wanted. "There are so many reasons. I'm not as free as you. I didn't shout my sexuality out in high school. Heck, I haven't even come out to my family. Besides, I hate drama. You kind of invite it in for coffee. And I guess the most important thing is that Buck flat-out told me that I couldn't date anyone on the team or he would fire me."

Parker said nothing.

The silence battered Carly until she wished she could pull her confession back like a loose thread on a sweater.

"And you're going to let him tell you what to do?" Parker finally asked.

"I have to. I really, really need this job." Carly rubbed her arm where Parker's hand had been. She missed her touch.

"You should have told me." Parker shook her head in quick jerks.

"I should've, but Buck was watching and I was afraid." She rubbed her neck. "But you know, in all honesty, I'm not sure it would've made a difference. The way you asked me out wasn't the most flattering proposition I've ever had."

Parker winced, and a flush crept over her cheeks.

"Sorry," Carly said. "I didn't mean to be harsh."

"No. I'm sorry." Parker cupped her own face, maybe to feel how badly she was blushing. "You kind of make me lose my words."

"Is that good or bad?"

"Both." Parker picked up the pads on the floor and hung them up in her locker. She adjusted a rivet on the neck and then swung back around. "So, how should I have asked you out?"

Carly's inner alarm bells blared. They were sliding into dangerous territory. She shouldn't play this game at all. But still she heard herself answer, "I don't know. Dinner, a movie, a hike. Something a little more thoughtful than asking if I was up for that kind of thing."

Parker's cheeks went rosy again, but this time the blush was accompanied by a charming smile. "Okay, okay, I get it."

Energy crackled between them, and Carly edged to the door. "Look. I need to get back. I know nothing's settled with Hill, but can we talk later?"

"Maybe over dinner?"

When Carly rolled her eyes, Parker threw up both hands and added quickly, "As friends. Only friends."

"Sure?" She hadn't meant it to, but her answer came out as a question.

Parker thrust her hand out for a shake. "Seriously. I promise. I'm not the one who's been lying."

Ouch. That stung, but Parker had every right to be upset. "Okay, if you promise…" Carly returned the smile.

Parker chuckled, and all awkwardness between them melted away.

As Carly stepped in, hand outstretched, to seal the deal, she stumbled over the mop that still lay on the floor. Her ankle rolled right, then left, and almost in slow motion, she began to tumble.

Parker grabbed her instantly, wrapped a strong arm around her, and pulled her close.

Carly knew Parker was tall. She had eyes, after all. Looking, however, was a lot different than being pressed up against her length. Her body was strong, her muscles chiseled, and yet somehow the whole package was warm and safe as if no harm would come to her as long as she stood in this embrace.

"I got you," Parker said softly.

"Yes, you do." Her voice trembled. "Your reflexes are fine. I guess you don't have a concussion."

"I told you." Parker looked down the exact moment Carly looked up.

They both froze, lost in each other's gaze. If either of them moved even an inch, their lips would touch. As it was, Parker's warm breath caressed her face, and she had to place a hand on Parker's hip to keep her knees from buckling.

God help me. Please don't bend down.

As if she had heard Carly's thoughts, Parker backed away, unpeeling her body limb by limb until only her fingertips touched Carly's elbow.

"You okay?" Parker asked. "Not hurt?"

Not trusting her voice, Carly shook her head and then nodded, confused on so many levels. She quickly gave up, reached for the door, and slipped out as soon as the opening was wide enough. "We'll talk soon. I promise," she called back over her shoulder. She had never heard her voice so husky.

Outside on the wall, the Rollers' mascot stared at her with its neon eyes as if it knew all her secrets.

"What are you looking at?" she said under her breath and rushed down the hall.

As soon as the door clicked shut, Parker slumped against her locker. "Fuck me," she said to the empty room. Her body tingled with desire. She had never wanted to kiss someone so much in her whole life. Carly had been right there, in her arms for the taking, and yet she hadn't made a move. What the hell was that about?

The truth came to her in pieces, like a puzzle sliding together of its own accord. Carly was actually becoming a friend. She had shown up, almost magically, twice when Parker needed her the most and so far had stuck around when the going got tough. For the first time, she might have a real ally in her life. It felt good.

As good as a kiss?

Maybe not. But she didn't want to blow it, and she had promised.

Yep. For the first time since middle school, she would try to be friends with a woman…a woman she was attracted to. It would be challenging, maybe even as challenging as being the first woman in the NFL.

The next day, Carly paced in the employee bathroom down the hall from the training room. For the moment, she was alone in the all-gender restroom, but it might not stay that way. She glanced to her phone and the unsent message on the screen.

Dinner? It will have to be late. You up for it?

The last part was a joke, of course. Would Parker think it was funny? Or just be annoyed by the reference to the awkward proposal at her father's hotel? She bit the inside of her cheek. Who knew?

She deleted the message.

She shouldn't joke about their moment in the locker room anyway. The last thing she wanted was for Parker to think she was asking her out as more than friends. That would be a colossally bad idea.

She typed out the invite again, minus the *you up for it* part, and hit send before she overthought the action any more.

As if Parker had been waiting, the reply came almost immediately.

Yes!

Don't know when, Carly typed. *Where can I meet you?*

Come to the hotel when U R done. I'm in Sky Villa 6. No, wait. Just text me the time. I'll be in the lobby.

It was settled; she couldn't take it back now. Butterflies rolled in her stomach all afternoon and were still there when she cleared the hotel's revolving doors. She zeroed in on Parker as if a quantum force drew them together.

Parker lounged against a column, dressed in black jeans, a crisp white blouse, and black kick-ass boots. Her attention was on the phone in her hand, and her thick hair, for once freed from its ponytail, swung in front of her face. Even relaxed, Parker's body was one long, lean, sexy line.

This is a bad idea. I should go and text her that I got held up.

Then Parker laughed. It came from low in her belly, so free and unrestrained that a group of tourists gave her a wide berth as they exited the elevator.

Carly couldn't help it. She smiled in response, and something deep inside unknotted. She took one step and then a second, and before she knew it, she was at Parker's side.

Parker looked up and met her gaze. "Hey. You're here."

Her warm smile made Carly's stomach flutter.

171

"What are you looking at?" Carly pointed at the phone, hoping to direct Parker's attention away from the nervousness that must have been obvious on her face.

"Oh, my nephew's latest Instagram post. He and his friends recreated some of Hekekia's trick snaps or tried to at least. Look." She held out the phone so Carly could see.

A handsome, blond teenager who looked surprisingly like a male version of Parker bombed the snap every time. Clever editing made each try more idiotic than the one before. Soon, Carly was laughing too.

"Wow. Your nephew's really talented."

"Yep. Look here." She pointed to a post by an ad for Wilson footballs. "He's invited Hekekia to weigh in on their skills. They might really have something here. You hungry?"

Carly nodded even though she was sure she wouldn't be able to eat a bite at dinner.

"Good. I'm starving. Someone told me about this great Thai restaurant just south of downtown. The Lotus Bloom. Heard of it?"

Carly shook her head.

"Well, I've got the address. Can you drive?"

"Um, I don't have a car." The tips of her ears went hot. She should have just suggested coffee, but she stupidly had wanted to be cute and reference dinner.

"Neither do I," Parker said as if it didn't matter. "We'll take a Lyft, then."

The driver, a chatty older man, dropped them off in a worse-for-wear strip mall just south of East Sahara Avenue. *The Lotus Bloom* in green letters, probably the only non-neon signage in the entire valley, hovered above one of the storefronts and invited them inside. The place was crowded for late on a weekday, and thankfully, no one gave them a second glance. They opted for the bar and were seated immediately.

As Carly climbed onto the tall stool and the menu was placed in her hands, the nervousness returned. The closest she had come to Thai food was the Chinese fast-food place near the library at UNLV. The Pad *this* and Tom *that* on this menu made little sense to her.

Parker, on the other hand, flipped through the menu, cooing at the endless choices. "You know the chef here got a James Beard award. Can you believe that? I read it on the website. Honestly, I don't think we can make a wrong choice." Parker gave her a quick glance and added, "We could get a few things to share if you'd like."

Carly nodded and wondered what her expression had said to warrant the shift in ordering strategy.

When the waitress arrived, Parker ordered off the menu as if it was a contact sport—fast and furious.

With the first bite of the garlic prawns, a house specialty, Carly had found her new favorite restaurant. Split down the middle, sautéed in garlic sauce and then deep-fried, the prawn appetizer melted in her mouth.

"I can eat this too?" Carly held up a shell.

"Let's try." Parker grabbed one, took a healthy bite, and nodded. "Good."

Carly nibbled at hers. "Oh my God! They taste like potato chips." She dropped the rest of the shell in her mouth. "That's beyond delicious."

In fact, everything was. She warmed to the experience and spooned a bit of everything that Parker ordered onto her bowl and plate—from lemongrass and coconut soup, to a green papaya salad, to a drunken noodle dish.

"Your first Thai meal?" Parker asked as Carly scooped up the last prawn.

"How can you tell? I can't stop eating."

"You don't have to. But you should know that I've spoiled you for every other Thai restaurant. This is something special." Parker's voice curled under the last few words, reaching out like a caress.

Goose bumps rippled on Carly's skin. Was it? Was *this* something special? Before she could formulate an answer, a stocky man with a High Rollers sweatshirt touched Parker's shoulder.

"You're Parker Sherbourne, right? Can I have your autograph?" He thrust a blank piece of paper and a pen in front of her. "It's for my daughter. She made me set up a kicking net in the backyard when the Rollers signed you." His face shone with pride. "She's pretty good."

Parker grinned and picked up the pen. "What's her name?"

"Ann."

Parker scribbled something on the page and passed it back to the man.

"Dear Ann," he read. "Keep your head down. Find your sweet spot. And I'll see you in the NFL." He folded the paper and slid it into a jacket pocket. "This will mean so much to her. We'll be watching when you score."

"Thanks. I won't let her down."

As he walked away, Carly studied the two pieces of rice left on her plate as if her life depended on it.

"You can look up now. He's gone." Parker reached over and patted Carly's hand. "He doesn't know Buck. No one is running back to tell him you're on a date with a player. Because you're not."

It wasn't that. Actually, it was just the opposite. She had been having so much fun with the new food and easy back-and-forth conversation that the idea of being something more with Parker hadn't seemed quite so alarming. The man with the Rollers sweatshirt had turned up like a bad penny to remind her just how long the organization's arm was.

"Actually," Carly forced a smile to her lips, "I think Buck said *fraternize*." She had wanted it to sound like a joke, but the words came out flat.

"You know, I've been thinking about that." Parker's voice turned serious too. "Do you think Buck would have said the same thing to you if you had been male and the players female?"

Carly thought back to her first moments in Buck's office. "I don't know. Why?"

Parker shrugged. "I'd like to think it was all about professionalism in the workplace, which is always a good thing. But did he tell Allen not to go after me? I mean, I'm queer and everyone knows that, but if I weren't, would he have?"

"Probably not," Carly said finally. "He would have just trusted that the men would be professionals."

"Right. That's what I'm thinking too." She bit her bottom lip as if she was weighing her next words carefully. "Hill may not be the only misogynist in the organization. That's the real issue here. They don't think we belong anywhere in that stadium. Unless we're signing the checks like Marina."

Carly twisted the fake Fitbit on her wrist. In many ways, this conversation was far more dangerous than dating a player. Parker's statement called for real action, much more than tattling on Hill for being homophobic, although that would be dangerous too. Sadly, she was not in a position to rise to any challenge. "It's like that everywhere, you know."

"Well, it doesn't have to be." Passion rose in Parker's voice. "We can be so much more than a publicity stunt or a distraction."

Carly pushed her empty plate away. A clinking noise sounded as it bumped against the water glass. "True. But I want Buck to realize that too, and that means I can't do anything he can call unprofessional."

Parker watched Carly's eyes cloud over.

"What do you mean?" Parker asked.

She licked her lips and swallowed. "I can't make waves at work. You don't know how it is for me. It's so different for you. You'll land on your feet wherever you end up. So you can have a voice. You got the Fire, your name, and your father—"

"You're right. I don't know anything about your situation. I'd like to, though."

Carly pressed her lips together and shook her head.

What did that mean? Parker was beginning to think that conversations with Carly were like kicking a point after: you threw out the words on faith and hoped they sailed through the uprights. Before, she might have given up, called the evening a bust, and asked for the check. But there was something about Carly that made her want to drop her own guard and open up. She was starting to understand that being vulnerable was not the same as being weak.

"You know, sometimes, despite what I told Lily, I can't make my voice heard in my own life." Parker struggled to find the right words, but she wanted to show Carly that she trusted her with her story. "Sometimes, my dad can be...overpowering. He doesn't listen much."

Carly's face softened. And so did Parker's heart.

"I mean, everyone's got issues. I know that. We just have a hard time connecting. He didn't have a whole lot of time for us, what with his plans for world domination and my mother. Basically, he thinks that I can't settle into things." Her throat went dry, and she gulped down a sip of water.

Across the table, Carly was still. Her gaze locked on Parker, silently encouraging her to go on.

Parker took a deep breath. "And he may not be totally wrong on that. But sometimes he's more about putting me in my place than letting me find my own footing."

"I'm so sorry," Carly said.

"Me too." She raised one shoulder in another shrug. "But I'm used to it."

A busboy came to clear the dishes, and they both fell silent. As he walked away, Carly picked at her napkin. "And you think that's what Hill and Buck are doing? Putting us in our places?"

Parker bit back a smile. Carly had made the leap in her argument without Parker having to spell it out. That was sexier than anything. *Whoa, don't go there.*

"Yep, they're silencing our story. And not just ours. Lily and that guy's daughter, Ann. Theirs too, if things don't change." It surprised her how passionate she sounded. God, did she really believe in all this? Had her new convictions crept up on her so slowly that she only now realized they had her in a tight embrace?

"You're right, in theory." Carly smoothed the napkin out and didn't look up. "But what can we do? I told you, I can't do anything to jeopardize my job."

"You're not going to believe this, but neither can I."

Carly cocked her head. "Really?"

"Yeah, another life lesson from my father. He cut off his financial support totally out of the blue. Which is his prerogative, but it makes going back to the Fire nearly impossible. So, I need to be careful too." She crossed her arms in front of her chest, feeling as if she was on the verge of revealing too much. Even on a first non-date, you needed to walk that line carefully. "The season doesn't end till January. We have plenty of time to figure out what to do."

A waitress slid behind the bar and cut the conversation short by pointing at the dessert menu. "Will you two be having a sweet ending to your meal?"

Parker glanced at Carly, who shook her head. "No, thank you." In a whisper only Carly could hear, Parker added, "We're just friends."

The corners of Carly's mouth twitched, and then she chuckled.

Her soft laugh was sweeter than anything the restaurant could serve up anyway.

CHAPTER 9

"Training room. Carly Bartlet here." She picked up the landline mounted on the back wall with the first ring.

"Hi, Carly. This is Becky in lobby reception. There's a woman here to see you."

Carly chuckled under her breath. Was this something Parker had set up so they could see each other on the sly at work? Dinner had been fun, and truth be told, she had thought about her nonstop since they'd said their chaste goodbyes in the Lyft car the night before.

"What does she want?"

"Well, she asked for a Carolina Lee, and it took me a moment to realize that's the name on your badge. So I'm not sure if she really knows you or not."

This maneuver seemed a little complicated even for Parker. "What's her name?"

"Belle."

Her heart leaped in her chest. "Did she…did she give a last name?"

"No. She said you would know who she was and you would want to see her. Do you?"

Carly squeezed her eyes shut as her heart continued to pound. This couldn't be happening. "I'll be right there." She turned to Allen. "I...um...need to step out for a minute. I'll be right back."

"Ah, okay." He studied her, and she could feel his questioning gaze linger all the way to the door.

The lobby was just on the other side of the training room, but Carly trod through metaphorical quicksand to get there. The receptionist pointed to a woman sitting straight-backed on the cushioned bench by the potted palms. She flipped through the pages of a magazine from the coffee table as if it were a high-intensity workout.

Carly didn't need an introduction. Even after so much time, she would have recognized her anywhere. Her pounding heart felt as if it someone were reaching into her chest and squeezing it. She walked up to the person responsible and took a deep breath. "Hello, Mom."

The woman looked up from the magazine. Her eyes were as blue as Carly remembered, much bluer than Minnie Lee's, and her white-blonde hair fell straight to her collarbone in fine, sculptured wisps. She glanced around the empty lobby. "Shhh. Call me Belle. I don't look old enough to have a daughter your age." There wasn't even a hint of a Southern accent in her voice. In fact, it rang hard, as if the years separating them had not been kind to her.

"Okay...Belle." Carly spread her fingers out like a fan against her breastbone and willed her heart to slow. It didn't. She had to be calm. Not give her mother any power. "How'd you find me?"

"From the newspaper. You're kind of famous now." She uncannily mimicked Teddy. "You were easy to find."

When you wanted to. Carly tried to push the thought out, but it refused to leave.

"You grew up pretty. Prettier than me." Her mother raised a hand as if to touch Carly's face but dropped it before there was contact. "No surprise there. That's your father in you. He was the handsomest man I ever met. You've got his eyes."

Her father? The subject twisted around in her head like a whirlwind. "Who…who was he?"

She had asked the question so many times in her mind, she almost couldn't believe she had said it out loud.

"An asshole."

Carly flinched. Not the response she had waited years to hear.

"He slept with me. He couldn't wait to get in my pants, but that was it."

Carly swallowed hard. She longed to reach out and comfort her mother. Everyone should be treated with respect, but this was about her too. "Where'd you meet him?"

"At the Luxor. The hotel had just opened, and he was there for a medical convention. I forget what kind. Maybe the one that deals with bones."

Her father was in medicine too? Carly sucked in a breath. Her mother was shooting facts at her like bullets, and they were all hitting their target. "He was an orthopedist?"

"That's the surgeon who puts bones back together?"

"Yes."

"Well, he wasn't a doctor that night. He was just out for fun. I was too, but, you know, he could have treated me better."

Carly nodded to keep her talking. She would unpack being a product of a casual one-night stand later.

"We were going at it, and his watch kept scratching me, so I asked him to take it off. He did, but he didn't put it on the bedside table like a normal person would've. He stopped, got out of bed, and put it in a drawer all the way across the room. As if I was going to steal his gold Rolex when we were done. I almost got up and left right then."

"Why didn't you?" It was as if she was two people—one having this crazy conversation as calm as could be and another fighting down the shock and anger that threatened to overtake her at any moment.

Belle shrugged. "I'm a sucker for a pretty face, and he knew his way around, if you know what I mean."

Carly almost choked. Her parents in bed was not an image she wanted to unpack at all. "Did he tell you his name? Or maybe where he lived? Or why he chose medicine?" That last question was a long shot, obviously, but the answers were so close she could almost taste them.

Belle snorted. "We weren't exactly talking much."

"So do you know anything at all about him?" Even she heard the desperation in her voice.

Belle studied her face. Her gaze circled from her eyes to her chin and back. "I think he was Indian."

"Like Native American…or the country India?"

"How the hell should I know?" A vein in her mother's neck pulsed, and Carly instinctively took a defensive step back. "He was darker than you. You could do that DNA test thing if you're so keen."

"I've thought about that, but it's about so much more than my genetic makeup. I want to know who my father was as a person."

Belle glanced over her shoulder, and her stare extended beyond the room. Carly was losing her. She had dreamed about this moment for so long, but in her imagination, her mother had looked lovingly into her eyes and had whispered one legitimate reason after another about why she had left. *Get it together*. Who knew how long she had? Carly had to ask what really mattered.

"And Teddy? What about his—?"

"Who?"

"Teddy."

Belle shook her head as if she had never heard the name.

"Your son?"

"Oh, Theodore." Belle laughed thinly and ran her fingers through her bangs, fluffing them out. "His nickname was supposed to be Theo."

Carly clenched her hands. *Then you should have stuck around to tell us that and a million other things.*

"How'd you get Teddy?" Belle asked.

"Grandma." She swallowed hard and tamped down the urge to tell her mother off. "Do you know who his father might be? He's been asking lately."

A hard glint entered her mother's eyes as her whole face tightened up. "Yeah, I might know a little something about that." She shrugged with a forced casualness.

Carly's knees almost buckled. Finally, they were getting somewhere. "This information could change everything for Teddy. Please, can you tell me?"

"Yes, of course." Belle leaned forward into Carly's personal space.

For a wild second, Carly thought she was reaching out for a hug, and she raised her hands, ready to latch on.

"For a price," Belle whispered when her mouth was only inches away.

"What?" Carly's arms slammed to her sides. Surely, she had heard wrong.

"Let's say…" Belle glanced around the ritzy lobby and then gave Carly the once-over. "Ten grand?"

"You…You're kidding, right?" Her stomach dropped. This couldn't be happening.

"Look." Her mother chuckled and took a step back. "I'm not out to con my own daughter. Let's get that clear from the start. I'm just a little down on my luck right now."

"So you didn't come here to ask for money?" Carly could kick herself. Belle didn't want to connect with her daughter; she just wanted cold, hard cash.

"Not exactly, but when an opportunity presents itself…"

"But ten thousand dollars? That's an insane amount of money for us."

"Maybe you know someone who might lend it to you. I mean, you're hanging out with the top one percent now."

Was her mother really selling information? She couldn't give it freely out of love or even duty? Her gut told her to turn heel and bolt for the door. But then there was Teddy. He wanted to know so badly. "Belle, I need to think about this."

Her mother's face fell. Surely, she hadn't thought Carly would whip out a checkbook on the spot. "Don't think too long. You never know with me where I'll end up."

"Right." Carly pulled her phone out. "I hear you. If you give me your number, I'll—"

"No." Belle reached for her own phone. Her jeans were so tight that she had to wedge it back and forth to free it from her back pocket. "Just give me yours."

"Okay. 702-555-6414." Here she was again, waiting around for her mother to contact her, just like when she'd been a child.

"Great." Belle plucked the magazine off the bench and headed out without another word.

Carly watched her wind her way through the luxury vehicles in the parking lot with a stolen magazine. Half of her longed for her mother to turn around with a little goodbye wave or a smile. The other half was terrified she would.

———————⊰✦⊱———————

Parker's foot hit the top step of the stadium stairs. Her breath came in ragged gulps, and she bent down to rest her hands on her thighs. She hadn't done a double-step stair run for weeks. *Use it or lose it.* So true, so true.

Mental note: she couldn't let her cardio suffer anymore. She wasn't, or shouldn't be, married to one sport. It was the joy of movement and pushing her body to the limit that called to her. She jogged along the uppermost walkway, pulling air into her lungs, and eventually, slowed to a walk. A few hamstring, chest, and core stretches completed her cooldown.

Way up here in the nosebleed section, the field below looked like a page from a playbook. Fans in these seats probably watched more downs on the jumbotron than on the field. More observers than part of the game. She pulled her arm across her chest to stretch out a kink in her shoulder. She got how that felt.

Plopping down in a seat, she pulled out her cell, and her heart sank. No texts from Carly. She didn't know what she had been expecting. They'd enjoyed a good meal, a few laughs, and a fun couple of hours away from the stadium. Nothing more. Sometimes friends could go days, even weeks, without contact and without either one getting upset.

Fuck that. We work together.

She took the steps in twos and threes on the way down as a plan came together in her mind.

But not a good one. She stood in the parking lot for what seemed like an eternity, just waiting for Carly to leave the stadium. She dropped her chin to her shoulder and stretched a crick out of her neck. Her scheme had been to pop up as if they were coincidentally exiting at the same time, but her lower back cried out in protest from standing in one place for so long. She could be here all night, or Carly could have already left the stadium.

Just as she pulled out her phone to get a Lyft driver, the staff door opened and Carly stepped out.

"Hey." Parker raised her hand, not caring if she looked like a stalker. A warmth circled in her chest when Carly returned the greeting, and her aches and pains disappeared. Something about Carly always smoothed out her rough edges. "I've been waiting for you."

"Oh, I'm sorry." Carly pulled out her phone. "I didn't get the message."

"I didn't send one." Parker studied her face. Carly's mouth was drawn tight, and tiny wrinkles pulled at the corner of her eyes. "Hey, you okay?" She didn't know what was going on, but it felt good to be giving her support for once.

"Yes."

Parker cocked her head and raised her eyebrows. "You wouldn't take that from me. Are you sure you're okay?"

A ghost of a smile rose on her lips. "Not really."

"So, what's up then?"

Carly rolled her eyes toward the darkening sky. "I'm not sure it's a conversation for the middle of a parking lot."

"Then come back to the hotel with me. We can have dinner, room service even, and all the time we need to talk." Shit, that sounded too desperate. Simple truth was Carly had helped her through a lot. She only wanted to return the favor. She should have said that instead.

Carly sighed deeply. "I can't. I need to get home. Teddy and my grandmother are waiting." Her gaze darted all around Parker's face, from her eyes, to her mouth, to her forehead, as if she was rolling around a hard decision in her mind. "Walk me to the bus stop?"

By unspoken consent, neither said anything until they cleared the last car, a brand-new Range Rover, in the parking lot. As they strolled, Carly had drifted closer to her, and when their shoulders bumped for the third time, Carly said, "My mother came to see me today." Her voice cracked.

"What? That's great."

Carly winced, and a pained expression settled on her face.

No, that would have been great if it were my mom. Parker mentally stepped outside of her own experiences. "Sorry. It's not great?"

Carly shook her head.

"So, what did she want?" Parker asked.

"Nothing good. I stupidly thought she had come to see me."

"She didn't?"

"Nope. She just wanted money."

"Ooh." Parker reached over and gave her an awkward one-armed hug. "I hope you said no." Carly leaned into her touch. They fit together perfectly like two halves of a circle. *Like we're made for each other.* The thought jumped into Parker's head, and she let go of Carly as if to step away from it.

"I wanted to say no. I really did." Carly wrapped her arms around herself. "But she offered to trade the money for information on who my brother's father is."

"Wow. And you want that, right?"

"Oh my God. So bad. Teddy's been talking about his father since the beginning of the school year. I don't know what it is about eighth grade, but he's really trying to figure out who he is, and this is a huge missing piece."

"How much is she asking for?"

"Way more than I have."

Parker didn't think before she answered. "I can give it to you or lend it to you. Whatever you want."

Carly stumbled. Desert dust from the road's shoulder rose into the air around her feet. "No. No. No." Her head jerked back and forth with each *no*. "I didn't ask for that."

"I know." Parker couldn't keep the hurt out of her voice. "I offered."

"Look." Carly stopped altogether, her feet spread in a wide stance.

Parker had to backtrack to face her.

"Okay. This isn't how I wanted to bring it up. But I'm sure you figured it out by now anyway. I take the bus everywhere; we drive thirty minutes to trick-or-treat in better neighborhoods. And I let you pay for dinner last night."

Parker tapped her fingers against her thigh. She had thought they had handled the check situation pretty well last night. "That's okay. You paid for the Lyft."

"Which was a fraction of what the dinner cost. I should have paid my full share of both. But I can't even begin to compete with you."

"This is a friendship not a sports game where we are competing against each other. There are no rules. We get to make them up as we go along."

Carly ran a hand through her hair. "There are rules, and the first one is I can't have expensive nights out with you and take care of my family when things like this come up. I have to be ready for the unexpected."

Carly's gaze pierced Parker to the heart. Her golden eyes were completely unforgiving.

"I don't know what I was thinking," she added.

Parker took a step back and waited for what she was sure was coming: she didn't want to be friends, much less anything more. A well-known feeling of rejection welled up. *Walk away,* the familiar voice in her head said. *Shut the door on this before she does.*

No, she answered. She willed her feet to stay put. Her whole life she had waited for these moments with first her mother and then her father. They had become almost a self-fulfilling prophecy, but she wouldn't allow the same to happen with Carly.

"Are you sure this is about who paid the check last night?" Parker's voice was timid and not at all sure, but it felt like the right move. And Carly was worth the risk.

Carly shook her head again, sighed, and then started up the road again.

Parker held her breath. Was Carly walking away or just moving to think? Should Parker say something or just give her space?

After a long moment—too long—Carly turned back and said over her shoulder, "You're right. I'm sorry. It's just that I've been dreaming about her coming back for a long time. This isn't what I thought would happen. I didn't mean to take it out on you."

Parker exhaled and jumped forward to match her pace. "That's okay. I get it. Parents make you crazy whether they are there or not. And I shouldn't have offered. I was channeling my father, who uses money like a baby's pacifier to solve problems." She pulled Carly to a stop and turned her body so they were facing each other again. "Look. I want this to go both ways. Us being there for each other as friends. That's all I mean." She added the last part quickly when Carly furrowed her brow. "Yesterday, you were there for me. And right now, I'd like to be here for you. I'm just not sure how. It's not really in my playbook." She licked her lips and waited. The evening could still go either way.

Finally, Carly's brow smoothed. "Teddy says that some people just fill your empty spaces." Her voice was soft and low. "He says it can happen without people even trying. He calls it the electron dance."

A sudden lightness rose up in her. Carly wasn't ditching her. "You know, I kind of believe that. Look what happened on the table the other day." Parker started walking again. They had rounded the corner, so to speak, but Parker couldn't shake the feeling they were somehow heading into even more dangerous territory.

Carly followed. "I know. That was crazy. But Teddy would say it's simple physics."

Nothing simple about it. Parker pursed her lips so she wouldn't say it out loud.

They fell in step with one another as they moved up the road.

"Do you've any ideas about your mom?" Parker asked. "I don't mean to pry. Do you have the money if you decide to go that way?"

"No, of course not." Carly hurried through the explanation. "And even if we did, that's not the way we'd want to spend it, but it's so important to Teddy. Boy, her just showing up like that is totally screwing with my head."

"I can only imagine. Is there someone you can talk to? Your grandmother maybe?"

"Maybe."

They came to the end of the main road, and Carly pointed to the covered steel-and-glass bus stop across the street. "That's my stop."

"Okay, I'll wait with you." Parker wasn't ready for the moment to end and headed over to the tiny bench seats inside the kiosk.

Surprisingly, once they sat down, they were able to chat casually about their day until the silver and white bus pulled up to the curb.

Parker got up with Carly, her fingers drumming on her thigh. Suddenly shy, she wasn't sure how they were supposed to say goodbye. If they were more than friends, she would have pulled Carly into a deep kiss, but if she was being honest, a kiss wouldn't have been as intimate as the conversation that had just passed between them.

Carly solved the problem. She encircled Parker in her arms and drew her back into that warm hug—this time with both arms. "Thanks for waiting for me tonight. I feel a lot better," she whispered into her ear, and her breath circled across her cheek like a caress.

Parker squeezed back. Hard. Damn, how could something so simple feel so good?

Teddy was wrong. It was much more than simple physics.

Tightening her core muscles, Carly slid the key into her apartment's door. After such a crazy day, she had no idea what the rest of the night would bring, and she had to be strong for what was coming. Parker was right. She should probably tell her grandmother about Belle. The question was should she take the leap tonight? Or did she personally need to figure out all the ramifications first?

Her grandmother, in her worn robe, and Teddy, still in his school clothes, sat at the kitchen bar, each with a plate of red beans and rice in front of them. Neither was eating, though. Minnie Lee had a hand on Teddy's arm, and he stopped talking mid-sentence when Carly stepped through the door.

"Ah, there you are." Minnie Lee waved her over. "Teddy was just telling me about his day. Do you want to start over, sweet pea?"

Teddy shook his head.

"Can I?" Minnie Lee asked.

Teddy nodded silently. He sat straight-backed, clearly fighting back tears…again.

"Mrs. Shantley," Minnie Lee began, "handed back the labs today. Teddy got an A, but Justin didn't. His math was all wrong, and I gather he said a few choice things to Teddy because of it. We were just getting to that exact part." She squeezed Teddy's arm as if passing on her strength. "Go on."

Teddy looked down at his food and took a ragged breath. "He told Frankie that the only reason I did good was because I cheated. And then he told me that there's no way that someone who looked like me could be that good at math."

"Seriously? Again?" Carly's blood boiled. She was ready to go down there right now and give everyone—Justin, Mrs. Shantley, the principal—a piece of her mind. Of course, no one would be there at this hour, but righteous fires burned fast inside her.

"Yeah. Again." Teddy sighed deeply as if the weight of the world had settled on his shoulders. "Grandma, it makes no sense. Why do people who look like you hate people who look like me? Don't they know that I've got your looks inside of me as well?"

"No, they don't. And I know you already understand what really matters is inside. But that doesn't really help right now, does it?"

Teddy cracked his wrist. "That's the point. I don't know what's inside of me. I mean, I know that Carly and I can make changes quickly; we're pretty flexible. And I got being reliable from you. But I'm the only one in this family who thinks stupid jokes are really funny, and I see numbers wherever I go. Where did that come from? I'll never know. And that just makes it that much harder to stand up to Justin."

Carly's hand flew to her mouth to stifle a gasp. She had the power to give Teddy precisely what he wanted. Life had hardly ever given her that kind of opportunity. But at what cost?

Her grandmother, who must have thought she was upset for Teddy, patted her shoulder. "Yeah, that's tough. I know it is. But you both have to remember that we're the author of our own stories. And you can't let anyone else write them for you, and that applies even more so if you can't look at all the cards you've been dealt."

"Huh?" Teddy scratched his cheek.

"Yeah, I heard it too. I mixed up lots of expressions there."

"I think what Grandma is trying to say is that in the end it's up to us how we live our lives, and we can't go around being what other people think we are or want us to be because it makes them feel more comfortable or better about themselves." The realization that she needed the advice as much as Teddy landed heavily on her own shoulders. If she had heard it earlier, she might have had a different response when Parker had brought up Buck and the misogynistic attitude at the stadium.

"Yeah, that," Minnie Lee said.

"Okay, I get it." Teddy's voice rang stronger as the redness in his eyes started to fade. "But easier said than done."

"Sometimes." Minnie Lee tightened the frayed belt on her robe. "But other times that's just an excuse people use."

"I'll have to think about that." Teddy sounded more mature than his thirteen years. "So what am I supposed to do tomorrow?"

No one said anything. Teddy, in his usual way, had come to the crux of the matter. Tough moments in life—and she'd been having a bunch of them lately one way or another—were much easier to deal with when they stayed hypothetical. What *was* he supposed to do tomorrow?

"Punch him in the snout," Minnie Lee blurted out, and her eyes widened in mock surprise at her own answer.

They all busted out laughing at the exact same time.

"Walk off to honors pre-algebra and ask him what math class he's going to." Carly smirked.

"Carly, that's mean. He's in regular math." But Teddy's smile lingered.

"Exactly." She raised her hands as if the implications were obvious.

"How about ignoring him for now?" Minnie Lee shrugged. "Maybe he'll stop if he doesn't get a rise out of you. Or going to see a counselor if it gets worse. Or one of us could come down."

Teddy picked up his fork and bounced the handle on the bar several times. "No, I'm going to try to take care of it myself. Write my own story." He glanced at Minnie Lee for her approval.

"Perfect. And if that doesn't work, we're here to help you edit it." Minnie Lee smiled, and Teddy let out a puff of air. She then pointed to his fork. "That, once again young man, is an eating utensil and not a drumstick."

Teddy rolled his eyes and dropped the fork.

Carly pressed a hand to her stomach. Her muscles were still tense. Any more drama and she wouldn't have to do sit-ups for a week.

Teddy and Minnie Lee ate dinner while he jabbered on about the free flag designer app he had downloaded at school that day. He laid out, in excited and excruciating detail, the colors, the placement, and the symbols of the zombie flag he was designing for the post-apocalyptic world of his new favorite book. If it turned out to be any good, he was going to send it to the author through his website.

Parker would totally get into this conversation.

Once again, Parker was everywhere in her thoughts.

When supper was over, Teddy happily disappeared to his room, claiming that he had homework. He hadn't even cleared the main room, though, before his phone was out.

"It could be worse." Minnie Lee gathered the empty dishes. "He could be watching that YouTube all the time."

Carly didn't tell her that YouTube took data or an Internet connection that they didn't have at home. "Grandma, sit. I'll clean up."

Minnie Lee pushed the plates to the edge of the bar and sank stiffly back down onto the wooden stool.

"Tea?"

"Please."

Carly dumped the plates in the sink and put the kettle on. With her back toward Minnie Lee and her hands busy, she had time to think, unobserved. How was she going to bring up Belle? Maybe she should wait until they'd had one day without a middle school crisis. She rotated one shoulder in a small circle, attempting to roll out the tension there. She had to be careful. Despite her fading eyesight, Minnie Lee could spot body language a mile away.

"You might as well tell me."

Too late. Carly was caught.

"You won't sleep if you don't get whatever it is off your chest."

Instead of turning around, Carly scraped the leftovers into the sink's disposal. "Is that how you got Teddy to confess?"

"Pretty much. When you're worried about something, you children are like an open book."

As usual, her grandmother had done all the heavy lifting and had given her the opening.

She turned almost all the way around. "Grandma, I've something to tell you."

Minnie Lee patted the barstool next to her as an invitation. "I know. Let's hear it."

Carly's heart leaped in her chest. Once she told Minnie Lee, she couldn't take it back. Her daughter's betrayal would sit between them forever, either pulling them together or pushing them apart. Her heartbeat thudded loudly in her ears.

"Look." She took two steps to the bar and ran her hand over its smooth surface. "This may come as a shock to you, and I want you to be prepared." She scooped up a tiny crumb, dumped it in the sink, and finally, met Minnie Lee's gaze.

"Sweetheart, don't worry about me. I've seen it all."

"I know. It's just that I'm afraid of hurting you."

"Well, if you do, I hope we can work through it together."

"Today at work—" A ragged coldness exploded in her stomach. It felt wrong. If she said anything, anything at all, Belle would pull them into a drama where money was the least of the issues. Maybe this had been her mother's plan all along— to reinsert her crazy energy into their lives and create a new mess on top of all the old ones.

"So?" Minnie Lee sliced into her thoughts.

No. She didn't want to tell Belle's story; she wanted to tell her own.

"So…" She grabbed the barstool with both hands. Was she really going to do this? "I'm gay." She squeezed her eyes shut so she wouldn't have to look at her grandmother.

"Have you met someone?"

Carly opened one eye and then the other. Had she misheard? Was there a hopeful note in Minnie Lee's voice?

Her grandmother had leaned back and was sitting casually on the stool, waiting for an answer. There was no hurt or disappointment in her gaze, only anticipation and a soft twinkle.

"You knew?" Carly asked.

"Of course. Like I said, I can read you and Teddy pretty well by now. Not to mention there was that one girl in college you talked a lot about. Felicia, right?"

Carly nodded. A thousand emotions swirled around her. She was surprised they weren't creating a windstorm. "So, why…why didn't you say anything?"

"I was waiting for you. I knew you'd tell me when you wanted to. When there was a reason." She leaned in and reassuringly dropped a hand on Carly's forearm. "Is there? Have you met someone?"

Her heart was still beating so loudly that she almost didn't hear her own answer. "No. I don't think so. Maybe."

"The kicker?"

Carly nodded as she basked in her grandmother's glow. She did know her inside and out. That was a comfort that few had and a luxury money couldn't buy.

"Yeah. Her name's Parker. But we're just friends. Nothing's happened." The near kiss in the locker closet, the hug at the bus stop, Parker's talking her off a ledge all could say otherwise—they were so intense—but technically, she wasn't lying.

"Tell me about her."

"Um, you know what she looks like." Carly waved a hand to the picture at the edge of the bar. "At first, I thought she was aloof and spoiled. But she's caring and smart and gosh, so tough. She never gives up."

"I would like to meet her. Teddy already has, right?"

"Yeah. At Halloween."

Minnie Lee drew her lips into an exaggerated pout. "I'm feeling a little left out," she said with a laugh.

Carly knew her grandmother was joking, but in every joke, there was a hint of truth. "We'll have to remedy that."

"Soon. I'll make dinner."

"Thanks, Grandma. She'll jump at that."

Parker would, with both feet and all of her heart—she never did anything by halves, Carly was beginning to realize. At first, she had seen that trait as chasing drama, but now she wasn't so sure.

Maybe she should try to grab what she wanted as well. Coming out to her grandmother had been a good start—much better than telling her grandmother about Belle, since there was no way to know how that story was going to end.

⚬⚬⚬

Poising the scalpel over the training table like an ER surgeon, Parker stood above her empty shoulder pads as if they were a disembodied torso. She poked the knife into the cushioning around the collar, cutting out bits and pieces to widen the neck and make the fit more comfortable. Lightness filled her chest. For the first time, she actually felt at home in the Rollers' stadium. She was working on her game, and, more importantly, Carly had sought her out, texting her to come over.

The training room was unusually busy; the Rollers were installing a full-body cryosauna in the back corner. Buck had decided to bring the big chill into the recovery program and fight the players' soft tissue injuries at the cellular level. Workers and curious players crowded the tall metal tube, which looked more like a time machine than a high-tech ice bath.

Hiding in plain sight, Parker and Carly spoke in low, but normal tones. With all the bustle around them, no one gave them a second glance.

"So you never told her about your mom?" Parker directed the question to the other side of the table, where Carly held down the pads.

"No. We never got around to it. Actually, we were too busy talking about you." A slight flush ran over Carly's cheeks.

"That sounds like a really fun conversation." Parker's voice dipped to a dangerous whisper, and feeling the heat on her own cheeks, she looked down. All she wanted to do was let one finger stray to Carly's hand on the edge of the table. The touch would be brief and featherlight, but the yearning to connect physically was so strong, Parker almost couldn't resist. She embraced the butterflies as they fluttered in her stomach. Would it feel like this to be more than friends?

"Hey, Sherbourne."

Parker's eyes popped open. Shit, was she caught?

In three long strides, Veris stepped up to the table and nodded repeatedly. "That's good work. We should get Hekekia over here. He's always complaining about his neck when he drops for the snap."

"Sure, text him." Her voice, low and husky, betrayed her.

A couple more players drifted over.

Carly stepped back from the table, either to let her connect with her teammates or because she was embarrassed. Either way, their cozy moment was over.

"I could use a little operation on my knee pads," a cornerback said. "You know, chop them down a little bit."

Forcing herself not to follow Carly's movement with a longing gaze, she plastered a broad smile on her face. "That's illegal, Jake. I don't want the uniform officials on me." She tried to make her tone light and not in any way judgmental.

"Those uniform police," he replied. "They're no better than fucking meter maids. Trying to strip whatever advantage I can get."

A true athlete's attitude. She knew it well. She had jumped off the line during penalty kicks now and again to get that edge. And if she was being honest with herself, she had leveraged the other advantages that life had given her, putting herself first.

Maybe not anymore.

Across the room, Carly moved to Allen's side and shook her head, laughing at something he had said. Her hair bounced around her face and shone under the fluorescent lights. Who knew there were so many highlights in brown hair?

The workman handed Allen a control pad. He punched a button, and the green light on the seven-foot-tall metal chamber lit up. Energy buzzed in the room. Everyone crowded in, wanting to try a cold nitrogen freeze or at least talk about the pros and cons of treatment.

Hekekia appeared at the door and caught Parker's eye. He held up his pads and swung them gently. "They tell me the doctor's in."

"Yep. Free clinic today." Parker tried to make her voice as atonal as his. She didn't want him getting spooked.

Hekekia dumped the pads on a trainer's table. "They always pinch right about here."

"Oh, that's an easy fix." She slid the scalpel into the foam padding and began to make tiny incisions. "You know, if you wear an extra Dri-FIT shirt with shoulder pads, it will lift these pads right up and give more room in the neck."

Hekekia grunted.

"Try it. You'll feel like a gladiator on Sunday."

He leaned in to study her work. "Not bad."

Two little words, but his shell had a few more cracks.

Later that night, Parker paced around the hot tub out on the balcony of the family suite. Round and round like a hamster in an exercise wheel. Nervous energy about the game, Hill's pronouncement, and a thousand other things coursed through her veins. Fuck this. She headed inside to grab her key card and a jacket. She had heard about this place just a couple blocks away that had pool tables, pretty women, and a casual vibe. The trifecta of diversions never failed to relax her before a game.

She had a hand on the door knob when she froze. Almost without thinking she had her phone out and called up Carly's contact info. They had talked in the training room just that morning. She dialed anyway.

"Oh, hi!" Carly's voice spun out of the phone's speaker. "Hey, Teddy? Can I have a few minutes?"

Parker didn't hear the reply, but a door closed, and then came a happy sigh. What did that mean? She shouldn't read anything into it. Sometimes a sigh was just a sigh.

"Perfect timing. Teddy and I are working on one of his *Dungeons and Dragons* campaigns. Boy, that game can go on and on and on."

"*Dungeons and Dragons?*" She hated when people just repeated a phrase and didn't ask a real question. But she also hated the fact that she was out of her element on so many levels. She paced around the shuffleboard table in the game room.

"Yeah. Old school with dice and battle maps. He usually plays with his friends. But sometimes when it's just the two of us, we get burgers from In-N-Out and try out his campaigns. He likes to make his own."

"How you doing?"

"Not well. I'm stuck in a cave at the moment with three goblins and my HP is only at two."

Parker chuckled and rounded the table's corner. "I meant with your big announcement to your grandmother and your mother just showing up. It's a lot to bear."

"Oh that. Surprisingly well. Yeah, better there than in the game, actually. Are you okay?"

Parker hesitated too long.

"Nervous about tomorrow?" Carly broke the silence.

"Yeah. Actually, I am." She held her breath and waited. She had been here before, and people—her father, her brother—had blown her off.

"How could you not be?" Carly asked, her tone both casual and caring.

Parker let her breath out with a soft whoosh, and the tension fled from her body. "I always get a little antsy before a game, but this time, it's so much worse because I don't know if I'm going to play or not."

"You never rode the bench in soccer?"

"Never. I mean, even mediocre goalies are hard to find. Unless I was injured, I played every minute of every game since AYSO. And even in football, my coaches put me in when they could. They had faith in me as an athlete."

"And as a person, I'm guessing."

"Yeah," Parker said softly. Carly had hit the issue on the proverbial head. Hill's dismissal felt a lot like her father's rejections. Personal on some level.

"I don't know if this means anything," Carly cut into her thoughts. "Hill's been actively coaching you since your talk."

Parker's heart skipped a beat. Somehow, Carly had been keeping tabs on her at practice. "You can smile and smile and still be a villain."

"Sorry?"

"I mean maybe he's setting me up." She pushed a blue puck down the shuffleboard table. It landed in the ten spot. "I don't know. Maybe he's being all coachy now so when he doesn't play me tomorrow, it won't seem so bad."

For a moment, the phone just sat in her hand as if the connection had been cut. Finally, Carly said, "That's giving him a lot of credit. Do you really believe he's thinking about you that much?"

She was right. Hill probably hadn't given her any thought since she closed the door to his office.

"I think mostly he just wants to win," Carly said so quietly that Parker pulled the phone closer.

"Maybe. But he made it clear in that conversation in his office, he doesn't like me for reasons that have nothing to do with my leg, and he pretty much told me that I am on the wrong side of our power differential. It's a hard place for me to be." Parker threw a second puck, harder than the first. This one slid right off the table into the tray at the end. "I hope I get a chance tomorrow, and God, I hope I'm as good as I think I am."

"I've seen you kick. You can do it."

Just four little words. Single syllables wrapped up in a ready cliché. Carly's voice, however, rang with belief. "Thanks. That means a lot."

She should say goodnight now. Finish the conversation on a positive note and not seem too needy. She opened her mouth, but nothing came out. Truth be told, she didn't want the conversation to end.

"Carolina Lee! Are you coming back? The goblins won't wait forever!" Teddy's shouting grew closer.

"Give me one more minute—"

"No. Go. I'll see you tomorrow," Parker said.

"Are you sure?"

"Yeah, of course."

"Okay. You totally got this. Bye."

"Night."

Easy breaths expanded into her chest as she hung up her jacket in the closet next to the door. Strangely, none of that crazy pre-game energy rolled through her muscles anymore. Whatever tomorrow brought, Carly would be by her side. Well, maybe not right next to her, but on the same sideline, and that, for the time being, was good enough.

She grabbed her phone again.

How's Mom doing? she typed into the text box in iMessage. Her finger hovered over the empty *send to* line. She hit *J,* and Jem's address popped up. She imagined him in his kitchen in Malibu, holding the phone up to his wife and making some remark. No, the elephant that was trumpeting was not in his kitchen. She chose her father's address and hit *send* almost in one motion—before she chickened out.

There went nothing. Probably literally.

She couldn't remember the last time she had initiated contact with her dad.

She wasn't going to run from him anymore.

CHAPTER 10

"FALSE START. NUMBER SIXTY-THREE. OFFENSE." The referee waved his arms in giant circles. "Five-yard penalty. Second down." His voice reverberated throughout the stadium.

The Rollers' defense celebrated, and Carly cheered along with the home crowd. She fell happily into the collective experience of the stadium and lost herself in pursuit of a bigger goal. This was what football was all about.

The Rollers' defense, playing fast and physical, had been the only bright spot of the day. Having spent the week studying film, they were reading the other team like a book. Denarius in particular seemed to know which way the ball would run even before it was snapped. They had kept Seattle out of the end zone, and with only two field goals lighting up the scoreboard at 6-0, the Rollers still had a sliver of hope, even this late in the fourth quarter.

Carly turned to the jumbotron at the far end rather than peer through the sea of bodies all around her. There, as big as a giant in one of Teddy's video games, Denarius dropped to the ground. *Oh no!* Carly pressed her hand to her mouth. Surely, he couldn't be injured! He was the spark plug of the defensive line.

On the screen, Denarius grabbed his right foot.

Buck tagged her on the shoulder, and the two of them raced onto the field.

"You hurt?" Buck asked, his voice gruff with concern.

"No. My shoe. It's untied." Denarius's gloved hands fumbled with the laces.

"For God's sake." Buck pushed the fanny pack bulging with supplies to his hip and bent down stiffly.

Like a shot, Carly dropped to the turf and grabbed the laces first. She knotted them off to the side, pulled in the slack, and then looped the laces into a tight double knot. "Done." She bounced up and led the way off the field.

Almost immediately, the referee blew his whistle, and both sides lined up. The Rollers' defense crowded the line of scrimmage in an attempt to close down running lanes.

As soon as the ball was snapped, Denarius jumped forward as if shot out of a cannon. His eye on the prize, he overpowered his blocker and drove into the pocket. Zooming up on the quarterback's blind side, Denarius drilled him in the back and somehow managed to get his right hand on the ball. Like the cork from a champagne bottle, the ball popped into the air and, unbelievably, landed in Denarius's outstretched hands. He took off, his legs churning as fast as they could, and streaked down the Rollers' sideline to cheers of both the players and fans.

Sixty-three yards later, Denarius rushed into the end zone.

Almost as one, the stadium erupted in screams and applause. The noise, deafening in its volume, filled the arena and overflowed into the desert. The Rollers were on the board; the score was tied at 6-6.

Back on the sideline, Carly jumped up and down with the rest of her team. Her racing heartbeat drummed in her chest as she sucked in the pure elation around her. Allen slapped anyone within a two-foot radius on the back. For a moment, he looked as if he wanted to high-five the Gatorade cooler next to him. Even Buck was grinning from ear to ear.

Carly pressed her hand to her chest. Surely, Parker's big moment was here. She glanced down the bench to share it with her.

Parker stood among the special teams players, clutching her helmet and twisting one way and then the other. Uncertainty and a thousand other emotions slid across her face.

Carly tried to catch her eye, but Parker's focus was downfield. And then her helmet slipped out of her fingers and dropped to the ground.

What had she seen? Carly spun around to look in the same direction.

Oh no. Hill was pushing Koch onto the field. The kicker tugged his helmet down as he ran toward the fifteen-yard line.

She took a quick step Parker's way and then shuffled back. A dozen cameras had to be focused on Parker to record this moment. Carly's heart dropped. Parker must be dying inside, but with half of Nevada watching, they both had to remain professional at all costs.

"Next time," she said under her breath as if Parker could hear her. Carly turned just in time to see the ball fly through the uprights.

The crowd's deafening cheer rose into the desert air.

The game continued until there were three seconds, two seconds, and then one. A piercing air horn rang out. The Rollers had won by only one point, but it was a win in anyone's scorebook—except for maybe Parker's.

The players on the Rollers' sideline erupted as if they had won the Super Bowl.

J.J. Ocean came at Carly with a swagger that made her cringe. She sidestepped him and grabbed the opportunity to move closer to Parker. Maybe there would be a moment for a quick word or a light touch in the surrounding chaos. Her grandmother had taught her that a burden was always easier when you shared it.

"There you are." Denarius grabbed Carly from behind, spun her around, and pulled her into a big, sweaty bear hug. "My good luck charm!" Brimming with happiness, he bounced his head up and down like a living bobblehead doll. "You'll tie my shoes next game and every game for the rest of the season."

"You did that all on your own. I had nothing to do with it."

"Maybe. Maybe not. But I don't plan on taking any chances." Another teammate pulled at his jersey, tugging him away. "For the rest of the season, you hear?" He pointed both index fingers at her as he sank back into the crowd.

Carly's grin faded as she scanned the sideline. Where was Parker? Nowhere to be seen. To her surprise, a tingling emptiness started in her core and spread outward. Was her connection to Parker that strong?

Son of a bitch. It was.

She looked for her in the team locker room and knocked on her private door. Nothing. Between treatments, she texted, asking if she was okay. Again, nothing. Finally, as she paced back and forth at the bus stop later that evening, she admitted to herself that she was worried. The question was: Should she do something about it?

She could get home in time for dinner with Teddy and her grandmother, whip the jersey that Denarius had signed out of her backpack and make his day. Sunday suppers, as her grandmother called them, were sacred and joyous in their house, always had been.

Or she could wait, catch the second bus, and head to the Sherbourne Hotel and all sorts of uncertainty.

She glanced at her phone. Still no response to any of her texts. Parker adorably called and texted for no reason at all. And now that there actually was one, nothing. Radio silence.

The bus, the one that went home, rolled up to the kiosk and stopped with a loud hiss of its air breaks. Like an invitation, the front door swung open. Carly hesitated. This moment was a true crossroads in her life.

Which ride should she take?

———◆◇◆———

Back in her suite, Parker lifted the bell-shaped cover off the meal she had ordered. The turkey burger with a watermelon-arugula-feta salad on the side looked appetizing, as did everything from the hotel's kitchen, but her stomach churned. Food was only going to make it worse. As she dropped the cover back onto the plate, it slipped out of her hand and clattered to the floor with a loud, metallic bang.

The noise echoed through the room, and she shuddered. She didn't know why she was so upset. Hill had pretty much told her he wasn't going to play her, and after the game, he had dropped a hand on her shoulder and had said, "Look, game-time decision. Nothing more. I went with the player who had the experience to grab the win."

She lurched from the table, leaving her meal untouched, and headed over to the wet bar in the back of the suite. She had one finger on the hydrogen-infused water in the minifridge but then jerked her hand over to a Shock Top beer.

She only deprived herself during the season. And if she was only practicing and not playing, what kind of season was that? She grabbed the beer.

Staring into the mirrored panels behind the sink, she froze with the bottle opener clenched in her hand. If she wasn't on the field, she wasn't in the game. And then it hit her: she wasn't in any game. Between being benched, her father not responding to her text, and the dry spell in her love life…what was destiny telling her? Game over? Thank you for playing?

The only thing that was keeping her grounded was Carly. With the way things were going, Parker wouldn't be in Vegas much longer. What would happen when she had to say goodbye?

A light tap on the door broke into Parker's thoughts. Someone from the hotel, no doubt, since only they had the special key card for this floor. Wrapped in her self-misery like a heavy blanket, she opened the door without looking.

Neon-green Nike sneakers scuffed the floor.

Parker's head jerked up. "Carly?"

She stood before Parker still in her khakis and Rollers windbreaker. She must have come straight from the stadium. "Are you okay? I didn't see you after the game, and I knew how much you wanted to have the chance to—"

Parker forced the surprise off her face. Did Carly have superpowers? Did she just appear like a guardian angel whenever she was needed?

"You know, we seem to ask each other that a lot. Are you okay?" Carly chuckled nervously. "I'm sorry. This is weird. I shouldn't have come."

"No. No. I'm glad you did," Parker said quickly. Carly must have thought her silence was from annoyance, not awe.

She swung the door back. "Come in. How...how'd you get up here?"

"I was in the elevator. I didn't know that you needed a special key card for the sky villas, but then this guy had one. He stared at me the whole way down the hall, though, like I was here to rob the place."

"Which one did he go into? I'll get him evicted." Parker almost skipped into the main room. Her mood had shifted like a tidal wave. "Do you want anything? I was just getting myself a beer."

"That sounds good." Carly glanced around the room. "This is unbelievable." Her voice cracked as she spoke.

Parker followed her gaze to the modern crystal chandelier, the gilded shuffleboard table in the next room, and the colorful flowers both in pictures and in vases. "It's my dad's suite. I'm just borrowing it until I get settled." She held up the Shock Top. "What about this? I've got a fresh orange to go with it."

Carly nodded, and soon they were settled, beers in hand, on the plush, white couch positioned to take in the incredible view.

"I'm so glad you came." Parker clinked Carly's beer bottle.

"Me too. I was a little worried. I texted and got nothing back...and that made me even more worried."

"God, I'm so sorry. I left my phone in my locker. I only realized it on the way here, and the last thing I wanted to do was go back to the stadium to get it. I didn't want to run into anyone. Stupid, huh?"

Carly shook her head. "Nah, I wouldn't want to go back either." There was no judgment in her response.

Parker leaned in. She couldn't help it. Most people looked at her critically, but not Carly. Her eyes were wide and warm and golden. Her gaze held such acceptance that Parker felt it on her skin, like the rays of a tiny sun. Unable to meet Carly's look any longer, she glanced down. Their knees were close, only an inch or two apart on the couch. Her fingers itched to touch that knee, feel her skin, which would be tender and soft, no doubt, and slide her hand eventually to more private places.

Stop. Oh my God. We're just friends.

She pulled her hand back and raised her head. "I'm not sure what to do. With Hill," she added the last part quickly in case Carly had gotten the wrong idea. "He's clearly homophobic, but you don't go against the coach. I mean, that's suicide. He told me after the game that he had made the best choice to grab the win. Funny thing, I agree with him. It was the right decision."

And staying just friends was the right decision with Carly. Whatever happened when she was around her was almost miraculous. Carly filled her with a calmness that bathed her soul. She didn't want to—no, she *couldn't* lose that.

"You would have scored."

She gave Carly a shy smile. No one had ever believed in her like this. Her mother had been absent, her father too busy; Jem had his own problems, and she had kept every girlfriend at arm's length.

"True. I hope." She grimaced playfully. "In the end, the team needed the sure win more than I needed the point after. I just don't have to like it. Hey, you hungry?" She motioned to the table with the uneaten burger. "I ordered but never ate."

"Um…" Carly hesitated. She looked around the room and out to the balcony with the million-dollar view.

"Come on." Parker grabbed her hand and dragged her to the table. "It's a turkey burger. We could split it, or I can get another or something else."

Parker followed Carly's gaze and with a start realized that her fingers were still wrapped around Carly's hand. She dropped it like a hot potato.

Carly stretched her fingers out and took a deep breath. "Let's split it. Will that be enough for you, though?"

She was talking about the turkey burger, right? Because if she wasn't... Parker couldn't go there. "Yeah, it's enough. I didn't work out today, remember?" She walked over to the bar and opened a cabinet beneath the sink. Every imaginable nut, chip, and candy were crammed into its shelves. "Besides, there's plenty." She grabbed two bags of chips and dangled them in the air on the way back. "Salt and vinegar or wasabi ginger?"

"Those are my only two choices?"

"My father has a very unique sense of humor. Both are actually quite good. We can split them too, if you want."

"Great." As if she had flipped a switch, Carly relaxed. She eased into the chair and threw her shoulders against its woven back. "This is really good," she said after the first bite of the burger.

"It better be. My father stole the executive chef from Burger Bar last year."

"You know, I do eat good things when I'm not with you. I mean, you must think I only eat bread and water."

"I never thought that." Parker laughed. It was nice that they were finally having a normal conversation about random stuff.

"My grandmother is actually a fantastic cook." Carly rubbed the back of her neck. "In fact, she wants to know if you would join us for supper." Red crept across her cheeks and mingled with her freckles.

Parker was charmed.

"Our place is nothing like this, though."

"I don't care," Parker said quickly before Carly changed her mind.

"I didn't think you would." Carly's shoulders dropped. "It's a date."

Parker searched her face. "I think you mean a not-date, right?"

"Right." Her face turned serious for a beat, and then she chuckled. "A not-date."

After dinner, they ended up at the shuffleboard table, and Parker divvied up the blue and red weights. "Come on. Let's play." As Carly glanced at her watch, she added, "Think of it as an act of mercy. There's no bench for me to be relegated to, and finally, we're playing something I might win."

"Oh, you think so?" Carly raised her eyebrows.

"Full disclosure. I've been playing on this exact table since I was a kid. My father thought he was saving us from a life of hustling by not getting a pool table."

"Full disclosure right back at you. I'm a fast learner, and I'll have you know, Parker Sherbourne, star of two sports, you are not the only athlete in the room. I went to UNLV on a partial softball scholarship. I wasn't a star, but I played."

"Ooh, you've been holding out on me, Bartlet."

"I have. Game on!" Carly laughed.

Her bold confidence sent a flutter straight to Parker's groin. "Blue or red?"

Parker won the first round handily, so she was a little surprised when Carly came roaring back in the second. Carly crinkled her face up in concentration with each shot. Somehow, it was sexy and adorable at the same time, and if Parker was honest, it might have put her off her game a bit. More to her amazement, she didn't mind. Just hanging out with Carly was a win.

The third and final game came down to Carly's last shuffle. She teed up the puck. "So, if I get this in the ten spot, I win?"

"Or you can knock one of my weights off the board. That might be easier."

Carly shook her head. "I'd rather win by skill, not strategy."

This daring resolve was a new side to Carly. Parker liked it—a lot. "Okay, then. That space is pretty small." She pointed to the triangle at the front of the scoring box.

"Just watch."

As if she could do anything but.

Carly leaned over the table. The soft material of her Rollers polo clung to her in all the right places. It hugged her breasts, fully outlining their full curves. Parker let her gaze linger and then jerked her head down. This was getting out of hand.

Carly launched the puck. It slid down the table and headed right for the ten spot. "Ha!"

"No, no, no." Parker bounded to the end of the table, hands outstretched as if to stop the puck.

"You cheater." Carly laughed and rushed after her.

Parker playfully lunged after the sliding weight.

Carly grabbed her hand at the last minute, pulled Parker away, and spun her right up into her body.

Parker gasped but didn't pull away, and Carly held on tightly. Parker looked down into Carly's eyes. Undefinable emotions swirled in their depths.

216

"I wouldn't have touched it." Parker's voice was husky. Their lips, again, were only inches apart.

"I know." Carly's tone matched hers exactly. "That's who you are."

This was absolute madness. The length of Carly's body was pressed up against hers. Her breasts, which she had been trying so hard not to see, were now pushed up right against her. All she had to do was shift her hand and—

She pulled back. "We shouldn't."

"I know that too." Carly held her tight.

Inner alarm bells were blaring, but Carly couldn't pull away. She had told herself on the bus that she was just checking up on Parker. Even then, deep inside, she had known she was lying. She had been thinking about a moment like this since their near miss in the locker closet days ago. Now she would do what her grandmother had said, write her own story.

Without another thought, Carly rose up on her tiptoes and found Parker's lips. They were gentle and warm, just as she had known they'd be.

Parker stiffened at the touch, and Carly's stomach tensed. Had she misjudged Parker's feelings all this time?

Then Parker trembled and slipped both arms around her body. "Oh God," Parker whispered against her lips.

The kiss became meltingly soft. Parker's hands, no surprise, were strong and gripped her body almost possessively. But the kiss…it stayed quiet and tender, brimming with discovery and passion.

Carly had never experienced anything like it before. She had assumed, in the moments she had let her mind wander in this direction, that Parker would be driven by lust. That she would attack lovemaking the way she did a ball on the field. That her need would overtake her and her desire would push them both hard and fast, but instead her touch was teasing... and patient...and totally intoxicating.

Their lips parted at the same moment. Parker's tongue slid over Carly's, bringing a sweetness to the kiss and the promise of what could come.

Parker moaned, and, in response, a slow tremor coursed through Carly's body. The kiss deepened.

"Well, well, well." A cold voice came from the far edge of the hallway by the front door. "What do we have here?"

Carly jumped back and broke contact. *What the...?*

Parker stepped around Carly as if to protect her.

Tall and proud, the woman walked toward them. Her heels clicked on the marble like tiny Gatling guns. She peered around Parker to give Carly the once-over. "Nice choice, Parker. Very nice." Her lips rose just at the edges in a decidedly unfriendly smile.

Nausea rolled in Carly's stomach at her tone, and for all her earlier bravado, now she thought she might throw up. Who on earth was this?

"How the hell did you get in here?" Parker glared at the woman.

"The blouse. Remember? You gave me access to your room then."

The party. She was with Parker at the party. The stranger was connected, in some way, to the Rollers. Carly's gaze darted around the room, looking for a spot to hide.

"Not to use whenever you wanted." Parker ran a hand through her hair and quickly glanced at Carly. "Tanya's my agent. Nothing more."

"That stings a little bit. You see, I had the evening off. Thought I'd surprise you. Didn't know I was the one in for the surprise." Tanya glared at Carly as if she were a dog marking her territory. "Oh, I see. You're the girl from the press photo. The trainer or something, right? Making house calls? That was some pretty interesting therapy. New technique?"

Carly swallowed hard. Coming here had been such a colossal mistake. This was what she got for stepping outside the lines.

"Tanya, stop. You've no idea what's going on." Parker took a step toward the woman.

"Oh, I think I do." Tanya rubbed her chin with her thumb and forefinger, playing up the theatrics. "But the question is: Do the Rollers?"

Carly's chest tightened, and she couldn't catch her breath. This was her worst nightmare. Not only had she been caught kissing a player, but soon everyone would know it. "I should go. You clearly have things to discuss."

"No. Please." Parker's plea was full of passion. "Don't leave." She grabbed Carly's forearm.

"Let her go, Parker. She's right. We've got to come up with an effective game plan for your future, which is far more important than whatever you're doing in this silly little hookup."

I have to get out of here. Carly slipped her arm out of Parker's grasp and fled to the door without another word.

Parker's legs wobbled, and she clutched the back of a nearby chair. How she had lost control of the situation so quickly was beyond her comprehension. The slam of the door echoed in the silent room.

Like a wild animal, Parker turned on Tanya. "What the hell? You totally fucked everything up."

"Yes, it did look like fucking was the number-one priority."

Parker shook first her finger and then her whole hand at her. "Goddammit. Don't move. Or better yet, just be gone when I get back."

When she bolted outside, the hallway was empty. How could that be? Carly had just left. She raced to the elevator and punched the button repeatedly until the doors slid open. On the way down, she tapped her foot against the flower inlay on the floor and gripped the handrail each time the elevator stopped to let in new passengers. By the time they hit the lobby, her knuckles were white.

Tanya hadn't fucked things up. *She* had. She shouldn't have kissed Carly back. Like any Monday morning quarterback, she knew that now. Here she was in the same old position, watching as someone walked away. The only difference was this time, she was chasing after her.

The lobby was empty too. Well, not empty; happy guests and tourists milled around the garden in the center. Ropes of colorful vines and flowers climbed to the ceiling, while petals and leaves tumbled down in a carefully controlled free fall. But no Carly.

Parker darted around the atrium until she was sure. Carly was gone. And to add insult to injury, Parker had no phone, she didn't know where Carly lived, and she had no way to get in contact with her.

When she returned to her suite, Tanya had made herself at home on the couch with a wineglass and a tiny wine bottle from the bar.

Parker curled her hands into tight balls and faced her head-on. "What exactly are you doing here?"

"Okay. Fine. I'll admit that I flew in tonight rather than tomorrow because I had hoped that we could have an instant replay of our night together. But I can see you've already moved in another direction." She jerked her head to the room on her right and grabbed a pretend steering wheel with her hands. "You up for a U-turn?"

"I am not. We need to keep this," she waved a hand between them, "strictly professional from now on. And I'm not even sure about that right now."

"You need someone to take control of this little farce. To get you back in the game."

"I've got it under control."

Tanya chuckled almost under her breath. "She walked out, you know? At the first sign of trouble, poof—she's gone."

"I think it was you who drove her out."

"Maybe, but how deep are her feelings if she flees at the first sign of trouble?"

Stop! Parker wanted to scream until Tanya was quiet. Truth be told, though, she wasn't wrong. Carly could have stayed, and they could have faced Tanya together. Instead she had fled.

"Forget her," Tanya said. "I've set up a meeting with Marina Fisher for tomorrow. You need to be out on that field and not in here with that trainer. That's the only way you're going to get those endorsement deals. Interest is already starting to dry up." She spread her feet out on the coffee table as if she owned the place. "I've got some ideas—"

"Great. Tell me tomorrow on the way in. I'm going to bed." Parker strong-armed Tanya off the couch and to the front door. "Please get yourself another room. I'll happily comp you."

Once Tanya was outside, she flipped the lock with a snap, loud enough to carry the clear message out into the hallway.

The question was: How was she going to get that message to Carly?

———— ◇◇◇ ————

An hour later, Carly sat on another, completely different sofa. This one had many more lumps, several unidentifiable stains, and huge empty spaces on either side of her. She sank back into the couch with a deep sigh.

"That good?"

Carly bolted back up. "Jeez, Grandma, you scared me. I didn't hear you come in."

"Were you at the stadium all this time?" Minnie Lee had stopped at the breakfast bar and leaned heavily against it.

She swung around to face her grandmother. "I think I may have really messed up tonight."

Minnie Lee patted the barstool next to her. "We can't talk if you're way over there."

Carly joined her, easing up onto one stool as Minnie Lee stiffly climbed onto hers.

"I'm sure it's not so bad. What happened?" Minnie Lee asked.

"I don't even know where to begin."

Her grandmother patted her hand.

Carly smiled thinly. "When I took the job at the Rollers, Buck, the head AT, told me point-blank I couldn't date the players or he would fire me. I thought fine. There's no way I'll want to date them." Her heart flopped against her ribs. She wasn't used to talking so freely about her sexual orientation with her grandmother. Was she really okay with it?

"And then Parker happened." Minnie Lee gently nodded.

Carly's heart settled back into a normal rhythm. "Yeah. I tried to stay away. I really did, but I don't know, Grandma, I just couldn't."

"My mother, your great-grandmother, always said that you can't find love where it doesn't exist, and you can't run from it when it does. She was a wise woman and might have known a thing or two about what you're going through."

Carly sucked in a quick breath. She wasn't too wrapped up in her own drama to let this little tidbit slip away. "What're you telling me? She liked women?"

Minnie Lee gave a one-shouldered shrug. "Looking back on it now, yes. Momma had," she curled her fingers into air quotes, "a special friend. We called her Aunt Effie."

"So she didn't run from it, but she didn't call attention to it."

"Yes, but we all knew, even if we couldn't put a name to it. Do you and Parker want to put a name to it?"

"I have no idea. I thought maybe I did." With some heavy editing, she recounted how Tanya had shown up at the worst possible moment. "And I don't think I'm reading the situation wrong, but she clearly has a thing for Parker. Now she knows about us, and she could use it at work to get me out of the game."

"Oh, I see." Her grandmother rubbed her forehead.

"So, what do I do?"

Minnie Lee looked around the kitchen as if she would find the answer with the plates and silverware on the drying rack. "Out yourself first," she said finally.

"Sorry?" Surely, she had misheard.

"You know what I mean. Do it before this agent or anyone else does."

The hair on the nape of Carly's neck rose. "I…I can't do that."

"Sure you can. Just go into Mrs. Fisher's office and tell her you like women and you're dating Parker." Her eyes lit up with an inner glow. "Figure out who you are, which you clearly have, and then do it on purpose. That's also something Momma used to say although she really didn't take her own advice, did she? You could, though."

Carly leaped from the stool and paced around the tiny kitchen. It wasn't the craziest idea she'd ever heard. Parker was already out and proud, and it might be easier for her with Buck if he knew about her orientation…unless he was homophobic like Hill. "I don't know," she said as she began a second turn, but her tone was less doubtful. "I'm not even sure where I stand with Parker."

"Two different issues, sweetheart. You need to find your own voice before you can share it with her. Crazily, she has nothing to do with this part."

"What if they fire me?"

"A company can make any policy they want, but you have a right to a private life as well. This rule, though reasonable, may not even be enforceable."

"And what if her agent doesn't say anything? What if she was just being vindictive in the moment?"

"So, what if she was? Marina hired you for a reason, and who you date doesn't affect that."

Her grandmother was right. Why sit around waiting for other people to write her story? Time for her to take the plot of her life into her own hands. Her pulse throbbed at her temple as she began to embrace the idea.

"What if they do fire me and UNLV doesn't take me back like they said they would? How will we survive?"

"We'll figure something out." Minnie Lee eased off the barstool with some difficulty, moved to Carly's side, and clasped both her hands in her own. "Life is tough, sweetheart, but so are you."

Carly's teeth raked across her bottom lip as she rolled her head first right, then left. Even thinking about it was scary. "Your mother said that too?"

"No, I read it in *People* magazine somewhere. Without the *sweetheart*, of course."

They both chuckled as Minnie Lee opened her arms for a hug.

"Thanks, Grandma." She rested her head on her grandmother's shoulder and wrapped her arms around her tiny waist. "You're always here for us."

Minnie Lee hugged her back, squeezing with surprising strength for such a small woman. "I wouldn't want to be anywhere else."

CHAPTER 11

"Carly? What are you doing here?" Marina asked as she stepped off the elevator to her office at the Rollers' facility the next morning. "It's awful early."

Not for someone who had barely slept a wink the night before. Carly rose stiffly from the sofa in the waiting room and faced her boss tongue-tied. In the cold light of day, everything she had practiced in the middle of the night seemed like whining.

"Are you here to see me?" Marina, dressed in an elegant pantsuit and a thick strand of pearls, breezed past her. "There was nothing in my book."

"I know. I'm sorry I didn't make an appointment." Carly raced after her. "Something's come up, and I was hoping to discuss it with you before everyone else got here."

"Yes, of course." She tilted her head down the hallway in an invitation. "My door's always open."

Carly followed her into her office and, despite her pounding heart, marveled how welcoming it was. A leather-and-wood desk dominated one corner, but two comfortable couches with a glass coffee table between them were the centerpiece of the room. On the coffee table, a decorative plate held fresh apples, and a thin wool blanket, as if from someone's living room, lay draped over one couch. The view out the wall of windows was not the Strip, as Carly would have bet, but instead, Mount Charleston and the lovely Spring Mountains range.

"Join me." Marina waved her deeper into the room and took a seat on the couch against the wall.

Carly swallowed heavily and eased down across from her. Here went nothing. "Thank you for seeing me." Her pitch rose with each word. Damn, practice did not make perfect. "I think you should know that I'm gay." Heat flushed through her body, and she tamped down the impulse to flap the collar of her shirt.

Marina's brows furrowed for less than an instant before smoothing out again. "Thanks for telling me, but I'm not sure that warrants a meeting."

Carly's mouth went dry. Here came the sticky bit. "I might be developing a relationship with someone in the organization."

"Oh." Marina studied Carly for a beat. "This is a human resources concern. Register your relationship with Joyce in HR, if it turns into one. If *this person* is not your supervisor or subordinate, and I don't see how she could be since you are the only woman in your department, and if you don't allow your personal relationship to adversely affect your work, I don't see it being a problem."

Carly took in a quick breath, slid to the edge of the couch, and leaned toward Marina. "Buck does." She hated throwing him under the bus, but since Marina didn't appear to be firing her, she needed to dodge the next bullet that was coming.

"Excuse me?"

"He told me that if I got involved with a player, I'd be fired."

Marina's eyebrows rose ever so slightly. "I can understand his concern. We're in uncharted waters here after all, but that's not company policy."

Thank God. Carly sank back against the cushions. *She won't let him fire me.*

As if Carly had spoken out loud, Marina got up, crossed to the phone on the desk, and hit a four-number extension. "Hello, Buck. It's Marina… Yes, we're both in early today. Could you join me in my office, please?"

What? Carly's heart began to pound. Couldn't she just have told him on the phone?

Rather than engage in small talk while they waited, Marina excused herself, listened to her phone messages, and fired up her desktop computer.

Carly was thankful for the silence. She stared out the window, following the red stripe of rock across the Spring Mountains range, and tried to calm her body. It didn't work. Her heart still thudded in her chest. *Not company policy. Not company policy.* She repeated the phrase like a mantra. That didn't work either.

Buck tapped lightly on the glass door, entered, and then glanced her way. Immediately, his forehead creased, and rather than joining them, he took a wide stance in the center of the room. "You wanted to see me, Marina?"

"Thank you for coming up." Marina left her desk to give Buck a friendly handshake and directed him to the couches. "Let's chat over here."

His stony expression gave nothing away as he sat heavily on the opposite end of Carly's couch. For several seconds, nobody said anything.

Carly glanced back and forth between her bosses as if watching a frozen tennis game, waiting for something to happen.

"Buck." Marina finally broke the ice. "Carly came in this morning with some surprising, but not disagreeable news."

He turned his attention to Carly, as did Marina with an exaggerated tilt of her head, clearly handing the responsibility for the conversation over to her.

With a jolt, she sat up straight. Surely, she, the most junior of the group, wasn't supposed to lead this discussion.

Then the truth of what her grandmother had really meant hit her. This was her story to tell, not Marina's. And with the telling came the ability to shape it. She had to walk inside her own story to control it. If she continued to stand outside, the ending would be written for her, as it always had up to now. Problem was, she hadn't practiced any of this, so she just blurted it out. "I'm gay, and I may be fraternizing with a player."

Buck's eyes widened.

"Of course, I'll not let my new status affect my work. Actually, I never would've." Her voice grew strong.

"I assume," Marina said softly from her side of the room, "that you do not have a problem with that, Buck."

Carly waited for the cartoon steam to pour from his ears. But then the unexpected happened. Buck smiled, and the first chuckle Carly had ever heard from him escaped his lips.

"No, I don't. Actually, that makes things much easier, or it will with the men in the training room." He looked at her as if he were seeing her for the first time. "My niece is a lesbian. Why didn't you tell me?"

"It's not something you announce to your boss on your first day," she said, surprised that her voice stayed steady.

"No, I guess not."

Marina's assistant popped his head into the room. "Excuse me, Marina. Your nine o'clock is here."

"Thanks, Ian." Marina stood, signaling that the conversation was near its end. "So, we're good here? I can send Carly back to the training room?"

Carly scrambled up as well. Nothing would make her happier, but new-and-improved Carly wasn't going to wait for his answer. "I'm needed there."

"Yes. Yes, you are." Buck lumbered up from the couch. "I'm big enough to admit when I'm wrong. She's a good trainer and will be even better once Allen's done with her. I still don't like the way she was brought on, but she's a fine hire, Marina." He spoke without looking at Carly once, but it almost didn't matter, the sentiment said it all.

"I knew that from the beginning." Marina smiled.

Carly almost floated after them into the hallway. The burden that had been sitting on her shoulders for weeks, possibly even years, lifted. She couldn't wait to call her grandmother, to tell her she had been right after all. No surprise there.

And the very next call would be to Parker to—

"Carly?"

Was that in her head, or—? She spun around. "Parker?"

Parker, who had been sitting with Tanya in the waiting room, leaped from her chair. She stared at Carly, her mouth open. "What are you doing—?" She clamped a hand over her lips as if she had just been caught with her hand in the cookie jar.

"It's okay." Marina crossed to Parker and patted her shoulder in her motherly way. "If you're here to come clean about you and Carly, she's beaten you to the punch."

Parker sucked in a quick breath. "She has?"

"I never actually said your name." Carly's legs went weak at the knees waiting for Parker's reaction. Things were happening too fast, her own fault for sure. They should've talked before she had gone in. But Parker's phone, she assumed, had spent the night in her locker.

Parker focused on her. Surprise turned into a gentle smile. "You could've."

Carly's heart melted.

Tanya uncoiled from her chair and joined the group. "No, of course, we're not here for something that trivial." The bitter tone suggested she was still upset about her surprise the night before. "We came with a more professional agenda."

"Then join me in my office." Marina spun back around the corner with Tanya close on her heels.

Parker followed haltingly and, before she was out of sight, cast a glance over her shoulder.

Tapping an imaginary screen in her hand, Carly mouthed, "Text me."

Parker nodded once and was gone.

The elevator doors behind Carly slid open with a scraping noise.

"Now," Buck said, turning her around to face the open door, "I hope we can put all this behind us and get back to work. We had the win yesterday and a bye this week, but there's still plenty to do."

Carly glanced at his face, which was grim as always. But did he sound a little less gruff, or was that her imagination? Maybe he had always spoken like that, and her perception of him had changed.

"I'm looking forward to it. Thank you." For the first time, she realized that there was nothing holding her back.

Striding through the open door, she moved into a whole new future, where her own narrative had authority and power… and with a little luck that story would include Parker.

Parker stepped into Marina's office, her mind in a whirl. Had Carly really come out to Buck? Of course, she had done it to save her own skin. Tanya's cruel barbs last night had put her in that position. Pretty bold. But maybe, just maybe, Carly had also been running away so she could run back for good. Parker's throat grew thick with emotion. It took everything she had not to fly out the door to find Carly.

"No, thanks. I'll stand." Tanya broke into Parker's thoughts as she answered a question she hadn't heard. Tanya had taken possession of the office with a hand imperiously on her hip.

Marina, from her position on the couch, shrugged. "Suit yourself." She spread out on the cushions as if it were a throne.

Parker quickly studied the office. Everything was positioned to give Marina the advantage. Her couch rose about two inches higher than the one across from it, and the placement also benefited from the view. In the distance, a mountain range occupied most of the plate glass window and presented Marina with a regal, commanding backdrop. Parker had seen the same effect in her father's Malibu office, where he had a huge desk chair set against the Pacific Ocean.

Tanya was not one to give an ounce of power away and rose up on her tiptoes. Even before the conversation had begun, owner and agent were like warring queens at a standstill.

"Marina," Tanya said, "we're not here to tell you how to run the Rollers, of course, but with all due respect, my client needs to play."

"I hire excellent coaches to make those decisions. You need to talk to Ethan Hill about that. But like most coaches, he's not very receptive to those types of conversations."

Shit. If Marina wasn't going to intervene, they would get absolutely nowhere with Coach Hill.

"Well," Tanya said, "we have agendas here that go beyond football and—"

"Which are?" Marina asked quietly, but her voice magnified as it traveled across the room. Another trick of the office. Marina was a sharp cookie.

"Celebrity endorsements. Nothing can build a company's brand like the first woman to score in an NFL game. But she needs to score." Tanya's words were punctuated with careful pauses as if Marina had never held a Rollers—or any other— balance sheet.

Parker cringed. Tanya's tactic wasn't a surprise, but Parker had been so wrapped up in Carly that she had given no thought to how her agent would present her case.

Marina smoothed out a wrinkle on her slacks.

Parker had seen her father do that same stall technique a million times. *Tanya's in the shit now.*

"So you've come in to talk about the bottom line? How extraordinary."

Tanya bounced one foot on the carpet, her feathers obviously ruffled. "What else is there?"

Marina snorted unkindly. "Character, integrity, inspiring a young girl to pick up a ball because it's empowering."

Parker went rigid and stared at Marina as if her words had taken a physical shape. That's exactly what she had been thinking lately. Not as nicely worded, but the sentiment was the same.

Tanya shook her head and laughed. "Of course, we want all that stuff too, but—"

"Enough." Parker stepped up and finally carved out her own space in the conversation.

Both women swiveled toward her. Tanya's eyes first widened with astonishment and then narrowed in fury. Marina's, on the other hand, gave nothing away.

"Parker. I've got this." Tanya's tone turned even more dismissive.

"No. You work for me. Not the other way around. Sit."

Grumbling under her breath, Tanya did.

"All my life," Parker spoke only to Marina, "I felt like I had to carry the ball myself, excuse the football metaphor, because no one else was really playing the game with me. Up in Portland, with the Fire, I was captain, and all the responsibility was on my shoulders. Since I've been here in Vegas, I see that you can hand the ball off. It's exhausting to always be—"

"What the hell are you talking about?" Tanya practically spat the question out.

Parker held up her palm to cut her off. "For the first time, I truly realize what it's like to be part of a team. To have someone's back while they have yours. It's a good feeling." She wasn't really talking about the Rollers. At least not yet.

"For God's sake, we're not in a sharing circle at kindergarten here." Tanya came to stand by Parker. "This is a straight-up business deal."

"Obviously, she's right." Parker took a step toward Marina. "You wouldn't have signed me if there wasn't a profit in it for you, and I wouldn't have signed if I weren't getting something out of it. But I'm beginning to believe you're right. There is a bigger game plan here, and maybe my playing for the Rollers is about what I can give, as well as take."

"Hmm." Marina shifted her body and cut Tanya out of the conversation.

"I know it's flat-out wrong for a player to ask, but can you tell Hill to put me in? Scoring's the first step to making a difference, I think."

Marina said nothing, and her gaze turned cold.

In response, a flush of heat rolled through Parker, and sweat dampened her shirt as she waited for Marina's reply.

Clearly punctuating the moment, Marina waved a hand in the air. "I could've done it yesterday," she said finally, "but I was waiting for you."

"For me?" The heat in her body turned downright uncomfortable.

"Yes. I want to make sure you're not just here to put the ball through the uprights and walk away. It seems to be your MO, after all. I want more than a publicity stunt or, worse, a joke."

So that was what Marina thought of her. Parker took a quick step back. "Why pick me then?" Had Marina copied a page from her father's book? Because suddenly this felt a lot like one of his attacks. Her throat began to close as she choked on another rejection.

"Because you have a lot more to offer to this community than a foot. But you need to take on that responsibility yourself. Are you ready for that?"

Parker fought against the familiar frustration and resentment at being confronted. She glanced at the door. A quick get-away? No. She couldn't always run away. Wasn't that what she was always accusing others of? And son of a bitch. Maybe Marina was right—walking away seemed to be her MO too.

"I can try." She swallowed hard. Maybe trying was all her father was asking for too. "And if you'll excuse me, I would like to go down to Coach Hill's office and tell him that there is more to this than playing time."

"Excellent. I think I'll join you, if you don't mind," Marina said.

All tension fled from Parker's body. "Are you kidding? Let's go."

"Don't forget the *Sports Illustrated* shoot next week." Tanya's plaintive call followed them out of the office.

When they arrived, Hill sat in his office, head down, studying films on an iPad.

"Ethan, do you have a minute?" Marina asked.

When he saw them at his door, Hill made a strange gurgling noise and jumped up.

I wonder how he likes working for a woman? Maybe it's the whole gender he has a problem with.

"Coach Hill," Parker started right up. She wasn't going to give him time to get the upper hand. "I'm here to tell you that I am a very good kicker. You put me in after a touchdown, and I'll score. That simple. You don't, you're missing out. But there's more to—"

"We've had this conversation. My feelings haven't changed." His focus shifted to Marina. "I don't know what Sherbourne told you, and frankly, I don't appreciate her going over my head."

"Actually, our meeting was mainly about how she's growing as an athlete and a person. She said nothing about you, Ethan, but I can guess what she would've said if she had gone there. Your reputation, good and bad, precedes—"

"With all due respect, Marina, there is no room in the NFL for political messages."

"That's where you're wrong." Marina's voice was hard as nails. "The league is so chock-full of messages that I'm surprised we all haven't choked to death. It's just that they speak to you as a white, conservative man, so you see them as the status quo."

"If we play her, fans will walk away, and some won't come back," Hill said.

"We don't want those fans." Strength radiated from Marina as if she were a superhero. Parker was proud to stand beside her. "Women make up about half of our fan base. Economically, the team that can tap into that dynamic first is in the driver's seat in this league."

"And you know, Coach," Parker said. "A serious, powerful female athlete is not a social contradiction. Just last week a girl in Texas was crowned homecoming queen at a halftime ceremony and then went out to kick a thirty-yarder to win the game."

"A publicity stunt."

"Maybe, but they got the win. Isn't that what you're all about? Ethan, you need to get on board here. Women are already here in the NFL—coaches, trainers, owners. A player was bound to come."

Parker had to bite back a grin. They were beating him down—together. Playing tag team with Marina was almost more fun than kicking a ball around a field.

"Yes, but was Sherbourne your best choice?" Hill asked.

"I thought you knew the Rollers' stance when you joined us. In the words of the legendary Vince Lombardi, there's *nothing but acceptance around here*. And just so you know, we're taking our support outside the stadium too. The Rollers are sponsoring both the Gay Bowl this year and The Center over on Maryland Parkway every year. We're active in NFL Pride, and we'll promote LGBTQ rights at My Cause, My Cleats this season." Without even stopping for a breath, Marina continued.

"I'll give you a chance to get on the right side of this, so we'll schedule you into a counseling session on social responsibility, and I want Sherbourne in the game at the earliest opportunity. That clear?"

A long beat and then Hill's shoulders rolled forward into his chest. "Yes, Marina." His voice was thin with defeat.

"Good." Marina tapped the doorframe twice and headed down the hallway. "I'll see you on the field, Sherbourne," she said over her shoulder.

"Thank you for everything." Parker followed, a lightness filling her chest. It was over. Hill had caved. It had almost been too easy. With anyone else, Parker would have felt compassion, but Hill was a bully, and seeing him get some of his own medicine was very satisfying.

She looked back to see how he was dealing with his takedown and gulped.

He sat completely upright as if his shoulders had been wound tight with a toy key. His gaze bore into the back of Marina's head until she cleared the hallway, and then he shifted his attention to Parker.

Oh, shit. That hard gleam in his eyes was back. He still had something up his sleeve. And sooner or later, it would be slithering out to bite Parker on the ass. She just knew it.

It was a lot to digest. She needed help. She rounded the corner, got out her phone, and typed a quick text. *Meet me by the Popsicle cooler after lunch.*

<hr/>

"We knew Hill was a snake. But now, thanks to Marina, we have permission to watch him like a hawk," Carly whispered and glanced around the cafeteria. Bad-mouthing a coach in public was not good form.

Parker nodded but scrunched up her face as if her strawberry Popsicle had suddenly gone bad. "I just hope we can figure out what he's up to."

"We will." Carly reached out to slide her hand down her arm—her usual gesture of sympathy—but froze before it got there. Technically, they didn't have to hide anymore, but coming out to her bosses in private was a lot different than coming out to the whole staff and team who were milling around the cafeteria as lunch ended. She had been hiding this part of herself for so long, and besides, she had used up all her daring earlier in Marina's office.

Parker glanced down at Carly's hand still frozen midway between them. "So how'd you end up telling Marina that we were...? I mean, after last night... You ran out so fast I was sure we were over before we really began."

Heat swept up her chest and across her face. "I took a chance and kind of implied that something might be on the horizon. I didn't know what Tanya was going to say, but it was more than that. I wanted to control my future for once and not just sit back and let others do it for me. Shape it the way I wanted it to be." She met Parker's gaze and held it. She couldn't read her at all. Had she made a bad call? "I'm sorry if—"

"No. I'm happy, just surprised is all." Parker cocked her head almost playfully. Her lips parted slightly before she spoke. "Does this mean if I asked you out on a date now, you'd say yes?"

"Well..." Carly regarded her with a teasing smile. "That depends."

Parker leaned forward. She was grinning too, but her gaze was somehow both hopeful and intent. "On?"

"On whether you find a better way to ask this time."

Parker chuckled. The sound was almost musical. "I've been thinking about it actually. There's this place I used to go as a kid, when my father was building the hotel. It meant a lot to me, and I'd love to show it to you now."

Perfect. That was perfect. Carly started to nod, but then her heart sank. "Oh shoot. I can't."

Parker frowned and lowered her head.

"No." Carly reached out and, no longer caring who might see, tipped her chin back up so Parker met her gaze. "I have to babysit. My grandmother's going out tonight. I got free tickets to a Vegas show, and Teddy will be home all alone."

Parker said nothing and just stared into her eyes.

She bit the inside of her cheek. "You…could come with me if you want."

"I would like that."

Carly's heartbeat quickened. "Me too."

Just then, a Pro Bowl safety muscled in between them to get to the cooler. "I hear there's fresh strawberry today. Move over, Sherbourne."

"I'll pick you up. Text me when you're ready to leave," Parker mouthed as she backed away.

Carly nodded, and they parted.

On unsteady legs, Carly headed back to the training room. Wow. What had she done? Dating Parker was all she had thought about since her tryout, even if she had just admitted that to herself, but thinking about it was a lot different than doing it. Their circumstances were like night and day, and, more important, who knew what Parker really wanted?

She was still considering the potential problems as she pushed open the stadium door to the parking lot later that night.

"Hey." Parker waved. Dressed in jeans and a Rollers sweatshirt, her long hair loose and flowing, she stood by a blue taxi sedan. She smiled and opened the door. "Your ride, milady."

Once Carly had slid in and scooted over, Parker settled beside her. Their thighs touched, and even through the jeans, Carly could feel Parker's heat.

"Where to, ladies?" the driver asked.

After hesitating briefly, she gave the driver her home address. She wasn't embarrassed, she told herself. If they were going to get to know each other better, Parker would eventually have to see where she lived. But as they drove through neighborhoods of one mini-mall after another, she admitted to herself that she was nervous. Parker lived in a palace on the Strip. Would she reconsider everything when she saw her apartment?

The car slowed, and Carly glanced up at her two-story building as if seeing it for the first time. The cream-colored stucco was dingy; the red awning over the front door was tattered and torn. Two scraggly palm trees soared out of a large brick planter in the front. A far cry from any installation at the Sherbourne Hotel. She glanced at Parker, who hadn't even given the building a second look. Instead, she handed the driver some money.

Carly's stomach tensed again. Should she offer to kick in? Would that offend Parker? By the time she had rolled the options around her head, the transaction was over. She had no idea how to navigate any of this.

On the way up the stairs, right outside her door, Parker grabbed her arm. She turned and, since she was on a lower step, looked Carly right in the eyes. "I…I should tell you… I mean, I want to tell you, and I didn't want to do it at work or in the car, that Tanya and I did have a little thing. One night, nothing more."

"Okay." A chill rolled through her body as she tried to stay calm.

"I know that kind of makes me sound like a jerk, but I hadn't even met you yet. I ended it for good last night."

Carly swallowed hard against a sudden tightness in her throat. She had been pretty sure that nothing was going on between them, at least not anymore. But... "Just last night?"

"No. I mean, yes. That's when I said the words, but we were over long before that. She just didn't know it until last night. A quick fling's not what I want anymore."

Here they were. At the point of no return. Carly pulled in a breath and released it slowly. "What do you want?"

"I want... I want to—"

Teddy swung open the front door and waved a big, white bag from In-N-Out. "I got everything set up. Let's go."

Parker turned from Carly to Teddy. "Dungeons and Dragons?"

Damnit, Teddy. We were so close.

"Good. You're playing too?" Teddy beamed at Parker. "Now we can play a real game. Come on."

Parker followed him inside and scooted around Carly to the center of the living room.

Wow, she had slipped out of that tackle way too easily. Whether Tanya was on the current playlist or not, Parker had a history of running through a lot of women. Carly didn't want to be just another song in that long catalog, but now, with Teddy around, there would be no way to bring the subject up.

So Carly just stood in the doorway and watched Parker. To her surprise, Parker didn't even glance around. Did she really not see the beat-up dreams in every corner? Instead, she crossed to the hand-drawn, colorful map already set up on the breakfast bar.

"This is amazing." She ran a finger across a multi-room tavern. "I am so in. You're going to have to teach me how to play, Teddy." She clapped him on the back.

"Um, I got your text too late. I only got two burgers." Teddy thrust the bag and the responsibility over to Carly.

Parker smiled. "We can split a burger, right?" she asked, echoing her own question from the night before.

"But will it be enough?" Here was Carly's chance, and she was going to grab it. But would Parker get the real meaning?

"Oh yes." Parker's voice was breathy and low. "In fact, I think it may be everything I've ever wanted."

Carly laid her hand over her heart and sighed. Maybe the differences didn't matter.

Teddy swung his head back and forth. "Are we still talking about the Double-Doubles?"

CHAPTER 12

PARKER WAS EARLY. SHE LOUNGED against the gray stucco wall of the Pinball Hall of Fame with a grin that couldn't be contained. Carly was coming. And this was a date. Had they really put all the trouble that the Rollers and Tanya had thrown at them in the rearview mirror? Would it be easy driving from here on in?

As the sun went down, she pulled out her phone to kill time while she waited. Her iMessage icon indicated four new messages. Two were spam, one was from the backup goalie on the Fire casually hoping she wasn't coming back, and one was from her nephew. It started *Hi, Auntie.* He knew how much she hated it, which was why he did it, of course. She hit the message.

Hi, Auntie. TU 4 connecting me with Pak. He's gr8. We're doin a podcast!

Pak? Oh yeah, Pakalani was Hekekia's first name.

Good for you. Can't wait.

Warmth spread through her body. Her brother was raising that boy well. She didn't know a lot of teenagers who reached out to say thanks. Hell, she didn't know a lot of people who reached out at all.

She checked on her father's texts, just to make sure. Nope, nothing. She gripped the phone more tightly. How could he just not answer?

Dad?

She sent the text before she could talk herself out of it. Full of regret, she raised the finger to her mouth and started tapping on her front tooth. Her emotions spun into a hundred jagged ends.

That was when she felt Carly before she saw her. Calm flooded her body and soothed her frazzled nerves. How did Carly do that?

"Pinball? This is where you hung out when you were a kid here?" Carly was at her side. Not one Rollers shirt or hat or jacket in sight. She had dressed for the evening. Just in jeans, a bright button-up blouse, and a cute jacket, but she had clearly thought about what she would wear. And now so did Parker. Her clothes clung to her as if they were haute couture.

She held open the single glass door for Carly. "Yep. I spent those three years with Medieval Madness."

Carly laughed and slipped inside. "Please tell me that's not some horrible disease."

Parker followed her into a warehouse filled to the rafters with old mechanical pinball machines and other novelty games. Little more than a bare-bones arcade, the Hall of Fame didn't quite deserve that name. Nonetheless, magic swirled inside. Parker took a deep breath. The place smelled of grease and old machine parts and many happy, wasted hours.

"Not even close. Medieval Madness is possibly the best pinball machine ever built. Certainly, the best I've ever played. Here, let me show you." Parker rounded the third corner and strode down an empty row of at least twenty machines. No one was in the place, and the heels of her boots echoed on the tile floor. She stopped at a machine where a crazed king flanked by two demons thrust out a flaming sword on the backglass. "Ta-da." She spread a handful of quarters onto its top.

"They let you play?" Carly asked.

"They do. It's not a museum or anything. Even better, they donate all profits to non-denominational charities."

"So you actually feel good about dropping quarters into the slots here."

"Exactly. You start."

Two quick drained balls later, Carly called out, "Help!"

"Don't take your hands off the flippers!" Parker slid in behind her and laid her hands over Carly's to catch the ball before it blew out to the left. "Hit the castle. Like this." She leaned into Carly's back as they directed the ball up into the castle's moat. Lights lit up on the display, and the drawbridge dropped. A voice shouted, "You stormed the castle."

"See?" Parker pulled back. "That's how you do it."

"No," Carly said. "Let's play together."

Parker gratefully nestled into Carly's body. They fit together well and played even better. One ball, sometimes two or three, zipped around the ramps and hit the catapult. Eventually, the demons popped up. Parker fought through the distraction of Carly's closeness and the fact that each time she lunged for the ball, Carly anticipated the maneuver and moved with her in perfect sync.

"We're a good team." Parker sounded raspy to her own ears when the round was over.

"We are." Carly turned toward her.

Hands resting on the flippers, Parker still had her pinned against the cabinet.

Carly made no move to wiggle away. "Funny how we keep ending up like this. I don't think we're playing any of these games right. Do you?" She reached up and touched the side of Parker's face.

Her fingers traced down her cheekbone so lightly it almost felt like a gentle breeze on Parker's skin. She closed her eyes and let the tingling sensation travel through her body, warming her neck and breasts, and settle below her groin, where a shiver spread out in waves.

"I think our gameplay is perfect." Parker's words almost hitched in her throat.

God, she wanted to kiss her so badly. Could she? Was this the right time to officially turn friendship into romance? To hell with it. Sometimes instinct and movement was all there was. She wrapped both arms around Carly and drew her closer. Carly's natural scent, fresh like summer rain, sailed around her. Delicate and barely detectable, somehow, it filled all her senses. Without another thought, she lowered her lips to Carly's.

Her touch was soft and gentle. Their lips moved against each other in an echo of the same rhythm they had found with the pinball game. Passion simmered right beneath its surface, but the kiss was comfortable and comforting.

"Hi, Parker." A large man in suspenders slid a wide mop up the tile floor and gave her a salute with one finger.

Caught in the act, Carly buried her head against Parker's shoulder.

"Hi, Jerry." She hugged Carly closer. "Okay. I still come here a lot."

"Did he see us?" Carly whispered as Jerry walked past them.

"Probably, but don't worry. What happens in the Hall of Fame stays in the Hall of Fame."

Carly laughed and relaxed. "What else happens here?"

"Oh, you'd be surprised." Parker nuzzled the top of her head. "But this is by far the best thing that's happened to me here."

After Parker beat her high score, they headed to the 7-Eleven on the corner of Tropicana and Spencer and sat outside on a bench, drinking fizzy water and sharing a 100 Grand candy bar.

"This is my favorite candy." Carly handed her half.

Parker bit into the gooey caramel with a soft moan. "There are so many things I want to know about you."

"Well, for starters, I have a big sweet tooth, just like my grandmother. My eyes really are this color. I don't wear contacts, and I can switch hit."

Parker almost choked on the candy bar.

"At the plate." Carly punched her leg. "Only at the plate. Get your mind out of the gutter."

"You went down there with me." She chuckled, and Carly, quick to laugh at herself, did too.

It felt easy, this date, first in a warehouse and now in a parking lot. A lot different from the way their friendship had begun. Until Carly threw the curveball.

"Are you going to stay in Vegas?"

Parker flinched. The kiss, the candy, the laughter had lulled her into a false sense of security. But the question made sense. Carly was not one to flit around.

"You mean will I go back to the Fire?"

"You said it yourself. You probably don't have a long-time career in the NFL."

"I did, and I can't imagine my life without sports, but for the first time ever, I'm thinking beyond it. Playing sports was always a way to get my father to notice me."

"Was it?"

Parker thought of her empty message box. "No, not really. He was wrapped up in work and whatever was going on with his and my mom's relationship. He hired a town car service to take me to all my games."

Carly opened her mouth, and Parker held up her palm. "I'm not looking for sympathy. Sports have worked out pretty well for me. It brought me here...to this bench...with you. That's a perfect place to be." She dropped her hand on Carly's knee.

Carly covered it with her own and squeezed gently.

The simplicity of the moment touched Parker to her core. A shiver raced through her. For a decade at least, she had been all about big, bold physical moves with women. Who knew a simple touch of hands in a convenience store parking lot would trump them all?

She glanced at Carly, whose eyes were luminous under the desert moon. Parker was so enamored, she almost didn't notice when Carly bit her lip and furrowed her brows. But withdrawing her hand and shifting a little farther from Parker on the bench was a clear sign. Of what?

And then it hit her. *Shit, I never really did answer her question.* In Parker's book, she had practically told Carly that her whole life had been leading up to this moment, to this bench with her. But obviously, Carly thought she had scooted around the response.

Parker opened her mouth and snapped it shut. No. She couldn't actually tell her she was staying. Who knew what would come after the NFL season? She didn't want to promise something she couldn't deliver, so instead, she told her the truth.

"I can't stop thinking about Lily standing on that porch." Parker glanced down at the ground. "What if she went home with the Hershey's Bar, and because of that, she never tried for a KitKat again?"

"That would be terrible. But she didn't. You were there." Carly's voice was even and gave none of her feelings away.

"By sheer luck. What if I wasn't?" She shook her head and pressed her lips together before adding, "When I was in Marina's office, she asked me if I wanted to be more than a kicker. The question terrified me, and…"

Carly went still. "And?"

Parker met her gaze and lingered. "No one's ever really asked me for more, at least no one that I ever wanted to. But I can tell you what I told her. I would like to try." She reached out for Carly's hand and intertwined their fingers. Their clasped hands fit perfectly together like an intricate Celtic love knot.

A quick glance told her that Carly was staring at their hands too. What if she wanted more assurances? What if a real answer wasn't going to keep them in the game?

Carly relaxed against the bench and squeezed her hand. "Okay. I can live with that. Let's see where that takes us."

And Parker, maybe for the first time in her life, also sank into herself and found that a place with no movement was good too.

———— ❦ ————

When Carly rolled into work the next day, she stifled a yawn. Thankfully, with the bye this Sunday, her workweek was light, but she couldn't keep burning the candle at both ends. After their big moment, she and Parker had sat outside that 7-Eleven for hours, just chatting about things. Nothing heavy anymore, just cute, little get-to-know-you tidbits. As it turned out, Parker loved Broadway musicals, had walked the entire Pacific Coast Trail over several summers, and had a weakness for stinky French cheeses.

Carly filled her coffee cup to the brim. She had promised Marina that her work would not suffer. That was one promise she intended to keep above all others.

Allen sat in his office right off the main room. Probably mired in paperwork, he didn't even glance up through his windows when she entered the training room.

Just as she was about to knock on his door and offer to take some of it off his hands, J.J. Ocean and two of his flunkies, decked out in Nike swag, blocked her path. "There she goes."

Had they been hiding in the back room, waiting for her?

J.J. hit his friend, a rookie receiver, on the back, and the man stepped up to Carly. "Can you tape me up?" He pointed to his right foot.

Carly hadn't seen him favoring it, but her job demanded that she play along. "Okay." She gestured to the nearest taping table. "Hop up, and we'll see what's going on."

"No." He glanced back at J.J. "I don't want anyone else to know I'm hurt. Table in the back."

Carly glanced around the room. Still empty. Something else was clearly developing. "Sure." Things had been going so well at the Rollers lately she had let her guard down. Sure enough, as she walked to the back of the room, the three men followed step for step. Her chest tightened. She was walking into a trap; she knew it.

The rookie hopped up onto the table. "Just a little tweak, but I don't want to take a chance. I need it taped."

That was the second time he had mentioned tape. As Carly reached for the drawer, J.J. and the other man crowded in. She pulled out the drawer and did a double take.

SEX in big, black letters drawn by a Sharpie pen was printed on every single roll.

"Get it? We made you a sex tape." J.J. gripped his stomach and burst into laughter.

The rookie reached past her, pulled a roll out, and sent it to J.J. with a casual toss. J.J. grabbed it out of the air with one hand and held it up to Carly with the word *SEX* in full view. "We could make a real one if you're down for that."

A bitter tang flooded Carly's mouth as her whole body tensed. She felt like Lily. Time to get the KitKat back.

She spun to J.J. "Seriously?" Anger laced through her words. "Let me be one hundred percent clear, here. I am not comfortable with this." She pointed to the roll of tape in his hand. "Unlike you, I am a professional. If you'd like medical treatment for any legitimate problem, I'll help you, but—"

"Chill." J.J. tossed the roll back to the rookie and threw up his hands, palms up. He smiled the dazzling smile that graced a billboard right outside the stadium. "We play practical jokes. That's what we do."

Allen was at their side, his brow furrowed deeply. "Is there a problem here?"

"Nah, no problem. Just fun and games." J.J. grinned again.

Carly's blood boiled. He honestly believed that sexual harassment was *fun and games* and that there was really no harm to his antics.

She dropped clenched fists onto her hips and puffed out her chest. "There's no problem here because I'm telling J.J. that if he or anyone connected to him asks for special treatment in the training room or a hug on the field or pulls a prank like this again," she snatched another roll out of the drawer and flashed it to Allen, "I'll report your letting off steam for what it is—sexual harassment—to HR, to Marina, and then to the media. Are we clear?"

Allen turned to J.J., his eyebrows raised with the same unspoken question.

The rookie had the foresight to push his own roll behind him on the table.

Carly clutched her roll so hard that her knuckles went white.

"Woah. You're wilding." J.J. took two steps back. "It's just a joke."

Allen opened his mouth to jump in, but Carly held out her palm to stop him. Not this time. She did not need rescuing. "I beg to differ. But I'll document this moment and any others and let the legal team decide."

"Fuck that shit. I'll get you fired before you fuck with my career." J.J. pulled the rookie off the table and dragged his little entourage out of the room.

As soon as the doorway was empty, Carly closed her eyes and brought a trembling hand to her forehead.

"That was intense," Allen said softly. "You okay?"

She turned his way and nodded.

"Good. Because you were great." He met her gaze and held it.

"Thanks." Her breaths came in tiny gasps. She sure didn't feel great. "I probably made it worse, but I couldn't take it anymore."

"Anymore?"

"Yeah." She barreled ahead. Might as well go for broke. "Remember ages ago when he asked for a groin treatment?"

"That…that was just—oh shit."

"See?"

"I thought it wasn't a big deal, but I allowed him to continue. I am so sorry. I should have stopped it. Said something to HR myself or maybe even Buck."

Carly reached out to touch his arm. "Thanks, Allen. I could have said something then as well and not let you handle it."

They stood in silence for a moment.

"Well, it's handled now. With a witness, no less." Allen nodded once for emphasis.

"Do you really think it's over?" Carly asked.

"It should be if he knows what's good for him."

Carly pursed her lips. Allen had been great, wonderfully supportive, but from his look, he had already moved on.

"Well, here's some good news," he said. "With the bye, Buck's giving us all a day off. Yours is Sunday."

"Wow, that's great." She tried to infuse excitement into her voice. Her stomach knotted, and *I'll get you fired* rang loudly in her ears. There was no question; if the Rollers had to choose between her and a star running back, they wouldn't side with her.

"Hey, you need help with the injury reports?" Carly followed Allen back to his office and tried to push the worry from her mind.

No such luck. It was still there when Parker called after dinner. "Excuse me," she said to Teddy and their grandmother. She slid out of the living room and onto the balcony for some privacy.

"No. J.J. hasn't said anything in practice or in the locker room," Parker said after Carly had explained. "I'll keep an eye out. He won't make a move I don't know about."

"Thanks." Just knowing that Parker was looking out for her took some of the sting off.

"That must have been so hard to do. I'm really proud of you."

"I didn't really have a choice, and I kept hearing you in my head, telling me to find my own voice. And Allen was great. Just being heard and believed was wonderful. I really felt like I belonged in that training room." She shifted the phone to her other hand. "But I'm afraid that it was a one and done for Allen. He thinks it's taken care of."

"You think J.J. will retaliate?" Parker asked.

"Don't you? I'm small potatoes, and it's his masculinity we're talking about. But for the time being, I just have to let it go." She needed to take her own advice. "Hey, I have Sunday off. There's this place I know."

"Your version of the Hall of Fame?" Parker laughed. She clearly meant it as a joke.

Carly's stomach rolled. She didn't want to turn every conversation into a declaration of intent, but at the 7-Eleven, she thought Parker had been trying to tell her she wanted to stay. Again, it wasn't the way Carly would have scripted it, but like on the steps of her apartment, something was holding Parker back. And if she wanted more from Parker, she needed to meet her halfway and that included sharing her favorite space. "Actually, yes. I'd love to show it to you."

"Can't wait."

"Good. I'll meet you in your lobby at nine. Until then, I'll see you at work. Is that good?"

"I'll be there with bells on."

Sunday morning arrived, and in a car that had to be as old as the rocks around her, Parker bounced down a desert road west of the city. The sun's rays dropped down through a cloudless sky to a panorama of limestone hills and muted browns and greens. It wasn't a view that Parker would have sent home to her brother on a glossy postcard, but somehow there was a real beauty in the starkness. In fact, the sparse vista called to her, showing her that an uncluttered life was actually possible and probably preferable.

A warm, dry breeze blew in from the open window to her right, washing the tension of the last few weeks away. Of course, it didn't hurt that Carly, smiling and as relaxed as she had ever seen her, was less than a foot from her.

"Where'd you get the car?" Parker asked.

"From a neighbor. She lets us borrow it now and again if we bring it back with a full tank of gas."

"Holy shit." Parker swept the hair out of her eyes. "I had no idea all this was here." She pointed out the window to plants that were half bush, half tree and all thorns and spiny leaves.

"Most people don't. They spend all their time at the-over-the-top shows and in the glitzy casinos." Carly took in a quick breath. "No offense."

"None taken."

"When I was growing up, most of Vegas was desert like this, and now it's houses as far as the eye can see. You should tell your dad the real splendor is out here, and, believe me, you ain't seen nothing yet."

Parker rolled her neck from side to side in an attempt to not let her father into her head. She hadn't heard back from him, and she wasn't sure where to go from here. She could hardly go on and on about grabbing your voice and then be silenced by two unanswered text messages.

They rolled past a small sandstone rock rising from the desert floor. *RED ROCK CANYON National Conservation Area* in big, black letters was carved into its face. Carly eased the car up at a fee station, passed over some cash, and continued down the road.

Parker looked around her. Nothing had changed. Sandy gravel ran to low, brown hills covered in shrubs. "I don't see any red rocks."

"Wait for it." Carly punched the gas. "Wait for it." She rounded a bend in the road. "Now. Look."

Out of nowhere, a burst of red, cream, and orange filled the windscreen. Aztec sandstone cliffs, thousands of feet high, sprang from the ground as if some ancient spirit had reached into the earth's crust and dragged them out. A cross between a drip castle at the beach and a gigantic layered cake, they dominated the horizon.

"Shit." Parker's voice was little more than a breath. "This is amazing."

Carly brought the car to a stop in the second turnout of the scenic drive. She pulled up the parking brake and patted the steering wheel as if thanking the car for a job well done.

Cute.

Carly swiveled in her seat and gave her an easy smile.

Even cuter.

Parker continued to study her face as she turned toward the back seat. The slight strain she had worn around her lips and eyes since the J.J. incident had vanished; her gaze was open and clear.

Not cute, breathtaking.

As Carly twisted toward a bag in the back seat, her breast brushed against Parker's side and sent shivers all the way down to her toes.

"Oh shoot. I forgot a hat," Parker said when Carly pulled out a Rollers hat from the workout bag.

"I brought two, just in case." She handed Parker an identical hat. "And I brought lunch too." She grabbed a small daypack. "Come on."

The trail began as a slot canyon, but soon they were scrambling up and around outcrops that jutted deeper into the formation. Parker fell into a meditative trance as she followed Carly's footsteps. Her senses intensified. A sweet, earthy smell—like sage, but not quite—enveloped her. A wild burro neighed in the distance, and the sound echoed around her as if she were in a high-end movie theater. The colors, which had already been brilliant from the car, soared to another level of intensity close up.

"It's like a Zen meditation walk." Carly broke the silence as if she had been reading her thoughts.

"What is this place?" Parker stumbled on a rock by her feet.

"It used to be sand dunes in the Jurassic period." Carly held out a helping hand to pull Parker up next to her on the ledge. "And before you get the wrong idea about me, I'm not a geology nut or anything. We came out here every year in middle school. They told us that the stripes that run across the rocks are because the wind would shift directions and eventually the sand lithified."

"Lithified?"

"I don't know. Maybe like petrified, but for rocks, not wood. The crazy thing is that when it rains, it all kind of melts again. Look how unstable it is right now." She scraped a rock in front of her and held out the chunks to Parker.

Carly's eyes sparkled, and their fingers brushed when Parker took the crumbling rocks from her. The jolt, welcomingly familiar, moved between them, and a warmth flowed through Parker's body.

Since the pinball dance, actually way before, if she were being honest, she had recognized a charge between them, a push and pull that seemed to govern her reactions.

When Carly jumped to the next ledge, Parker was right on her heels. Her heart thumped and not from the climbing. They hiked for much of the morning, following a steep trail that disappeared completely at times. Not an experienced climber, Parker mirrored Carly's technique, lots of hand and footwork and the occasional butt sliding, as they moved across expanses of horizontal and vertical rock. Parker marveled at how agile Carly was, how her body moved with an internal rhythm, and how she naturally found the easiest path through the rocks. Parker wasn't the only one who enjoyed movement. Carly did too.

Finally, to reach the peak, they shimmied up a cliff at a forty-five-degree angle and got their reward. The top was large and flat. A frozen river of red, cream, and bronze colored its surface and ran the entire length. It was the perfect place for a picnic.

The view stretched out in every direction. To the east, a small herd of wild burros ran across the desert floor, to the west a grove of prickly pear cactus grew, and to the southeast, the Vegas Strip snaked off like a creature from a sci-fi movie.

"Worth the climb?" Carly unshouldered the daypack and dropped it to the ground.

"Yes," Parker answered simply.

Carly pulled a checked vinyl tablecloth from the pack and spread it on the rock. Her shorts rode up on her thighs as she stretched this way and that to smooth out the cloth. Her muscles weren't the developed ones of soccer players; instead, her quads and hamstrings were long and lean as if she did yoga. Or maybe she was just made that way; it didn't matter. Parker was hooked.

"You hungry?" Carly gestured to the cloth.

Parker's heart gave a little stutter as she nodded. *Not for food, though.* She eased down to the ground and pulled her hand back when the rock felt hot to the touch. "It's warm."

"Yeah. Kissed by the sun, my teachers always used to say." Carly crossed her legs and sat down all in one graceful movement. "It's one of the reasons I come up here."

Parker slid her hand along the ripple of red rock outside the tablecloth. The delicate heat rose between her fingers in tiny waves. "It's almost like it's alive."

"And we're not the only ones who think so." She pointed below them and to the right.

Parker craned her neck but saw nothing, so she scooted closer to Carly to get a better view. "Oh, wow." Her breath stalled.

A couple of feet away and rising perpendicular to them was another bright red rock. This one, however, was covered in swirls and diamond patterns. In the center, herds of bighorn sheep ran toward giant lizards, and men with blocky heads stretched out their arms and legs. The designs were carved, seemingly without reason, into the sandstone and sat nearly on top of each other.

"Who did that?" Parker asked.

"The Native Americans. Hundreds of years ago."

"And they mean what?"

"No one knows." Carly pushed her damp hair off her face. "Some people think the animals are spirit guides painted by shamans, and the spirals are about time or evolution." She pointed to a cream-colored rock about a foot farther off. "But it is very clear what those mean, right?"

Parker craned her head.

Two red hands, a right and a left, rose off the surface, so bright and fresh it was as if the artist had heard them coming and had just dropped to another ledge.

Parker bumped Carly's shoulder playfully with her own. "Sure. It says, *I'm here. Look at me.*"

"Yep, that's a selfie if I ever saw one. Talk about finding your voice, right?"

Parker laughed. "Wonder what they were thinking when they made them." She leaned over Carly to get a better view. "They're so red. What did they use?"

"Iron hematite...ochre...ooh."

Parker swiveled her head to meet Carly's gaze. Once again, their mouths were only a few inches apart. Just like the rock art, the moment froze around them. Parker glanced away and focused instead on Carly's tan hand against the cream sandstone—a visual mirror of the ancient picture nearby.

I am here, Carly's hand said, just like the Native American one.

I hope so. Because anyone who falls as hard as I am falling usually breaks if there's no one there to catch them.

Carly took her fingers off the stone and burst whatever spell the rocks had cast. She cupped Parker's chin and tilted her head to close the space between them.

Parker's eyes fluttered shut as she leaned into both the touch and the moment.

When Carly's lips dropped, the kiss was fierce. Both a promise and a prayer.

Parker's body, already tingling with excitement, went hot with desire as Carly's mouth moved powerfully over hers. The sliding and sucking and nibbling played on nerve endings she hadn't even known she had. There was something so arousing about just letting go and allowing Carly to set the pace and the intensity.

"Come here." Carly pulled Parker into a more comfortable position in the center of the tablecloth.

Parker couldn't help smiling as she scooted across the material.

Carly tossed off first her own hat and then Parker's. She brushed kisses all over her face, starting with her hairline, moving to her cheek, and ending by nuzzling the hollow of her neck.

Parker moaned and then drank in Carly's fresh scent. She wondered if she was becoming addicted. "You sure you want to…you know…out here, in public and all?" The words were almost completely lost with Parker's face buried in Carly's shoulder.

Carly slid her hands under Parker's shirt. "It's a lot more private than your place or the pinball hall."

"True." Parker chuckled and leaned completely into her touch.

Carly's fingers were gentle and strong as they ran up her back but became demanding as they dropped, clutching at the hem of her shirt and tugging it upward.

Parker threw her arms up, wanting to be rid of the shirt as eagerly as Carly did. It took both of them to get Parker out of her sports bra, which stuck thanks to the exertion of their hike. But Carly's strong trainer's fingers worked their magic again, and Parker twisted under her hands until the bra, too, fell on the tablecloth, already forgotten.

"Oh, Parker." Carly's irises flashed. With a confident touch, she caressed Parker's bare shoulder and down one arm. At the same time, she buried her face in her chest and pressed her mouth between her breasts. Carly traced her nipple, and Parker's body contracted with a dizzying surge of pleasure.

Her body responded to Carly with an arousal she hadn't experienced in a long time. But it was more than that. Carly was here *with* her in this point in time, full of passion and joy, but, more importantly, Carly was here *for* her. She didn't know how to explain it, except she felt she could sink into this moment completely, with no fear of drowning.

Parker clutched at Carly's shirt and tore it off. Still kissing her shoulder, she slipped one bra strap off and then the other, freeing her breasts. They were full and round, as she knew they'd be, a perfect handful. Maybe it was the afternoon sun, maybe it was Parker, but Carly's body sizzled with heat. Wherever Parker touched her, wherever she tasted, a throbbing pulse jumped up to meet her hands and mouth.

Carly pushed her back and scooped a finger inside her shorts.

Parker moaned at the soft scrape of cloth down her legs, her skin bare and alive. Like a heated breath, a warm desert breeze blew between them, and Parker realized that her underwear had been part of that package. She was completely naked, and Carly was sliding a hand up her calf and around to her thigh—

the touch was both intense and soft, the fingers strong and agile. The featherlight contact shifted, lingering by the apex of her thighs for a tantalizing moment, and then in one long, continuous stroke swooped around her center to her behind. She caressed the muscles there with just the right amount of pressure. Tension released in both her hips and her lower back. When Carly finally eased her back down, she felt loose and fully open to what might come next.

Parker trembled. Carly's fingers, those magical fingers, explored between her thighs, and she arched with pleasure as Carly moved closer and closer to her center.

"Touch me." The words were barely two breaths.

Carly moaned and drew small circles around her clitoris, darting into the center with a flick here or a brush there. Her touch was electric, and just when the tingling became almost unbearable, Carly ran her hand up Parker's stomach, and the fluttering spread to her whole body.

"Ooh." Parker closed her eyes and lost herself in the experience.

With one finger, Carly slowly dropped inside and explored just the entrance with circular touches.

Parker arched her back and took Carly deeper inside with each stroke. She met Carly's rhythm with an equal motion and shuddered uncontrollably. She was close.

As if sensing her need, Carly slid her other hand around her clitoris, and Parker let herself fall completely into the give-and-take between them. Their bodies moved to the beat of their connected hearts.

She tensed as her release began to build. And yet when it came, the pleasure tearing through her body, she gasped in surprise. Nothing had ever been like that.

Parker's eyes fluttered open.

Carly stared back at her, her eyes as soft as her hands. Arousal swirled in their depths, but she was focused only on Parker. She withdrew so slowly that even though Parker was spent, another spasm of pleasure quivered within. Somehow, Carly caught it with her fingers, and as she slid her hands up Parker's body, the flutters of pleasure traveled with them. Carly feathered caresses along her sides. Parker sucked in a breath. Tingles ran the length of her body under Carly's touch.

"How can you—?"

"Shhh." Carly silenced her by dropping her lips to Parker's.

Parker wrapped her arms around her and pulled her close so that their bodies were touching all along their lengths. She couldn't get close enough. For the first time in her life, she didn't have one foot out the door—or off the mountain, to be more accurate. She was content to just lie in Carly's arms and be.

⇥ ⌑ ⇤

Carly snuggled up to Parker. The action should have been horribly uncomfortable. The vinyl tablecloth was sticky, the rock underneath was hard, and an unsatisfied yearning still gripped her. Not to mention, they lay naked in plain view. Although unlikely, anyone could stumble upon them at any minute. And yet...

The moment was anything but horrible. Carly's heart soared. Making love to Parker had been one of the most liberating experiences of her life. She hadn't driven out to the canyon with the idea of seducing her, but when the opportunity had come, she embraced it with no second-guessing. She was present in the moment, then and now.

The warm sun kissed her skin, and without thinking, she shimmied out of her own shorts and underwear and climbed back into Parker's arms.

She traced lazy circles on Parker's side until Parker gently grabbed her hand and studied her fingers.

"Wow. How do you do that? Is there magic in there? Is that your superpower?"

"No." Carly laughed. "They're just fingers." She wiggled them as proof.

"I beg to differ." Parker kissed their tips.

Butterflies fluttered below Carly's stomach with the simple touch. "Do you?"

"I do." Parker made the words sound like a promise. She sat up and let her gaze rove over Carly's body, lingering in certain places.

Goose bumps spread all over her body, and Parker hadn't even touched her yet.

A jolt of pleasure spun through her as Parker bent down without any preamble, sucked a nipple into her mouth, and rolled it around between her lips.

She surrendered to the magnetic pull between them and let her hands explore the muscles in Parker's shoulders and back. Even though she had been over every inch of her body just moments before, this, her hands sliding over Parker's soft skin, was for her now. Parker's body was beyond fit; the muscles tensed under her touch and then softened. The power she had over Parker made her shiver with delight.

She let out a moan, heavy with anticipation, as Parker trailed kisses from her breasts downward. She arched off the ground, and Parker slid a knee between her open thighs. Again without any preamble, Parker dove into her with her mouth. She moved around her clitoris with short strokes. This was the Parker she had dreamed about, the one who attacked lovemaking like a sport—and she was the prize.

"Oh God." Carly wrapped her fingers in Parker's hair, holding her in place as she sucked and licked, tasting her from the inside out—stroking all parts of her except the center. Finally, she touched the top of her clit with only the tip of her tongue.

Carly's body shuddered in response.

Parker stilled, and Carly sank into the thrill. Parker teased her again. She started slowly but flicked her tongue back and forth more quickly until Carly rocked with her. She couldn't tell where Parker's tongue stopped and her own body began. And soon it didn't matter. Parker slid two fingers inside and pressed upward into a spot so sensitive that just touching it nearly sent her over.

Parker backed off just in time, let her drop into a slow simmer, and then turned the fire up once again with both her fingers and her mouth. This time as the tension built, Parker said, "Tell me what you want." Her hot breath curled over where her mouth had just been.

"Please. Don't. Stop."

Parker took her clit into her mouth and sucked, while at the same time pushing in with her fingers.

Carly clutched the tablecloth, holding on while the storm overtook her. Pleasure rolled in like waves until she was powerless in its grip and release ripped through her body.

Parker stilled but didn't withdraw, and when Carly's orgasm billowed and she had come back down, Parker pressed her tongue along the underside of her clitoris while her lips covered the top.

"Oh my God." Everything was so sensitive.

Parker rested her head on her stomach, and Carly ran her fingers lightly through her hair until their breathing had returned to normal. Sitting up, Parker pulled the elastic band out of her ponytail and shook it free. The last time Carly had seen her do this had been on the field during her tryout. Then as now, the sunlight caught her hair.

"What?" Parker raised her brows.

Carly could only imagine the look on her face. "You're amazing. That was amazing."

Parker's smile was soft. "For me too. What are we going to do on our next date?"

CHAPTER 13

EVENTUALLY, THEY GOT DRESSED AND fed each other bits of lunch. Parker normally didn't like fried chicken and certainly not cold, but the stuff Carly had brought was delicious. Then, when the sun got too hot, they climbed back down the cliff to the real world. At the car, Parker turned back to the mountain for one last look.

With the sun just beyond the cliffs, the red of the rocks had dulled a bit, but the incredible connection she and Carly had shared up there was still dazzling, at least in her own mind. Could they bring those feelings back with them to reality, or would they have to leave them among the rocks, frozen in time, like the ancient handprints?

"Oh my God." Carly cut into her thoughts.

Parker spun to see her standing by the passenger side door, staring down at the phone in her hand as if it were a ticking bomb. The color had drained from her face.

"What's wrong?" Parker asked, stilling her first impulse to jump to her side to rescue her.

Carly thrust the phone out over the roof of the low car. A gray text bubble on the screen read, *We need to meet.*

"Who wrote that?" Parker's hackles rose. "Buck? Marina? Oh my God, J.J.?"

"No. It's not them. It's my… It's Belle."

"Your mother?" Parker's face tingled with embarrassment, and she tugged her Rollers cap down over her forehead. In the craziness of the last few days, she had completely forgotten about Carly's mother and the drama brewing there.

The offer to help—the loan of money or even some of her father's security people—jumped to the tip of her tongue again. She clamped her lips shut to prevent any suggestion from slipping out. That was what her father would do. Take the situation over.

Even this far away, though, Parker could feel the tension coming off Carly in waves. "Think what you're going to say. Don't give her the upper hand." Damn. Apparently, she couldn't help herself, but it was good advice, and it did put the ball in Carly's court. She could decide how to hit it over the net.

Carly tapped out her answer. Once her thumbs stopped moving, she cocked her head in an invitation to come over.

Parker was by her side in a heartbeat, and Carly angled the phone outward so she could read the screen.

Yes, we do.

"Ooh, that's good," Parker said. "Totally noncommittal and yet you kind of sound like you're calling the shots."

Belle's reply was almost instantaneous.

You got the $$?

Parker pursed her lips so she wouldn't let anything slide out. This was Carly's call. She had to navigate this on her own.

Carly's thumbs moved fast across the keyboard. *Give me a week.* She glanced up to meet Parker's look. "I've been thinking about it. I've got a little cash in the bank. Not the amount she wants by a long stretch, but she doesn't need to know that until I give her the envelope. Right?"

Parker swallowed hard and met Carly's gaze. Her eyes were wide and open, eager even. Did she really want to talk it over this time? The last time Parker had butted in on this topic had almost been a disaster. But Carly had asked, so Parker had to trust that she really wanted to hear her answer. Still, she chose her words carefully. "What if she counts the money before giving you the information?"

Carly rocked her head back and forth. "Um...good point."

Parker exhaled. They had brought some of that intimacy off the mountain after all.

"I'm going to have to stay strong," Carly added. "She's got to think that she wants the money more than I want the answers. Not true, of course, but I think I can do it."

"I think you can too." Parker's voice was soft. "You're totally in the driver's seat here. Maybe you don't even have to put any money in the envelope at all. Or put Monopoly money in. Seriously, you don't have to give her anything if you're going to play it this way."

"Yeah, I know. I thought of that too." Carly scrunched up her face. "But it's not going to be a lot of money. And what if this helps her out of a jam? I can't leave her with nothing. I don't want to be the one pulling the scam, here."

Of course she didn't. Parker wouldn't handle it the same way—she had too much of her father in her—but that didn't make Carly's plan wrong or bad. She was beginning to realize that Carly walked through the world with kindness. Maybe that was the better strategy.

Belle's next text popped on the screen.

No. Friday at 10:00. At the stadium.

This time Carly didn't even hesitate before answering.

Not the stadium. Somewhere neutral.

No. Stadium.

Fine. Noon. Better for me.

"It's not ideal, but let her think for five days she's got the upper hand," Carly said.

Parker nodded. Carly was kind, but she was clever and courageous too. A winning combination.

"Maybe I can sneak away at lunch, and no one will be the wiser, I hope, and we'll make sure that we get what we need for Teddy."

Parker's heart fluttered at every *we*. It was probably just an unconscious slip of the tongue, but at that very moment, she felt very much a *we*. A team of two.

They said nothing as the three reply dots circled endlessly on the screen. Either Carly's mother was writing a short novel, or she kept changing her mind.

K, the reply finally came.

"Perfect." Carly slipped the phone back into the side pocket of her cargo shorts. "I'll give her the last word. Or let her think she has it." Her brows furrowed. "You think this is going to work?"

"I do. Belle has no idea what's coming at her." Parker nodded repeatedly. "You're way tougher than she thinks."

And way tougher than I thought. You're someone for everyone to contend with.

"I don't feel tough. All my life I dreamed about my mother coming back to me." Carly gave her a sad smile. "She would appear one day and tell us why she couldn't be with us. I came up with a thousand reasons. In one scenario she was running from the mob. But none of them was because she couldn't be bothered. It really hurts."

Parker folded her into a hug. "Yep. I know it does. That's what makes you so tough," she whispered against the top of her head.

"Thanks. I needed that."

"Good, because I need this." Parker bent down and brushed her lips against Carly's.

It was their first kiss that wasn't also a relationship-defining moment, and Parker wrapped an arm around her back and pulled Carly closer. The kiss deepened. Carly was a good four inches shorter, but somehow, as always, Carly's curves conformed to Parker's athletic build.

Just an ordinary, simple kiss that somehow felt magical nonetheless.

"You going to tell your grandma about Belle?" Parker asked when they finally separated and caught their breath.

"I guess I'm going to have to. I might wait a day or two to figure out if I am doing the right thing." Carly shrugged lightly and rested her head on Parker's chest. "But I don't have any more deep, dark secrets that will rush out to save me."

"I don't know." Parker slid a hand down Carly's arm and brought her fingers to her mouth. "Does she know what these can do?" She kissed the fingertips one by one...again. Silly, she couldn't seem to stop doing that.

"No." A blush spread across Carly's face. "And let's keep it that way. Okay?"

Parker raised her brows playfully.

"Okay?" Carly wrapped her fingers around Parker's hand and brought it to her chest, trapping it there. When Parker said nothing, Carly squeezed even more tightly.

So tightly that Parker felt the soft thumping of Carly's heart and the comfort of her breasts on either side—the perfect place to be. "Okay, okay." She chuckled. "Besides, now we're even."

Carly sent her a questioning look.

"You know, when we were at the fountains at the Bellagio. I wanted something on you."

"Oh, and you think you have that now?"

Parker's answer was to pull her back into another anything-but-ordinary kiss.

<hr />

The next day, Parker's cleats clicked on concrete as she headed down the empty players' tunnel out to the field for the *Sports Illustrated* shoot. Tanya's texts, telling her to *hurry the fuck up* and asking *where the hell are you,* pinged to her phone one after another. Parker wasn't late, but Tanya, as a control freak, needed to have her finger on everyone's pulse.

Instead of rushing through the tunnel, Parker leaned against the wall and figuratively took her wrist away. Besides, annoying Tanya would give Carly a little more time to join her.

As if on cue, Carly rounded the corner and stopped in the center of the entrance. The late afternoon sun slanted in through the opening and dappled the floor at their feet.

"Hi." A warmth rolled through Parker. She was surprised how happy she was to see Carly.

"You ready for your big moment?" Carly's smile rose to her eyes.

"I am, if J.J. will stay away from it. He and those stupid rookies were all huddled in a corner talking shit about the shoot in the locker room." Parker instantly kicked herself when Carly's smile died. "I'm sorry. I just wanted you to know that he's just a loud-mouthed jerk to everyone."

"A jerk superstar who people listen to." Carly clearly couldn't keep the bitter tone out of her voice.

It was okay. Parker could talk them both out of this moment. "He's all mouth and no action. We'll fight him if we have to. You're not alone in this."

Carly lowered her head rather than answer.

"Come on." She raised Carly's chin with two fingers. "Marina had to know things like this would come up. She's already proven once she's on our side, and you have a lot of friends in this organization. Me for one."

Even though Parker lowered her voice, emotion rang in the response. She couldn't stop it. She wanted to take Carly into her arms and squeeze away the hurt and spend all day in this tunnel, trying to make her feel better. Maybe humor would work. "I mean more than friends, if you're up for that kind of thing."

Despite herself, Carly chuckled, and the spark that Parker had grown to love returned to Carly's eyes.

Was this the moment? The moment that every relationship supposedly had. Where you knew that you were a team no matter what was thrown at you. That she would stay in Vegas if that's what it took. *The tunnel moment...*

"Oh, for God's fucking sake. Can you step away from each other for one second?" Tanya was at the entrance, a black shape against the sea of light. "Seriously, the whole *Sports Illustrated* crew is waiting for you, Parker. Not to mention the team. A lot of them are hanging out. You need to show them you belong with them and not here, getting your rocks off with your girlfriend."

Parker opened her mouth to call Tanya out but closed it with a pop. She didn't want to give Tanya any power at all. Whatever was developing between Carly and her had nothing to do with this crass woman. "You coming?" she asked Carly instead.

"You bet."

Tanya wasn't kidding. It was a production in every sense of the word. A bigger crew than she would have thought stood on the sidelines with cameras, tripods, softbox lights, and reflectors.

A man with a barrel chest and a round face approached. "Hi, I'm Red." His voice twanged with a Nashville accent. He read as country as cornbread all the way down to his bright-red boots. "I'm glad to be here." He put an arm around her shoulder and directed her down the field. "Normally, *SI* would just go with a game-day photo, but we want to get ahead of this story a little since we heard it's about to break. We thought we'd position you up by the stadium curtain with the Vegas lights in the background."

"Right." Parker tapped her helmet against her leg and looked around at the players who were funneling off the field.

"Veris. Hekekia." She waved them over. "The shoot's this way."

Veris and Hekekia stopped in their tracks as the rest of the players filed around them.

Parker motioned harder and turned to Red. "You can get three in the shot, right?"

"Ah, yeah, I guess so." He looked toward an older woman with large, turquoise jewelry and designer sunglasses, who stood at the edge of the group.

"Wait a sec." Tanya edged between Parker and Carly. "What are you doing?" she whispered loudly in Parker's ear. "Do you know how rare it is for a woman who isn't in a bikini to be on the cover of *Sports Illustrated* alone?"

"No." Of course, Parker had an inkling, but she wasn't going to give Tanya that satisfaction.

"Well, it is. This is all about promoting Parker Sherbourne the brand and the person, not the event."

"For you maybe, but I've got a different agenda. There are three people involved in a point after."

"The cover of *SI*? This is unbelievable!" Veris, who wore his habitual grin, wagged a closed fist for a bump.

Parker met his hand and then raised her own to Hekekia, who hesitated.

"Come on, dude," Veris said. "She doesn't have to include us."

"No. She certainly does not." Tanya rolled her eyes. "And it's a huge mistake, if my opinion counts."

"It doesn't." Parker poked her fist out again to Hekekia. "Come on. We can turn our situation around three hundred sixty degrees if we want." She chuckled to make a hard truth funnier. She hoped like hell she could get through to him. Even with the *SI* cover, she needed him far more than he needed her.

"What the hell does that mean?" Tanya stomped her foot on the grass.

"Well, it's a joke, obviously, you know, three hundred sixty degrees is right where we started. But you know what they say," she turned her attention back to Hekekia, "football doesn't build character; it reveals it. I can show you the real me."

"We all thought that this was just a stunt for you. A way to get attention. So it's not?" Hekekia asked, but his voice had lost its harsh edge.

"No. Not anymore."

Hekekia finally raised his fist, and after weeks on the same field, they fully connected.

From that point on, the shoot went off without a hitch, except for the one moment when the makeup artist, after applying foundation on her face, slid Parker's uniform off one shoulder and wrinkled her forehead. "Odd. You seem to be a little sunburned everywhere."

A smile danced on Parker's lips as she shared a glance with Carly.

The shoot began. Red positioned them at the entrance of the stadium against the iconic Vegas skyline. His camera clicked as he put them through their poses: Parker in front, flanked by the two men.

Parker was surprised how much she enjoyed the production. Once he loosened up, Hekekia had a wicked sense of humor and an infectious laugh. And just as easily as they hadn't meshed before, they fell into a good-natured camaraderie as they all joked their way through the shoot. Even Tanya wore a genuine smile when she shook hands with the producer after the camera's last click. "This was great. I'm looking forward to the proofs," Tanya said.

Bumping shoulders with Carly, Parker walked away without a backward glance. Her mind was already on the upcoming game.

"To make that cover, we need to score on Sunday." Hekekia, one step behind them, echoed her thoughts.

True. So very true. Everything—from these emerging friendships to her new life purpose—was totally dependent on the point after that she had yet to make.

Wait a sec... Had Hekekia said *we*? Her second *we* in as many days.

She grinned and bumped Carly's shoulder again.

She was beginning to believe that there might be a silent *w* in team after all.

T-W-E-A-M.

Later that night, Carly sat on the couch at home, wrapped her hands around a mug of hot mint tea with honey, and let its heat flow into her body. Sighing, she stretched her legs out across the rickety coffee table. It had been an incredibly full and eventful day—so much still to unpack. After the shoot, she had returned to the training room to work out a new stretching plan for a running back with a tight Achilles, worried about J.J., and tied up other loose ends. Fourteen hours after her day started, the hardest part was still ahead of her.

"Grandma," Carly dropped her feet with a plop, "I've something to tell you."

Steam rising from her own cup, Minnie Lee shooed her feet from the table with her free hand and joined her. "What else can there be?" She chuckled and eased onto the cushions. "You're a zombie, no, an alien—" Her cup froze halfway to her lips when she must have seen Carly's expression. "What is it, sweetheart?"

As usual, she had practiced this moment all the way home on the bus, but now that it was here, also as usual, her tongue had tied itself into little knots. "Um…"

Her grandmother leaned in with an understanding nod. "If you don't let it out, it will eat away at you." It was Minnie Lee's standby line, but it always worked because it was true.

"Well…" Carly's heart sped up. Last time she'd been here, she had done a surprising one-eighty and blurted out her darkest, deepest secret. Was there another? She sucked in a breath. "Belle came to see me last week." No, apparently not. Maybe this was the last secret eating away at her.

"Heavens to Betsy." She glanced around as if Belle might be there in the room. "She did? Where?"

"At the stadium."

"What did she want?" With shaking fingers, Minnie Lee placed the cup on the coffee table and wrung her hands, squeezing so hard that the tips of her fingers turned white.

Carly mentally kicked herself. She was letting her grandmother do all the heavy lifting, forcing her to ask questions. When was she going to grow up? "Grandma, I'm sorry to tell you this. She wanted money."

Minnie Lee let out a long breath and deflated on the couch.

"I know. When I saw her, I thought maybe she'd come to meet me. To see how I'd grown up. What kind of person I was. But she was just looking for an angle."

Minnie Lee shook out her fingers and ran a comforting hand down Carly's arm. "She's got some gumption. I'm so sorry."

"Me too."

They sat there for a moment, each lost in her own thoughts.

"I think it was good that I finally saw the truth," Carly eventually said. "For most of my life, I wondered why…how she could've left first me and then Teddy. Now I finally know it has nothing to do with us. It was her all along. She's just not a good person. You were so right to protect us."

Minnie Lee nodded heavily.

"Grandma, there's more. I am going to meet her tomorrow."

"Surely, you're not going to give her the money." Her Southern accent grew deeper as it always did when she was upset.

"Not all of it. But yes, some."

Before her grandmother could open her mouth to object, she told her everything—the dead end with her own father, the possible leads about Teddy's, and the conversation with Parker.

Minnie Lee continued to gently rub her arm but shifted her gaze down the hall toward Teddy's room. What Carly didn't have to say was that they would both endure a lot of pain for Teddy's sake.

"Do you want me to come with you?" Minnie Lee asked when Carly had finished.

Carly took a deep breath and let it out through her nose. "Parker asked the same thing. And I so appreciate it. From both of you. But I think I want to work this out on my own. I need to figure out where I stand with her, even if it is a complete disaster. Is that okay?"

"Of course. You know me, though. I'll worry." A soft smile played at the edges of Minnie Lee's mouth as she squeezed Carly's arm and let go. "You better call me afterwards."

"The second I'm done. Will you pick up your phone?" Carly could envision her grandmother's cell phone buzzing and bouncing on the bar with her nowhere in sight.

"As quick as a tick jumping on a hound."

Carly laughed, more from the sudden lightness welling up in her than anything else, and settled back on the couch. That had gone way better than she had expected.

Minnie Lee retrieved her mug from the coffee table, and the smell of mint filled the room. "Is Parker still coming over for dinner tomorrow?"

"Yeah. Is that okay?"

"You tell me. Do you want her here if things with your mother go badly?"

"I think so."

"Then, yes, let's still have dinner tomorrow and end the day well, no matter what happens in the middle."

"I'll leave some cash on the bar before I go. You don't mind cooking on your day off?"

"For this? Absolutely not."

Carly rested her head on her grandmother's shoulder. "You making Sweet Luck for tomorrow?"

"Of course. I've got something from the diner for the morning and my world-famous pecan pie for dinner. Not that you'll need it."

Unfortunately, that was where her grandmother was wrong—maybe for the first time, as far as Carly could remember. Despite a few bites of cobbler from the rose-colored tin during breakfast, the next morning in the training room—hours before the main event of squaring off with Belle—was horrible. Everyone who dropped in for treatment reported that something was wrong with J.J. He was going off in the locker room about countless things.

"He said that this organization doesn't give a fuck about its players." The backup quarterback pedaled on a recumbent bike and chatted to his favorite receiver on the next one.

On the other side of the room, Carly barely looked up from an injury report she was reading. That was innocuous enough. There wasn't a locker room in the world where players didn't complain about management.

"And then he said medical is garbage."

"Really?" the receiver asked.

"Well, not all medical. He was just talking about the, quote, new bitch."

The report swam before Carly's eyes. This was clearly about her.

"Yep. He told everyone to boycott her." The quarterback didn't even look her way when he said it. Backup or not, this was his kingdom, and she was invisible. "Then that's where Sherbourne got involved. She marched over and told him to stick it where the sun don't shine. You should have been there. She threw some serious shade. Man, the dude was pissed."

Not good. Not good at all. Parker's defending her was wonderful—it felt crazy good to have her so squarely on her side—but had it made matters worse? Football was just a soap opera with shoulder pads, and now all the drama was directed at her. Carly's stomach went sour.

Soon everyone took off for lunch. She hung back, waiting for her mother's call. Exactly at noon, the wall phone vibrated with a shrill ring.

"Tell her I'll be right there," Carly told the receptionist.

Belle stood in the lobby, staring out the plate glass windows into the parking lot. Light flooded in, outlining her from head to toe and glittering off her ice-blonde hair.

"Hello, Belle," she said only loud enough for her mother to hear her.

"Carolina." Belle turned and smiled just with her lips. "You have the money?"

"I do." Carly pulled a plain white envelope out of her back pocket and waved it.

"Excellent." Belle let out a ragged breath and reached for it.

"No, no. I need the information first." Carly clutched the envelope to her chest and crazily fought back an urge to laugh. They sounded like a B movie.

Belle rolled back on her heels, eyeing Carly. "You're sure you want to find Theodore's father? He dumped me and wouldn't take my calls when I tried to tell him I was pregnant."

"That might be about you and not Teddy. So yes, I'm sure."

"Fine. I don't know much. His name was Ricardo Castro or Colon or Chavez. It started with a C. I know that for sure."

Carly squeezed her eyes shut and dropped her head. Her hair fell in front of her face. What had she been expecting? That Belle would wave her hand and Teddy's father would walk around the corner—a big smile on his face and arms open wide? Shame whirled up in her. Yeah, she had.

She slid the envelope around her body and back into her pocket. "Come on, you must know more than a first name and an initial."

Belle shrugged. "Honestly, I don't. He just went by Ricky C. I saw his license once, and the full name was definitely something from south of the border. But I don't remember it exactly. It was a long time ago."

Carly bit her lip. She didn't know where to go from here.

Belle shuffled her feet and eyed Carly's back pocket. "He was from North Las Vegas, born here, I think. Before he dumped me, he had just applied for a job in a casino."

"Do you know which one?" Carly jumped on the lead.

"I'm not sure. Maybe the Sherbourne."

Carly's heart froze and then began to pound. "The Sherbourne?" she repeated in case she had heard wrong.

"Yeah. Why? That mean something to you?"

Carly dug a nail into her palm to prevent any further reaction. "No. Anything else?" Clearly, Belle hadn't made the connection. If she had, there would be more demands for money and who knew what else.

Belle shook her head and held out her hand. "If there is, I'll get back to you. My money, please."

Carly once again slid out the envelope and held it over Belle's palm without releasing it. "Are there any other...?" She tried to fight through her nervousness. To no avail. She couldn't ask the question.

"Spit it out." Impatience crept into Belle's voice.

"Do Teddy and I have any siblings?" Her lips pressed together into a grimace.

Belle laughed. "No. I got the free clinic to knot me up. Believe me, two was more than enough."

The comment hit Carly in her gut. She had to get away from Belle's toxicity. She dropped the envelope into her mother's open palm.

Belle clutched the money tightly. "You know, I might be able to come up with some information about your father. For a price."

Carly met her gaze.

Greed tugged at the edges of Belle's eyes.

Would she do anything for a buck? Clearly, lying to her own daughter was on the long, long list. It was an unkind thought, but Belle had said she didn't know anything about Carly's father. Carly would follow the first lead and hope, for Teddy's sake, it worked out, but other than that she was done with this woman. Her mother was on her own now, exactly the way she had left her and Teddy. "No. I'm good." She turned and walked away.

"Hey!" Belle called after her. "This isn't what we agreed on."

Of course, she would have stopped to count it right then and there. "It's all I have...Mother." She stepped into the private hallway of the complex without looking back.

"We had a deal." The cry was plaintive.

"Ma'am," the receptionist said. "Ma'am, stop. Only authorized personnel are allowed in there."

She should go back to help. But security was only a phone call away. This probably wasn't the first time someone who didn't belong in this part of the stadium had gotten in. Carly kept walking.

She knew she hadn't heard the last of her mother, but she had heard all she needed to move on.

Sweet Luck had worked after all. She shook her head. How had she ever doubted her grandmother?

CHAPTER 14

PARKER'S FIST TOUCHED THE DOOR of Carly's apartment, ready to knock, when she pulled back. Did she have everything? She rifled through the bags on her arm and on the floor in a mild panic. Everything accounted for, just as it had been when she had checked at her suite and during her Lyft ride. It wasn't like her to be so nervous. And there was no reason for it. That glorious morning out at Red Rocks, their *tunnel moment*—even though that was only from her side—and then the easy conversation when Carly had told her about her successful meeting with her mother earlier. Yes, something real was happening here.

Which could all come crashing down in tiny shards if Carly's grandmother had any reservations.

Here goes nothing. She tapped softly on the door.

Scuffling came from inside. "She's here, sweetheart." A Southern lilt drifted through the closed door.

Footsteps approached, and then Carly pulled the door open. As soon as she saw Parker, her eyes crinkled with a broad smile. "Hi."

"Hi." Parker smiled back. For a brief second, she couldn't breathe. It was as if the air was richer around Carly and her body had to readjust each time they were together.

"You moving in?" Carly gestured to the bags.

"Huh?"

"That's a lot of stuff." Carly grabbed a bag and pulled the door back in invitation.

"No…um…I just kind of got carried away."

"My favorite kind of person." Carly's grandmother scooted around Carly to hold out her hand. "I'm Minnie Lee."

Parker had to look down over a foot to meet her eyes and more than that to shake hands. She was a tiny little thing with snow-white hair and wide blue eyes that seemed to carry a world of comfort in their depths. With the shake, Parker sensed that some of those good feelings were directed at her. "So nice to meet you."

"And you too, honey." Minnie Lee grinned.

"Hey, Parker." Teddy appeared in the living room and waved his hand back and forth enthusiastically. "What's in the bags?"

"Everything." Parker dropped her bag on the coffee table and pulled out a large takeout box. "I didn't know what to bring. Carly said nothing, but I didn't want to come empty-handed. So here is a goat cheese and pomegranate salad." She handed Minnie Lee the box and then took out another. "And here are some appetizers that the restaurant does really well. We don't have to eat them if they don't go with the meal."

Minnie Lee peeked into the second box. "Goodness gracious me. What are they?"

"French cranberry cheese boxes."

She tipped the box to Teddy and Carly. "Look, it's a present that's a present." The square-shaped cheeses were wrapped up with a cranberry spread that looked like wrapping paper and green onions and fresh orange peels as ribbons.

"They're gorgeous," Minnie Lee said.

"I didn't make them."

"But you brought them."

Teddy eyed the other bag on the coffee table. "Is that food too?"

"Teddy!" Carly and Minnie Lee said in warning at the same time.

"As if." Parker pulled out a rust-colored hoodie with a black hammer on the front.

"No way." Teddy gave a small yelp and danced for the sweatshirt. "Oh my God. It's from *Deadication*." He twisted the shirt around to show the TV show's logo. "Shawn is going to freak when he sees this."

"There's more?" Carly asked, looking in the bag.

"Just this." Parker handed Carly a white box with a red bow.

Carly unwrapped it, revealing a simple votive candleholder made of red sandstone.

"Cool, a candle," Teddy said, clearly much happier with his own gift.

Carly bit her lip and glanced at Parker. Her eyes sparkled from within as they locked gazes. "Thank you," she said softly.

Minnie Lee tilted her head back and forth as she considered first Carly and then Parker. "More than a candle, I think. Shall we eat?"

A flush crept up Parker's throat. She thought she was being so clever with the candle, but Minnie Lee seemed to understand the implications and, incredibly, didn't seem to mind.

Dinner was delicious. Smothered pork chops with homemade biscuits, collard greens cooked in pot liquor— Parker didn't ask, she didn't want to know how unhealthy it might be—and black-eyed peas.

They sat at the bar. There was only enough room for three, and Carly ate standing on the kitchen side, serving up the food and generally making sure that everyone had what they needed. Parker had spent her childhood dinners at a twelve-foot table, where the space between her and her family was actually bigger than Carly's bar. This setup was so much better. Lots of laughter and talking and happy clinking noises when crowded silverware, plates, and serving dishes ran into each other. And the best part: football didn't even come up once.

During a natural lull in the conversation, Teddy grabbed the second-to-last biscuit and asked, "Hey, you know what happened today?"

"No, what?" Minnie Lee handed him the butter before he asked.

"Molly came up to me after school."

"And?" Carly added.

"She said that she liked what I did with Justin. More like how I did it, she said. That I was cool. She's cute."

"Oh?" Minnie Lee looked down at her plate, clearly avoiding eye contact.

"Yeah," Teddy said with forced casualness. "I might ask her out."

Parker held out her fist for a bump. "Way to go, Teddy."

"Yeah. If things go well, maybe we can all go to a game or out on a double date."

Everyone at the bar froze. Carly's fork, halfway to her mouth, hung in mid-air.

Parker bit her lip. She hadn't seen that coming. It was one thing to make veiled references to their relationship with a candle, but a whole other ball game to announce it to a teenager.

His shoulders visibly tightening, Teddy's glanced at each of them before he spoke. "You…" He settled on Parker. "You are with my sister, right?"

Her stomach knotted. "Um…" She looked to Carly.

Her eyes, at first as wide as the salad plates on the bar, softened with a smile. "One voice." Her tone was tender and quiet.

Together they turned to Teddy and said, "Yes," completely in sync.

Minnie Lee slid Teddy's butter plate deeper onto the bar. "They'd be lucky if you and Molly joined them on a night on the town."

Teddy's shoulders dropped a foot. "I have to ask her first. I don't know if I'm going to or anything."

"You've plenty of time to decide, sweet pea."

Teddy nodded, sat back on his stool, and picked up his fork. "Knock, knock?"

Parker smiled. "Who's there?"

"Cash."

"Cash who?"

"No, thanks, but I'll take some pecan pie."

Parker's laugh was almost as loud as Carly's groan.

"Meet my brother, the bottomless pit. For puns or food. Take your choice."

———— ✦◇✦ ————

After dinner, Parker and Carly stepped out onto the tiny balcony off the living room. The sliding glass door was broken, and Carly had to yank on it a couple of times. Parker's heart went out to her. She knew how hard it must have been to invite her out here the first time. People always tried to impress Parker with things or big talk to prove they could run with the Sherbournes. Carly had never been like that. With her, she was just Parker. Her last name could have been anything.

The cool night air swirled around them, announcing that sweater weather and winter had officially arrived. Of course, neither of them had brought a jacket.

Carly shivered, and Parker slid an arm around her waist. "This okay?"

After glancing back at her grandmother and brother still at the bar, Carly snuggled into Parker as her answer.

"Your brother's something else." Parker held her close. "How do you think he knew about us?"

"I talk about you all the time." A flush crept across Carly's cheeks, and she laughed softly. "And he's wise beyond his years sometimes. Hey, Parker?" She spoke quickly as if she had just remembered something. "Can I…um…ask you a favor?"

"Always."

"You know I told you that Teddy's father works, or at least worked at some point, for a casino here in town. What I didn't say was that Belle thought it was the Sherbourne, and I was wondering if…well, maybe you could…"

Her heartbeat quickening, Parker rushed to finish the thought. "Help?"

Carly was reaching out to her. Parker's heart bubbled over with… God, she didn't want to put a name to it in case she would jinx it. But she knew she wanted to stand with Carly like this every day—sharing moments, big and small. Maybe this was the defining moment for their relationship: *the balcony moment*. It certainly had a better ring than *the tunnel moment*.

Carly cocked her head and fixed a puzzled gaze on Parker. "Oh, you mean now?"

"Yeah, start the ball rolling, if it's not too much trouble."

Parker rubbed the back of her neck. She hadn't heard from her father since she had texted him outside the pinball hall.

She had checked her phone almost obsessively at first. After the Red Rocks date, not so much. She could use this to reach out again. Her father had never been good at real emotions. Now she would be giving him a problem to get his teeth into…if he cared.

"No, it's not too much trouble." Even she heard the hitch in her voice.

"If you're sure." Carly waited for Parker's nod before she said, "Thanks, I'll give you some privacy."

Parker nodded. She wanted her to stay, but she was too nervous. If things went south with her dad, she would need to process that alone.

Carly labored to open the patio door and slid inside.

Parker stared at her phone. Her fingers trembled as she dialed. His line rang and rang. She was composing yet another voice mail in her mind when he answered, "Parker?"

"Hi, Dad."

Nothing but silence on his end.

Goddammit. How hard is it to ask how I am? Was that part of their problem—that she was always disappointed before they even began? She took a deep breath and hoped her voice would sound normal. "Hey, did you get my texts?"

"I did."

"And?"

"I'm sorry for not responding." After another long beat, he said, "I wasn't sure what to say. Your mother checked herself back into the center." His voice turned thin.

Parker started tapping on the top of the stucco balcony. This was the second time this year, and she hadn't even known. She glanced inside. Carly and her family sat at the bar, all of them laughing at once. That's what she wanted, laughter not blame. And she did blame him on some small level. Maybe if he hadn't been gone so often, her mother might…

Inside Teddy got up and started handing dishes to Carly, who stood at the sink. The two of them moved like a well-oiled machine, and Minnie Lee scooted around them to put the kettle on. They danced around each other in the small space as if they had done it a million times, which they probably had. Her family—she, Jem, their father—all just quietly sat in the corners, alone, blaming themselves and each other. There had to be another way.

"You could have just told me." Parker's voice wasn't quite as gentle as she had hoped. She cleared her throat and tried again. "Maybe I could have helped somehow."

"There's no way to help. I—"

Of course, he was right, technically. The man who could navigate any business problem couldn't negotiate this personal one. None of them could. But teamwork came in all shapes and sizes, she was beginning to realize.

"Maybe I could just listen, then. Take some of the pressure off and… I don't know." It had sounded better in her mind.

Silence spread along the line. Had they been disconnected? A squeaking noise as he shifted in his chair announced his presence. "Yes," he said finally, "we could try."

"I would like that," Parker said, her tone as compassionate as she had hoped for earlier.

"I would too."

Another silence, but this one didn't have any harsh edges.

"So," her father broke in, "when are you going to score?" It wasn't his usual challenge, just an easy question about her life.

"I think I might get into the game on Sunday," Parker said, happy to be just talking with her father. "If, of course, someone scores a touchdown and there is an opportunity for a point after. And if I'm put in, I'd love to have you there. I mean, it might be a complete waste of your time, but—"

"Honey, I'm sorry, but I have—"

"Look, Dad." If she was going to get this ball into the end zone, she would have to carry it herself. "It's not just about the game. Actually, that's the least of it." She took a deep breath. It was one thing to announce her plan to Carly and her punting team, but her father was a whole other ball game. "I've been thinking about my future, like you asked. I have an idea, well, really whatever comes before an idea." Her heart started pounding loud enough for her to hear it.

"I'm listening," he said finally.

"I would like to give young girls power and teach them how to find their voices. Through sports at first. I know it's not a new idea or anything, but we could get Marina involved. I think between the Rollers and Sherbourne Worldwide, we could really make a difference. The how is something I would like to work out with you. Maybe we could be…I don't know… partners or something."

Despite the cool breeze, heat burned in her chest, and she clutched the phone like a lifeline as she waited for her father's response.

"Is this for real?"

"This is totally for real, and I know I'm going to have to prove that to you."

"And you'll be in it for the long haul? Not just something to kill time until something else comes along?"

Everyone was asking her that. She thought of Carly and how she had evaded the question then. Here was a second chance. "Yes."

She waited for the desire to run from the answer and from the walls she had always felt around her. But it didn't come. With a jolt, she realized that she had been running from her father for most of her life. She hadn't wanted to give him the chance to hurt her the way her mom had. All that had changed. Being with Carly, even for this short time, had taught her that sometimes you had to rush toward possible heartbreak. It was worth the risk if it brought you to where you wanted to be.

"So, you'll come?" Without waiting for a reply, she jumped to the next point. "There's also someone special here I want you to meet."

"How special?"

"Pretty special." She glanced up to watch Carly move. "She's great. I think you'll like her."

"Really? This is the first romantic interest you've asked me to meet since high school."

"Like I said, she's pretty special."

"Okay, I could fly out there for the game." Her father's voice was strong and clear. "And fly back afterwards."

"Great. I'll send Patti the info," she said quickly before he could change his mind. "Oh, and Dad? I've got a favor to ask."

"What is it?" He sounded cautious.

"It's not for me."

She explained that she just wanted to check some personnel files and got permission to call the hotel's HR the next day. After they said their goodbyes, she dropped the phone onto the stucco wall and blew warm air into her hands. Her father was coming! That was surely something to celebrate. With Carly.

The three Bartlets were inside at the bar, still goofing around and laughing. For some reason, Teddy was waving his napkin above his head as if he were a rodeo star, and Minnie

Lee was giggling so hard that she almost fell off the barstool. Carly stood off to the side, watching, with an expression of love that lit up her entire face.

Parker grabbed her phone and slid the door open.

Carly waved her over.

Parker hurried to join them to share her news.

All of it.

Sunday morning. Game day.

The thought flipped through Carly's mind even before she opened her eyes. One by one, other sensations entered. Early-morning light barely made it through her closed eyelids. The softest sheets she had ever slept on. A mattress with plenty of support. Gentle fingers fluttering up her side, drawing circles on her skin and sending shivers all the way to her toes.

"You awake?" Parker's voice was low and throaty.

"I am now," she said with a chuckle and opened her eyes.

Parker was right there, looking down at her; a soft smile played at her lips, and her silky hair brushed against Carly's temples, tickling her and sending those shivers into overdrive.

"Morning." Parker bent even closer. Happiness swirled in her gaze.

Carly's own eyes fluttered closed again just as Parker pressed her lips to her mouth. The kiss was full and tender, and when Parker slid her tongue inside to take possession of her, Carly melted. How was it possible? Each time was like the first time—her emotions completely overwhelmed by what her body felt.

Carly tangled her fingers in Parker's hair, crushing her even closer. "You excited?"

"Like Christmas morning." Parker moaned and then pulled away. "I'm glad you woke up because I have something I want to show you."

"I thought we showed each other everything last night." Memories of their lovemaking and an orgasm that had rocked her to her bones washed over her.

"Oh God, I hope not."

Carly shivered. A quick glance at the alarm clock told her they had time; it was still early.

Parker slid out of bed, letting cold air under the covers. "But for this, you need to actually put your clothes on." She strode across the bedroom in that confident stride of hers. "Your work clothes. Do you have them here?"

Carly could only nod. The sight of Parker completely naked took not only her voice but also her breath away. To think she'd had total control of that body just last night. Watching Parker's orgasm ride over her had been as exciting as her own moment.

"You coming?" Parker asked over her shoulder as she disappeared into the bathroom.

"Yes." With the sensations of the night before still very much swirling around her, she almost was.

But Parker had different ideas. They showered—together, although after soaping each other up, it was all business— dressed quickly, and took a Lyft to the stadium.

"Okay, this is really dumb. And I usually do this by myself. I hope you don't mind joining me." Parker raised her eyebrows, and a smile curled the corners of her mouth.

"No. I'm honored," Carly said.

They stood at the Rollers' end zone. Parker moved to the goalpost and slid a hand down the padding as if she were comforting a friend. She leaned in, dug her hand inside the padding to get to its heart, and whispered to it. Then she nodded, patted the goalpost twice, and turned to smile at Carly.

Cute and just a tad weird, which made it even cuter.

When Parker came to her side, Carly raised her eyebrows in an unspoken question.

"Denarius and those guys aren't the only ones who have game-time superstitions," Parker said with a chuckle.

"Oh God. If this has anything to do with bodily fluids, I don't want to hear it."

"Urine luck, then, because it doesn't."

"Ha, that's Teddy-worthy. How long have you been sitting on that one?"

"Since about twenty minutes after that dinner before the Buffalo game. Actually, I came up with it on our ride up in the elevator that night. Too shy to tell you then."

"But not now?"

"No." She grabbed Carly's hand and took her to the goalpost and put her hand on the padding right below the NFL logo.

"You see, in soccer, if you play for a good team, the position of goalie can be a little lonely. If the game is going well, the play is on the other half of the field and your defense is way up. So, I got into the habit of talking to the goalposts to keep myself occupied."

"What would you say?"

"Just the usual. I'd tell them about the game, the strategy, to grow large when the shots came. Bounce the ball away from the net when I couldn't."

"Did they answer?"

"No, of course not. But in a weird way, I thought they might be listening. Not really, but maybe. So, with so much on the line today, I just went out to introduce myself to them, thinking that maybe if I do get on the field, they might help me out. Kind of embarrassing, right? But you should know what you're getting into."

"I don't think that's weird at all." She was lying a little. But they were in that honeymoon stage, and it was also totally adorable. Standing there with her hand on the goalpost, she gave Parker her heart. "It's your own Sweet Luck."

"Hey, Carly!" A call coming from the players' tunnel broke into their moment.

She turned to see Denarius waving them over with both hands.

"You on the clock, girl?" he asked when they were close enough. "You got customers."

That was an understatement. When they arrived at the training room, the entire starting defensive line was backed up in single-file out of the main door.

"What's this?" Carly stopped at the back of the line.

"They all want a piece of my lucky charm. I told everyone how I got the first touchdown of my career, and the only thing that's different is your tape job on my ankle."

"I told you that's mostly in your head."

"Whatever. The stats speak for themselves." Denarius shrugged, and almost a dozen men nodded hopefully.

Just then J.J., decked out in an expensive suit and enough bling to sink a ship, strolled by on his way to the locker room.

"Hey. What's going down, big D?"

"We're just showing Carly here the right kind of love."

Carly's hand popped up to her mouth, and she caught Parker's eye. Denarius had done this for her!

J.J. stepped up to him. A deep scowl creased his face. "Don't cross me."

"You may be a big player on the field, but in here you're a small, small man." To prove his point, he ran his hand above J.J.'s head. It was a good foot lower than his own. "Carly's a Roller. Just the same as you and me. Family has to treat each other right. Get it?"

J.J. rolled his eyes and snorted.

"Get it? Cuz if you don't, you're going have to deal with me."

Carly sucked in a breath. J.J. went rigid with tension. She could literally feel the energy change in the hallway.

Parker caught her eye and nodded.

"And with me, in case you've forgotten." Carly stepped up to Denarius. Her fists were balled at her side.

Then the D-line and Parker moved as one to join her. Even Allen appeared at the training room door and crossed his arms over his chest.

J.J.'s grimace dropped off his face like a mask. Underneath was a grin. What had Parker said? You smile and are still a villain. Here was living proof. J.J. strolled off in an empty swagger as if the conversation had been just about the weather. "I don't know why you all are making such a big deal about this. I'm just heading to the locker room," he said over his shoulder.

Carly shook her head, slowly and full of disbelief. *Thank you,* she mouthed first to Parker and then to Denarius.

"Didn't want to lose my lucky charm. I am not peeing on my hands. All right, boys." Denarius waved them into the training room. "She's open for business."

Carly had a busy morning, to say the least, and she had to take a minute in the training room to stretch and unwind fully into the excitement of the game. She rushed to the field as the stands erupted into a loud cheer. The game was about to begin.

Immediately, she turned to the seats behind her. Teddy and her grandmother sat in the place normally reserved for the players' families. Marina had once again delivered.

When they saw her, Teddy waved his foam dice high in the air, and Minnie Lee tipped her silver-brimmed baseball cap.

On the sideline, Allen rolled back on his heels and patted her shoulder. "I got a feeling about this game. Mark my words."

"From your lips, Allen. From your lips," she shouted over the noise of the crowd and glanced to Parker, who sat on the bench between Veris and Hekekia. As usual, her foot was tapping on the turf. So much hung on this game. Carly pressed a hand to her churning stomach. Some feeling, for sure, was swirling in the pit of her belly. Was it good or bad?

Three quarters into the game, Parker's butt cheeks were numb. Hill hadn't even looked her way. Not that he should have. The Rollers hadn't put a single point on the scoreboard. Surprisingly, though, they were only down 10-0. For thirty-six grueling minutes, the Rollers' defense had turned in a stifling and dominating performance. Flying around the ball as if they had wings on their cleats, they had stuffed one running play after another, pulled down two interceptions, and celebrated a fourth-down stop.

Parker's own troubles loomed large, however. Her father was up in the owner's box. She had seen his shock of blond hair towering over everyone, even from this far away. Or at least she had up until halftime. When the team raced back from the break, he was nowhere to be seen. Either he had retreated to the back of the box to work or could have left altogether. If his private jet was standing ready, he could be halfway home to L.A.

She needed to get into the game, not only to prove something to her dad and to herself, but also to have any chance at this new future she was envisioning. No one would listen to a spokesperson who was a failure at the one thing she was promoting.

She wasn't the only one who was antsy. J.J. Ocean jumped around on the sidelines, bumping shoulders and waving his hands in full, excessive circles. He was averaging 4.1 yards a carry and was just 17 yards off his 1,000-yard record for this year. Clearly, he was itching to get back into the game.

When J.J. ran onto the field with eight minutes left, Parker leaped off the bench. Of course, she wasn't the least bit excited for him. J.J. was a pig, especially after what he had put Carly through, and she was more than a little sick that her fate was tied to his. Nevertheless, she jumped up. If he scored, she needed to stay loose. She moved around and visualized her leg swinging at full speed and the ball rising off her foot.

The roaring crowd brought her focus back to the field. The quarterback handed J.J. the ball. Sidestepping a hit, he finally found some open space. His legs churned as he sailed into not only the end zone but also the record books.

The stadium went wild.

With all the focus on him, he held the ball high and then brought it down for an exaggerated air kiss, only to flip it to the ground, where it spun on one end. Preening like a fool, he held out his hand and pretended to take a selfie.

Parker's heart stilled. Surely this was her moment. She took a step toward the field when Veris's heavy hand clamped down on her shoulder, stopping her forward motion.

What the fuck?

The offense was still on the field. No way! The Rollers were going for the two-point conversion. Adding insult to injury, the ball was handed off to J.J., and he zigged and zagged his way into the end zone. Again.

Win or lose, he would be unbearable in the locker room, but maybe, just maybe in all his success, he would finally forget about Carly.

Parker looked down the line to Carly, who stood with Allen and Denarius. She turned immediately as if she had sensed Parker's attention and mouthed, "Sorry."

Not replying, Parker glanced down. She couldn't take the comfort of that one word. She needed to be tough now.

Another great defensive stop. And the Rollers got the ball on their thirty-yard line with only 2:34 left on the clock. The team hadn't led all day, but with just a field goal, they had a chance to win the game. The Rollers, inspired, drove down the field. At 1:07 and 3rd and 2, the backup quarterback, with the Miami defense draped all over him, still somehow found the receiver up field—bam! First down and much more as the receiver went out of bounds at midfield.

The clock was ticking down: forty-five seconds left. On the blitz, the quarterback went over the middle. The receiver snatched the ball from the air, spun toward the sideline, and was forced out close to the fifteen-yard line. Then two plays in a row where J.J. couldn't find a hole, and with only four seconds left, a thirty-five-yard field goal was the only play.

"Dammit," Parker said under her breath and plopped back down onto the bench.

"Sherbourne." Hill was at her side and pulled her back up, his fingers digging into her shoulder pads.

"Me?" She tapped her chest in disbelief.

Steely-eyed, he met her gaze. "Don't choke." The threat was painfully clear in his voice.

Parker looked down at Hill's bald head. "You wish," she said, sounding much cockier than she felt.

Her insides quivered, and she adjusted her pads as she ran out to the field. No doubt about it. Hill was setting her up. If she made the field goal, he was the genius who sent her out to grab the victory. If she didn't, his point—that women did not belong in the NFL—was made for him. And she was sunk with her father and all her future plans.

Her breath came in quick, shallow bursts as she watched Veris and Hekekia set up. The quivering in her stomach was now officially nausea, and a tightness that had started in her shoulders also gripped her neck like an iron vice. Everyone was watching—the players and coaches, the fans and her father—and, of course, Carly. So many people to disappoint.

Parker shook out her hands, trying to clear her body of all this negative energy. She had to reach that Zen space where kicking was an art and not a skill.

"Ready. Ready," Veris called.

Hekekia fired the ball between his legs. A textbook-perfect snap. Veris's hold was laces out.

Parker stepped into the kick.

Thud! The ball rocketed off her foot and began to climb. In response, her body rose up and her left foot skipped toward the goalposts.

Soaring in the air as if a breath of wind were carrying it, the ball rotated end over end.

The crowd rose to their feet, their cheers thundering in the stadium. Time clicked off the clock as the ball sailed higher.

This was it—make it or miss it—the last play of the game and maybe of Parker's NFL career.

The ball sailed right through the middle of the uprights.

The crowd went wild.

She had done it.

She was the first woman to score in the NFL. Her insides burst with a thousand emotions.

And the Rollers had won the game.

That felt even better.

Hekekia was on her in an instant, tapping helmets in what would become a tradition between them.

She glanced up at the owner's box. Her father was still here after all. He held both arms up in victory and then clutched Marina to him in a big bear hug.

Parker searched the sideline. Players and press were running out to the field. J.J. stood forgotten by an overturned cooler. The sour expression on his face said this was supposed to be his day.

Someone thrust the ball into her hands as she continued to scan the sideline.

There she was.

Standing still in a sea of commotion. A hand on her hip, much like the first time Parker had seen her. So lovely, so calming, and that soft smile was all for her. Not for what she had done—that was just a swing of a leg—but for her.

All of the commotion dropped away. The stadium full of screaming fans and the people pressing in on her from all sides. None of it mattered. Just the woman who raised her fingers to her lips, brushed them, and then threw the kiss out to her.

It fell on her cheek as if it had been physical. And then she knew. She had been wrong. This was their moment. Everything that she had been searching for her whole life was waiting for her on the sidelines and not going anywhere. And neither was she.

The field goal moment.

Parker had scored in the best possible way.

EPILOGUE

Carly squeezed Teddy's arm above the elbow. "Just be yourself, T. You're going to be great."

Teddy sighed deeply and crunched the rocky ground cover under his feet. "Here goes nothing." He stepped up to a cream-colored front door and raised a fist.

All of them—she, Teddy, Minnie Lee, and Parker—stood in the yard of a one-story stucco house on the far edge of Paradise Valley. A Thanksgiving flag, a goofy turkey holding an *eat only chicken* sign, swung out over the porch.

Carly rubbed the back of her neck and stilled her tapping foot. The flag was a good omen. It was totally Teddy's sense of humor. Maybe this meeting would work out after all.

HR at the Sherbourne Hotel had worked fast, not that it was hard with dates, initials, and a home location. Teddy's probable father, a Mr. Rico Cortez, still dealt on the casino floor. And when Carly had finally gotten enough nerve to call, he had taken the unexpected news of a fourteen-year-old son surprisingly well. He wasn't convinced that Teddy was his. After all, Belle had been with a bunch of men at that time, but he was willing to take the DNA test and the first step to meet.

The door popped open, and a fit man with a round face and a goatee stood before them. He scanned the group and smiled. "Did you all fall out of my family tree?"

Carly laughed and put an arm around Teddy's shoulder. "No. Maybe just this one."

Teddy raised a hand awkwardly in either a wave or a handshake; Carly couldn't tell.

Rico smoothed out the moment and clasped Teddy's hand firmly. "Teddy, right?"

"Yes." Teddy's voice cracked, and Carly's heart went out to him.

"I'm Carly, his sister," she said to help him out. "And this is Minnie Lee, our grandmother. And Parker, my girlfriend."

Girlfriend rolled off her tongue so easily now. Just a few weeks after Parker's big moment, but so much had solidified in that end zone that day.

Standing next to her, Parker touched her back, just for a beat. It said volumes, though. Yes, girlfriends. They were a real couple now.

Teddy twirled his wrist as he always did when he was nervous. The popping noise sounded louder than it should have in the silence.

"Ay, madre mía." Rico stepped back in the doorway. "My brother does that. All the time. He even gets the same expression on his face. Come in." He opened the door wider. "Come in."

They talked for an hour in Rico's living room. Carly stared at the family pictures on the mantle, finding Teddy's high forehead on one woman and his dimple on another.

Teddy relaxed as the afternoon wore on, eventually enough to crack a stupid pun. Rico laughed loudest, and Carly fought back the tears that sprang to her eyes.

As they got up to leave, Rico said, "We should get together again soon." The warmth in his voice suggested he meant it.

Before Carly could respond, Parker said, "Actually, how about Christmas Eve?" She looked at everyone crowded into

Rico's entryway. "I mean, I know it's just a few weeks away, and you probably have somewhere to go, but I was thinking about doing something at my father's hotel. Yes?" Her gaze lingered on Carly, and Parker nodded excitedly.

Carly was tongue-tied. Christmas Eve was a big deal in their house, and she didn't know how her grandmother would feel about giving it up.

"Sounds wonderful," Minnie Lee answered for her. "I'll bring the dessert."

"Could you come?" Parker asked Rico.

Hope shining from his eyes, Teddy leaned in, held his breath, and waited for his answer.

Parker proudly surveyed the Christmas table. It could've easily been a celebrity spread in *Vanity Fair* magazine. Red and white tulips with evergreen accents sat on either end. In the center, candles burned in pine cone and holly topiaries. The biggest ornaments at the table, however, were the smiles on everyone's faces. This dinner party, the first that Parker had ever thrown, was a huge success.

The dining room table in the family suite was set for fourteen. The sidebar held delectable dishes, ranging from beef tenderloin and a Christmas ham to truffled mashed potatoes, loaded cauliflower bites, and a corn pudding that came straight from the hotel's celebrity chef. Laughter and talking and ugly Christmas sweaters—Parker had insisted—screamed success.

"You were worried for nothing. Everyone's getting along wonderfully." Carly leaned over and tugged on the sleeve of Parker's sweater. A plump cartoon finger across her chest pointed at Carly, and bright letters underneath announced: *All I want for Christmas is her.*

"Yep, everyone's having a great time."

Carly waved her fork at the corn pudding. "Don't tell my grandmother, but this is the best thing I've ever tasted."

Parker glanced down the table at her guests.

Hekekia, his wife, and their young daughter sat next to Jem and his family. Jem and Hekekia had discovered a shared love of surfing, and over a third glass of wine from her father's personal reserve, Jem had invited the long snapper's entire family to the beach house in Malibu as soon as the season was over after New Year's. Mateo had already booked time for three podcasts in his home studio.

At the other end of the table, Minnie Lee hung on Keaton's every word. Wearing a green Papa Elf sweater, Parker's father had pulled out all the stops and was beyond charming. What they had to talk about was beyond her, but she had seen a different side of her dad since they had sat down to hammer out a business plan for the new Sherbourne/Rollers foundation, Kick It Up. Parker tingled all over when she thought about it. Kick It Up would bring sports and opportunities to underprivileged girls all across Las Vegas.

The best grouping was Teddy and his father—the DNA test had confirmed what they all already knew. Teddy wore a T-shirt with a gingerbread man who had a broken leg. *Oh snap!* rose in a speech bubble. He and Rico chatted, inclining their heads in mirror images of the same angle as they listened to each other.

Parker glanced at Carly, who watched them with a half-smile. Carly was obviously thrilled that Rico had taken to her brother. Even Parker could tell that Teddy seemed happier, more complete somehow. She wished she could give a loving parent to Carly.

As if she could hear her, Carly turned to her, and the half-smile became a full one. There were other ways to find family in this world, it said.

Parker also wished her mom could be here, but the center probably was the best place for her right now. Holidays had always been a hard time in their house. The center had suggested that they visit in early January. She already had it on her calendar, and Carly said if she could get the time off she would come with her.

Her watch beeped. She rose, stretching her arms as she went. "Come on, everyone. Get up. We'll miss the show."

She led the group into the bedroom and to the plate glass window, which overlooked the lake. Down below, crowds gathered on the shore and on the Holly deck as red and green lights flashed across the rolling lake.

Her father, who had hung back by the doorway, flipped a switch, and a French horn version of "O Holy Night" drifted out of speakers in the ceiling.

Parker slid her arm through Carly's, directed her to a spot by the window, and then pointed down to the carpet. The letter C in black Sharpie was written on a piece of blue painter's tape. "For you. Here." She positioned Carly over the C and pointed to the lake. "And there."

"Oh, Parker." Carly's voice, so soft, was for her ears only.

Stories below, a red package rose out of the foaming water. The lid opened, and images of children celebrating winter holidays all over the world flew from the box—a girl in a crown of leaves and light, a boy spinning a dreidel, another boy lighting the kinara, a second girl holding up a bread wreath and a tiny baby Jesus. Parker couldn't even pay attention to the story that followed. She was waiting for the end, when the present would rise once more. All week after practice she had spent hours with the engineer for the show, adding a few frames.

Parker squeezed Carly close as more holiday images climbed from the box. A candy cane, a snowflake, a star, and then…

Carly gasped.

Two red hands, the exact likeness of those at Red Rocks, floated out of the box. They curled and twisted together, forming a huge heart that floated over the lake. On the mountain top, a white sparkler burned bright, and as the music built, one lone spark shot through the air and landed in the heart's center. The white fire began to carve letters into the surface.

Butterflies rolling in her stomach, Parker felt faint. She had totally committed and couldn't take it back. Not that she wanted to, but why had she chosen to let all this play out so publicly? What had she been thinking?

I love you appeared on the heart and, after a beat, swirled into a new message: *Happy holidays.* The music died, the present returned to the water, and the show was over.

Carly hadn't moved. It was as if she were frozen to the C on the carpet.

"I love you?" Jem spun around to his father. "That's a weird ending."

"I don't think it was meant for you, son. Who wants dessert?" He crooked his arm to Minnie Lee. "I hear your pecan pie is the best thing that's happened to Christmas since Santa Claus."

"Well, I don't know if that's true," she said as if nothing had ever been more accurate.

With the promise of dessert, everyone else hurried after Keaton and Minnie Lee, leaving Parker and Carly alone in the bedroom.

"They're going to get Sweet Luck," Carly said, finally turning from the window to face Parker.

"You want to join them?" Parker searched her eyes, looking for an answer in their golden depths.

"Nah. I don't need Sweet Luck anymore." Carly slipped her arms around Parker's waist and pulled her close.

"Really?" Parker's heart skipped a beat. She wanted to spend a lifetime in quiet, tender moments just like this one. It really didn't get much better.

And then it did.

"Yes, really," Carly whispered and raised her lips to Parker's. "Because I love you too."

ABOUT CATHERINE LANE

Catherine Lane started to write fiction on a dare from her wife. She's thrilled to be a published author, even though she had to admit her wife was right. They live happily in Southern California with their son and a very mischievous pound puppy.

Catherine spends most of her time these days working, mothering, or writing. But when she finds herself at loose ends, she enjoys experimenting with recipes in the kitchen, paddling on long stretches of flat water, and browsing the stacks at libraries and bookstores. Oh, and trying unsuccessfully to outwit her dog.

CONNECT WITH CATHERINE
Website: catherinelanefiction.wordpress.com
E-Mail: claneauthor01@gmail.com

OTHER BOOKS FROM
YLVA PUBLISHING

www.ylva-publishing.com

THE SET PIECE
Catherine Lane

ISBN: 978-3-95533-376-8
Length: 284 pages (70,000 words)

Amy gets an irresistible offer: Become engaged to soccer star Diego Torres to hide that he's gay and in return get a life of luxury. The simple decision soon becomes complicated. Diego is being blackmailed, and Amy needs to find the culprit. It doesn't help that Casey, his pretty assistant, is a major distraction. Will Amy watch her from the sidelines or find the courage to get back into the game?

FOOD FOR LOVE
C. Fonseca

ISBN: 978-3-96324-082-9
Length: 276 pages (96,000 words)

When injured elite cyclist Jess flies to Australia to sort her late brother's estate, the last thing she wants is his stake in a rural eatery. She'd rather settle up, move on, and sidestep the restaurant's beautiful owner, Lili, and her child. Given her traumatic life, Jess isn't sure she'd survive letting her guard down. A lesbian romance about how nourishment is much more than the food we eat.

CODE OF CONDUCT
Cheyenne Blue

ISBN: 978-3-96324-030-0
Length: 264 pages (91,000 words)

Top ten tennis player Viva Jones had the world at her feet. Then a lineswoman's bad call knocked her out of the US Open, and injury crushed her career. While battling to return to the game, a chance meeting with the same sexy lineswoman forces Viva to rethink the past...and the present. There's just one problem: players and officials can't date.

A lesbian romance about breaking all the rules.

DEFENSIVE MINDSET
Wendy Temple

ISBN: 978-3-95533-837-4
Length: 276 pages; (100,000 words)

Star footballer and successful businesswoman Jessie Grainger has her life set, and doesn't need anything getting in the way. That includes rebellious rival player Fran Docherty, a burnt-out barmaid with a past as messed up as her attitude. So when the clashing pair find themselves on the same Edinburgh women's football team, how will they survive each other, let alone play to win?

Romancing the Kicker
© 2018 by Catherine Lane

ISBN: 978-3-96324-129-1

Also available as e-book.

Published by Ylva Publishing, legal entity of Ylva Verlag, e.Kfr.

Ylva Verlag, e.Kfr.
Owner: Astrid Ohletz
Am Kirschgarten 2
65830 Kriftel
Germany

www.ylva-publishing.com

First edition: 2018

Credits
Edited by Sandra Gerth and RJ Samuels
Cover Design and Print Layout by Streetlight Graphics